T0166681

DOUBLECROSSED

BY

SUSAN X MEAGHER

DOUBLECROSSED

ISBN (10) 09799254-9-5
ISBN (13) 978-0-9799254-9-8

THIS TRADE PAPERBACK ORIGINAL IS PUBLISHED BY BRISK PRESS, NEW YORK, NY 10023

EDITED BY: LINDA LORENZO
COVER DESIGN AND LAYOUT BY: CAROLYN NORMAN

FIRST PRINTING: OCTOBER 2010

By Susan X Meagher

Novels

Arbor Vitae
All That Matters
Cherry Grove
Girl Meets Girl
The Lies That Bind
The Legacy
Doublecrossed

Serial Novels

I Found My Heart In San Francisco

Awakenings: Book One
Beginnings: Book Two
Coalescence: Book Three
Disclosures: Book Four
Entwined: Book Five
Fidelity: Book Six
Getaway: Book Seven
Honesty: Book Eight
Intentions: Book Nine
Journeys: Book Ten

Anthologies

Undercover Tales
Outsiders

If you judge people, you have no time to love them.

— Mother Teresa

Acknowledgements

Great thanks to Linda Lorenzo for sharing her wisdom.

As always, for Carrie

CHAPTER ONE

CALLIE HEARD A faint metallic squeak as the front door opened. The force used to close it was slightly more than needed, and her ears pricked as her attention focused completely on the sounds from the foyer. Automatically, she checked her watch. Marina was three hours later than scheduled—never a good omen.

Even though the foyer was thirty feet away, Callie could tell exactly what Marina was doing. First, she went through the mail, tossing each piece back onto the table if it failed to hold her interest. Then she emptied the pockets of her trench coat, dropping her keys and her change onto a silver dish placed on the table for that sole purpose. Finally, she hung her coat in the closet and started to roll her suitcase down the long hallway.

As Marina got closer, Callie rose and checked her face in the mirror, then put her hand in front of her mouth to make sure her breath was fresh. The act jolted her and she stopped to consider her behavior. When had this started? She wasn't normally the type of woman to act like a puppy trying to please her mistress. Most people tried to figure out what pushed their lovers' buttons and steered clear, right? But she'd never had to do that with Rob. She shrugged off the annoying thought.

Maybe women were just harder to please. God knew that was one thing most men agreed on.

She went to the door of her office and smiled when she saw Marina start to make the turn to her own office. "Tough flight?"

"Always," Marina sighed, giving her a wan smile. "The bastards are determined to make my life a living hell." She continued into the room and Callie debated her next move. Marina always needed a wide berth when returning from a trip, and when she'd had a bad flight that berth sometimes needed to be the size of a football field. But Callie'd missed her after the week-long absence, and she had a palpable need to at least look at her carefully. So she ventured into the room, lingering near the door.

Marina started to unpack, as she always did the minute she returned home. She took out her laptop and plugged it in, then took her PDA from her purse and put it in its charger. Next a bunch of files landed on the desk, followed by receipts of all sizes and shapes. Callie knew an expense report would be finished by the time Marina went to the office the next morning. She envied her lover's organizational skills. Marina often said that every piece of paper should be touched no more than twice, but Callie tended to nearly caress everything that came across her desk, loath to part with the slightest bit of ephemera.

"What's up?"

Startled from her reverie, Callie knew the question wasn't a genuine inquiry. It meant "why are you watching me?" Time to back away. But maybe… Hunger made her grumpy. It was worth a try. "Do you want a snack?"

Marina stood still for a moment, then shook her head. "Nah. It's too late." She zipped up her briefcase, put it by her desk, then headed towards Callie. Her suitcase rolled quietly across the carpet and, when she reached the doorway, she placed a kiss on Callie's cheek. "Thanks for the offer, though."

She went towards their bedroom and headed directly for her closet where Callie knew she would unpack and sort her dirty clothes into the proper hamper. She was still tempted to watch, but was out of reasons to follow her, so she asked one more time, "A piece of fruit? Cup of tea?"

"No, thanks," Marina replied from deep in her closet. "I'm just going to unwind for a few and then head to bed. Anything on TiVo?"

"I saved the Cowboys game for you."

"Some jerk on the plane announced the final score. Bastards lost again…at home. How do they think they'll make the playoffs?"

Callie didn't have an answer for that, so she treated it like the rhetorical question it was. "You probably know who won the awards, but I saved the Golden Globes. I know you like to see the plastic surgery failures."

Marina emerged from the closet and went into the hall, giving Callie a genuine smile. "Thanks. I really do like that. That was nice of you to think of me."

"I always think of you." Callie extended her hand and put it on Marina's cheek, pleased when her lover leaned into the touch.

"It's nice to be home." Her eyes fluttered closed and they stayed in just that position for several seconds.

It was time to make a move. She'd feel a hundred percent better after they had sex. Moving closer, Callie let her hand drop to Marina's neck and give it a light tickle. "It's nice to have you home." She saw Marina's cautious gaze momentarily travel to her hand, and when she didn't pull away, Callie put the slightest pressure behind her touch.

Suddenly, Marina's arms were around her and a pair of brown eyes almost touched her own. "What are you up to?" She was playful, only slightly suspicious.

"Nothin'," Callie said, making a show of her innocence.

Marina kissed her, nearly overwhelming Callie with the force of the embrace. "I'm keeping my eye on you," Marina growled before releasing her hold and backing into the bedroom, holding her index finger up to her own eye, then pointing it back at Callie.

Everything was good. She wasn't all that grouchy. If she could tease, they'd have a great night. Marina kicked off her heels, then removed her jacket. Callie approached her from behind. "Let me get your necklace."

Marina dropped her hands and let Callie slowly remove the gold chain, making sure no hair was snagged. "And your blouse," Callie murmured, her lips close to Marina's ear. When no protest was forthcoming, Callie unfastened the single pearl button at the back of Marina's neck, then reached around and pulled the blouse from her lover's pencil skirt.

Her fingers tickled across Marina's belly and that earned her another wry smile. "What are you up to?"

"Nothing. I'm just helping you get undressed." Her smile was guileless.

"I think you're up to something." Marina wrapped an arm around her waist, and pulled her against her body with surprising strength. Her grin took on an evil intensity that Callie loved. "I think you're craving a good, hard fuck." She moved her head closer to Callie's, so close that her eyes almost crossed. She squeezed tightly, demanding, "Tell me. Tell me what you want."

"I want a good, gentle fuck," Callie said, unable to contain her laugh. "I'm not as tough as your usual trade."

Marina laughed as well, releasing her hold and slapping Callie on the ass. "You're tough enough. Let me get undressed and we'll see how tough you are."

Callie tingled with anticipation. She would have liked to continue to undress and tease her lover, but Marina didn't have the patience or the interest in being seduced. She liked to get down to business, and Callie had come to believe the end result was worth the compromises she'd had to make.

She sat on the bed and watched Marina neatly and methodically remove and fold her clothing. She loved the way Marina dressed, particularly getting off on the dichotomy between her stylish business attire and her dominant personality. Marina was a true steel magnolia, tough as nails inside but lithe, graceful and very womanly outside. Looking carefully at Marina in her suit, one would think she was a high-powered executive with her mind focused on just one thing—business. But Callie knew better. She knew that her lover was a sexual dynamo with needs greater than anyone she'd ever met. Needs that probably would have been overwhelming if Marina were home for more than a week at a time…but she rarely was.

When Marina was naked, she approached Callie and loomed over her. "Take off your clothes." It was a soft command, but she rushed to comply. "All of them. Right now."

Callie's skin tingled with untapped need. She was naked in moments, then sat back on the bed, looking up, waiting for instructions.

Marina reached between her legs and patted her vulva. "Did my favorite pussy get a workout when I was gone?"

Callie thought for a moment, showing her dimples while she tilted her head in a seductive way. "Twice, I think." She spoke cautiously, wanting to get it right. "Monday and last night."

Marina put her fingers under Callie's chin and lifted it so their eyes met. "What did you think about?"

"You." Callie slowly blinked her eyes, trying to look sincere.

Chuckling, Marina said, "Tell the truth."

"I am telling the truth, about last night, at least. I thought about you and Cynthia, and I wondered what you were doing to her."

"I could show you." Marina grinned, showing her teeth. "But you don't want to have a replay."

"If it's good I would."

Marina jumped onto the bed and hauled Callie up to the middle of it. Then she grasped her legs and hooked them over her shoulders and knelt in front of her.

"I like it so far," Callie said, her voice turning low and sultry.

"She'd been teasing me forever...making me crazy for her." She flopped down onto her belly and hovered right above Callie's vulva. "And right when I thought I was gonna get what I needed..." She grasped Callie's legs and pushed until her knees bracketed her head, rendering her spread open and helpless. Marina bent her head and bit down hard on Callie's leg. Marina ignored Callie's squawks of pain and pressed her mouth between her legs, nuzzling her mouth against her.

Callie fought to break free, winding up on her side. She reached down and tenderly touched her thigh, checking for blood.

Marina lay next to her and pulled her into her arms. "It was just a love bite."

"You could have broken the skin," Callie grumbled. "Worse yet, she could have broken yours. If you bring home hepatitis..."

"You know I'm safe. That's non-negotiable." She took Callie by the chin and looked into her eyes. "Right?"

Callie nodded forcefully. "I've never been unsafe."

"I haven't either." She pulled away and sat up. "Now, let's get back to business." She was sitting back on her heels, her legs spread wide. Her hair was mussed just enough to be rakishly attractive, and Callie felt herself getting wet just looking at her. "I liked having her bite *me*, but I'd never do that to anyone but you. Too risky." She tried to force Callie's legs apart. "Don't be afraid. I might not do it tonight. It's the threat that makes it hot."

She knew Marina would never press her advantage, but Callie didn't want to refuse outright. Instead, she grasped Marina by the shoulders and pulled her down onto her body. "Don't do it. Tell me about it." She nibbled on her ear until Marina squirmed. "Make me hot. Tell me every detail."

Marina settled down and let her weight rest on her lover. She started to kiss Callie's face and ears and neck, getting down to her breasts before she began to tell the tale. "She had me pinned so tight that I almost couldn't breathe. I don't normally like being at someone's mercy, but having her bite me a couple of times felt fantastic. Really fantastic."

"More," Callie breathed. "Tell me more."

"It felt so wrong," Marina said, her eyes shining with desire. "Just something you know you shouldn't be doing. You know how hot that is."

"Mmm, I do." They were grinding against each other, their bodies warm and tingling with anticipation.

She kissed Callie gently on the mouth. "Don't worry about me bringing anything home. I care about you. I love you." She kissed her again, slowly and softly. "I only love you." Another gentle kiss.

Their faces were an inch from each other and Callie gazed into Marina's expressive eyes. "I missed you."

"Do you love me more than any other woman?"

"Yes. No question. How about you?"

"I do. You're the only woman I love, baby. When I'm with you I'm happy." She put her hand over her heart and gazed at Callie with tenderness and affection. "I'm home."

Marina was up and out of the house before Callie was thinking in complete sentences. She was on her second cup of coffee when her phone rang. Seeing it was her best friend made her smile. "Where have you been? I haven't talked to you in days."

"It's been like two days and you texted me twenty times yesterday. Thanks for that, by the way. I was bored to tears."

"Don't you know you're supposed to be available when Marina's out of town? Can't you schedule your hours better?"

"Wish I could, but my boss doesn't ask about Marina's schedule when he sets mine. He just makes sure I work the worst hours so I can make as little in tips as possible."

"Hey, are things really that bad? You could always move here, Terri. There are more bars and restaurants than you can count."

"No, things aren't that bad. I'm just complaining. Besides, I could never leave Phoenix. At least in the winter," she said, chuckling. "Ask me in August and I might be more flexible. So, did Marina finally get home last night?"

"Yeah. Like an hour after I texted you last. But she was in a surprisingly good mood. We had a great night."

"Oh, Callie got some. Good for you."

"Callie gets plenty. And we have fun in other ways, you know."

"Can't say that I do. Other than sex, I still can't figure out why you're together."

"Hey! It was your party that brought us together."

"Unh-uh. You brought her. She wasn't my friend."

Slightly stung at her tone, Callie said, "That was harsh."

"Oh, damn." Terri took in a breath. "I didn't mean it like that. I'm just bitchy today. Don't take me seriously when I'm in this kinda mood."

"I know you're not crazy about her, but it hurts my feelings when you make it clear how much you dislike her."

"I'm sorry. Really, Cal. I am."

Callie exhaled slowly, reminding herself that Terri didn't know Marina well enough to have a well-thought-out opinion of her. "It's okay. I still love you."

"I hope you always will, 'cause I'll always love you. And I don't dislike Marina. I've just never thought she was the right woman for you."

"I know that. But I think I'm in just a teeny bit better position than you are to pick my girlfriends. Remember, you're the one who convinced me to give women a try. If not for you, I'd probably be married and working on churning out a couple of kids."

"You were on the ledge. I barely blew on you and you fell into Marina's lap. If it was always that easy to convince girls to be gay, I'd have a lot more girlfriends."

Callie laughed at how accurate her friend's analysis was. "You get your share."

"I'd prefer a nice, steady girlfriend, and I'm not going to settle for another pretty face with an empty head."

"Jess's head wasn't empty. It was…sparsely furnished, but not empty."

"You're being kind, and I'll never complain about that. I've got to get going now. I just wanted to hear a friendly voice before I have to get ready for work."

"This early?"

"Yeah. I'm working lunch today and tomorrow. Call me if you're bored."

"We're going out tonight, but I might have time tomorrow night."

"No rush. Whenever. Where you going tonight?"

"Out for cocktails with some friends of Marina's."

"Cocktails, huh? Does that mean a fifteen dollar drink?"

"Usually. Ugh. I have to make one drink last all night." Callie let out a grunt. "Don't remind me of how I'm running through my money."

"You don't have to go."

"I want to be with her. I enjoy her company."

"Really?"

"Yes, really. Why is that so hard to believe?"

"She's never…well, you don't talk about doing much together. I know I've only been with her a few times, but she's not very friendly and she's not…oh, shit. Ignore me."

"I don't want to ignore you. I just don't think I can make you understand why I like her. I know she doesn't show her best side all of the time, but she's private and kinda guarded with people she doesn't know well. Around her friends she's very outgoing."

"Are you outgoing around her friends? Or do you act bored by them like Marina does?"

"We're in a relationship, Terri. I try to make her happy, and getting along with her friends is part of the deal."

Terri was silent for a moment and Callie heard her unasked question. *Why doesn't Marina do that for you?*

"I've gotta go. Think of me when Marina's doing you like mad."

Callie laughed. "Don't take this the wrong way, but when Marina's doing me, I wouldn't notice if the apartment was on fire."

CHAPTER TWO

TWO WEEKS LATER, Marina was rushing to get ready for an evening flight to Boston. She'd just gotten in the shower when Callie heard a phone ring and recognized it as her own. Puzzled, sure she'd left it in her office, she followed the distinctive sound of a xylophone to the foyer. Her head tilted in confusion. Why was her phone in Marina's coat pocket?

She reached inside and pulled out the device just in time for it to stop. Staring at it perplexed, she started towards the bathroom to ask Marina why she'd taken it. After just a few steps, a text message showed in the window. "I can't wait to see you. I've been counting the days."

Now even more confused, she stared at the message for a moment. Why was the name Angela Kirkland so familiar? Then it hit her—Angela worked for Marina's company in the Boston office, the office Marina was traveling to.

She turned the phone over in her hand, checking to verify it was her own. It was the default screen saver, not the photo she'd loaded. But Marina didn't have this brand of phone. In fact, she made fun of the phone and the company, called her a fan-girl who bought everything that fell from the corporate tree. Callie clicked on the contacts button and saw just a few—all friends of Marina.

So this had to be a phone Marina bought. That didn't make sense, but nothing else added up. Suddenly, a cold, dark tendril of suspicion coursed through her body. Something—a force outside herself—compelled her to act. She wouldn't have believed anyone who claimed she'd have the nerve or the desire to do what she did next. Fingers shaking, stomach turning, she texted back. "Me too."

Her pulse was hammering so loudly it seemed to envelop her. It took just seconds for the response, but they were dramatically long seconds.

"I've been dreaming of all of the things I'm going to do to you."

Automatically, Callie wrote back. "Me too. Gotta go." There was no need to look when the last message came in. It didn't matter what it said. There was nothing Angela Kirkland could say that would stop the shaking, the rage, or the sorrow. She wasn't aware of her body, didn't notice when it slid down the wall and left her slumped against it like a discarded doll.

It could have been seconds or minutes, but Marina started to roll her suitcase down the hall, calling, "Callie? I'm taking off."

When she reached the foyer, she gasped and let her suitcase fall to the floor as she lunged for Callie. "What's wrong?" She was clearly panicked, and her hands slid along Callie's arms and legs, trying to ascertain how she'd hurt herself. "Can you hear me?" she asked, her voice tight with fear.

Unable to speak or even to focus, Callie extended the phone in Marina's direction. Nonplussed, Marina took it and started to toss it aside. But Callie's thin voice said, "Look at it."

Confusedly, Marina did, switching her attention between the phone and her lover. But as soon as she read the messages all neatly lined up in one window, she shifted her weight and plopped onto her ass, almost mirroring Callie's pose.

"Ah, damn," she muttered. "I know what this looks like, baby, but that's not what it is."

For some reason, it occurred to Callie that Marina's faint Dallas accent got thicker when she was trying to get out of a jam. She idly wondered if that was intentional or if this was the way she spoke when she was unguarded.

"Come on, Callie, talk to me."

"Why?" She finally felt like she was at least tenuously connected to her surroundings. "Why? Why hurt me like this? Why?"

"It just happened. I didn't want it to, but Angela came by my room one night when we were at a conference and she..." She took in a breath. "I don't want to make her sound like an asshole, but I felt like I had to go along."

Callie couldn't think of a response.

"I know it sounds bad, but I didn't want to have sex with her. I never like to mix sex and business." She grasped Callie by the shoulders and squeezed her tightly. "I should have told you when it happened, but I felt...stupid. I did it because I didn't want her to vote against me when my promotion comes up."

Callie looked at her. How had they ever been intimate? "Is that supposed to make it all right?"

"No. I know what I did was wrong, I know that. But I was ashamed to admit it. I know I shouldn't have done it and I should have been an adult and admitted it. Then I wouldn't be in this ridiculous position."

Another long stare didn't make Marina seem any more familiar. Maybe this person had wandered into the wrong apartment. She was definitely speaking an indecipherable language. Confusion filled her mind. But it was her turn to talk. "I don't know."

"You don't know what, baby? Tell me." Marina was nearly pleading now, her accent so pronounced she might have just jumped off her horse to come in and sit on the floor.

"I just don't know." She slid down a little further. It took too much energy to stay upright.

"I know I made a mistake, but it wasn't..." Marina ran a hand though Callie's thick red hair, pushing it from her eyes. "I swear I've been one hundred percent committed to our agreement—except for this one time. And this wasn't really cheating. It wasn't like that. I didn't want it; I didn't like it. I was just doing what I thought I had to do. But I was wrong. I should have quit. I'm so sorry I didn't."

"Fine." She would've agreed to anything to get her to leave.

"I've got to go, baby. Come on. Please!" Marina got to her feet and grasped Callie by the arms. She tried to pull her into an upright position, but was barely successful. "Sweetheart, I can't leave you like this. Come on. Please, stand up."

Realization slowly dawned that she had to give in to these insistent demands to be left alone. Slowly, she got her feet under her and allowed herself to be pulled upright.

"Are you all right?"

"Sure." She craved solitude in a way she could almost taste. "Goodbye."

"Aww, you know I can't walk out on you when you're acting like this. God damn."

"Go." If she could sound like herself, Marina would leave. Easily. "It's fine."

"Are you sure?" Marina's head was bobbing up and down as if willing her to agree.

"It's fine."

"Okay." Marina took a quick look at her watch. "I'll call you as soon as I can." She hugged her tightly, whispering. "I'm so sorry."

"It's fine." Her voice was automatic, computer generated. "Bye."

"I'll call." Marina took one last look, grabbed her coat and gloves, picked up the handle of her suitcase and eased out of the door. The sound of her running footsteps echoed down the hall.

The hours passed with Callie doing nothing more than going over and over the last year and a half. How had they gotten here? Had Marina lied about everything?

She hadn't eaten, and her stomach was empty and sour. Marina's betrayal was just starting to reach the rational part of her brain, and she had to stop before it knocked her to her knees. She was so sad and lonely. Bracingly lonely. She didn't want to be alone for another minute, but she didn't want to talk to anyone either…especially anyone who knew Marina. So she put her shoes on, combed her hair and quickly washed her face, then drove to her favorite local bar.

Talking would only have made things worse, so she was relieved to see no one that she knew. Ordering a beer and a burger, she sat at the far end of the bar, waiting for her food. After a few minutes a woman approached and tentatively asked, "Mind if I join you?"

Callie snapped out of her fog and saw a woman who'd previously caught her eye a couple of times. "Uhm, sure, but I'm not very good company tonight."

"Something wrong?" the woman asked, signaling the bartender for a beer. "I'm Linda, by the way."

"Hi. Callie. Nice to meet you." She took a sip of her beer. "I just found out my girlfriend cheated on me."

"Ooo. Every time I've seen you here you've been with a group. I thought you were single."

"No, I'm not…at least not yet. That might change. Soon."

"Well, I don't want to wish you bad luck, but…" Linda smiled, her face made all the more attractive by a warm, somewhat shy expression.

Taking another drink, Callie surveyed the woman quickly. She was just her type and she knew she could easily take the woman home without a twinge of guilt. But she also knew she'd be doing it to even things up between her and Marina. And she would never, ever use another woman like that. "I'd love to hang out if I wind up single. But tonight...well, tonight I don't know what in the heck I am."

By the time she got home Marina had called her fifteen times. She'd also sent an e-mail, obviously written on her PDA while waiting at the airport.

Callie,

I don't have a good excuse for what I did. I know it was wrong, and I knew it was wrong at the time. All I can say is that I screwed up and I'm sorry. I know that isn't much, but it's all I have.

I don't know if it matters, but I don't have feelings for Angela. She's just a co-worker, a co-worker I let myself believe I had to make happy. I know how stupid that sounds now, but that night it seemed like my only option.

I didn't think of it as cheating, even though it obviously was. It didn't seem like it because I didn't think it would put our relationship at risk, and that's the basis of our agreement, right?

Angela lives a thousand miles away, she's in a relationship, and she's a co-worker. I'm not seriously attracted to her and I know she feels the same about me. For her it was just a way to blow off some steam after a mind-fuck of a client dinner. For me it was a way to make sure I hadn't wasted the last 3 years of my career.

The facts don't excuse what I did, and they certainly don't make it any less hurtful for you, I'm sure. But I want you to know what happened, for what it's worth.

I love you, Callie, and I desperately want your forgiveness. Please give me the chance to explain this all better.

Marina.

She looked at the note for a long time, but realizing how detached she felt, knew she was wasting her time. Time she could have spent in bed, where the big, fluffy pillows were practically calling her name.

After twelve hours of a near-coma, Callie finally dragged herself out of bed. She tried to go about her day, but it took an hour to manage a shower and a bowl of cereal. Making coffee was out of the question. It was too complex for the brainpower she had available. She surprised herself a little by picking up the phone and making a call.

"Dad?"

"Hi." He sounded sunny and wide awake. "What's up?"

"Can I come see you?"

"I'm playing golf at one, but…I can cancel. Is everything all right? You don't sound like yourself."

"I've heard that a couple of times in the last day or so."

"Let me come to your place. I'm playing golf not too far from you."

"Okay. If you don't mind."

"I'll be there in a half hour."

Callie sniffled with the certainty that her father's love was one thing she never doubted. He had his faults, plenty of them, but she knew he loved her.

They'd been talking a long while when Jeff Emerson leaned back in his chair, looking more than a little stunned. "I've gotta say, you've given me a bagful of information here, Chicklet, and it's gonna take some time to sort through it all."

"I know it's weird talking about sex, but I just had to unload and I don't have anyone else I trust as much as I do you. Are you really sure you don't mind?"

Jeff shook his head, his pale, straight hair moving around his head when he did. "No, no, not at all. My friends all complain that their kids never tell them anything important." He scratched the back of his neck, shyly grinning at his daughter. "Maybe they should count their blessings."

"I can talk to Gretchen or Emily about this, Dad. Really."

He gazed at her for a minute, then shook his head again. "No, if you wanted to talk to them, you would have. Do they know about your... what do you call it?"

She shrugged. "No, they don't. And we call it our arrangement. Our agreement."

"They called it swinging when I was your age."

"No, that's a different thing. We're monogamous when we're in Dallas, but when we're away from home we can sleep with someone else as long as we get permission. We both have to agree."

He scratched his neck again, more forcefully this time. He'd never seemed so frazzled. "What's the difference between that and swinging?"

"Swingers usually bring another couple in to have sex with both of them. We don't do that."

"Why? Isn't this...worse than swinging? At least you'd be together."

He didn't get it. It was probably too much to expect him to. "I don't want to be together and watch her have sex. That would make me sick. What she does on her own time is her business."

"Right." He nodded, still looking confused. "You only cheat when you're out of town."

"It's not cheating!" How could he ever understand? "What Marina did was cheat."

"Okay. Okay. I don't see how you can cheat when you're allowed to have sex with strangers whenever you're out of town, but if it makes sense to you, that's what matters."

"It does make sense when we follow the rules. It does." That sounded like begging. She had to show she was convinced for him to buy in.

"This has worked for you? Until now?"

"Yeah. It has."

"And you've been doing this the whole time?"

"We talked about it before we got together, so yeah."

"Is this…uhm…common for…you know…girls like you?"

"I think it's more common for guys like you." She wished she could have prevented that last sentence from leaving her mouth, but it was out. Maybe it was time. She reached out and grasped his hand, squeezing it. "I didn't mean it like that. I just think more straight couples have open relationships than lesbians. I think it's harder for women to get their heads around it." Pain etched his features and she hurried to add, "I know you regret what you did."

"Worst thing I've done in my life," he said for what Callie estimated was the thousandth time. "I thought I was just having a discreet little fling, but it cost me my family and my whole way of life." He sank down in the sofa, looking utterly defeated. "If it hadn't been for you and Emily, I think I would have ended it all."

That would have been just perfect. Having him leave the house almost killed her. What would have happened if he'd killed himself. She couldn't stand even the thought. She got up and sat next to him, pulling him into a tender hug—the kind he'd given her every night before he was booted out. "Don't even think about that. We need our dad and I'm darned happy I finally live close enough to see you more often. Emily's jealous," she said, showing the happiness sisters seem to get from having something the other doesn't.

"Gretchen's not. She doesn't care if I live or die."

"That's not true. She just…she's just like mom. Things are black or white for her. It's not just you that she judges. She's not wild about me being with Marina."

"Because of the open relationship?"

"No. Because Marina's a woman." She chuckled. "It seems that still matters to some people. My narrow-minded sister, for one."

"That's ridiculous." He frowned. "How do you turn your back on family?"

He was so clueless sometimes. How could he ask that question when he'd moved to Dallas—just to escape the bad memories of Phoenix. To save himself from pain, he'd made it worse for them. So much worse. He had called every night to read to her, but that hadn't make a dent in the loss.

"She hasn't turned her back on me, she just lectures me about how childish I'm being. She thinks my sexual orientation is a sign of my inability to be in a mature, fully developed relationship. She thinks I'm taking the easy way out."

"I never should have paid to send her to school to study psychology. She cherry-picks all of the things that support her views and ignores the rest."

Callie leaned back and looked at him, trying not to dwell on the fact that her father paid for Gretchen to go to a private school, while she had to go to a state university. Even worse, Gretchen had completely wasted the money. She had a degree from a good school and had never worked full time. "That's remarkably accurate. How do you know so much about her?"

"Just from things you and Emily tell me. She does sound a lot like your mom."

"Too much. They get together and figure out what to complain about that day. It's too much."

"You know, I think I'm a sharp guy, but it just dawned on me why you wanted to talk this over with me."

"I called because I respect your opinion, Dad."

He straightened up, assuming his normal posture, looking like the middle-aged systems engineer that he was. Intelligence radiated from his blue eyes, and his gaze was sharp. "Yeah, I know. But I think you're hoping I can tell you what goes on in a person's mind to lead him, or her, in this case, to cheat." His eyes got bigger. "Especially when she practically has carte blanche to sleep with whoever she wants to."

"It's not quite that broad of an agreement, but she certainly has a lot of freedom."

"If I'd had just a snippet of that I'd still be with your mother."

"Yeah, you probably would. But for mom to give you a little leeway would have killed her. She's just not the type. Never was…never will be."

He patted Callie's knee. "I wish I knew why Marina screwed up, but I still can't explain why I did it. I wanted a little variety, the opportunity came up and I jumped at it. I knew it was wrong, I knew your mother would never forgive me if she found out, and I did it anyway. A real recipe for disaster."

Callie wished he would stop admitting he knew how wrong it was. That made it hurt more. Wouldn't anyone know that?

"Marina certainly didn't need variety, so that's not it. She claims it just happened—that she didn't stop to think."

"That's kind of what happened with me, honey. I could make a case for how the woman chased me for months and kept making offers that

I had a harder and harder time refusing. But it wasn't her fault. I was married and I gave in to temptation. No excuses."

Callie chewed on her lower lip, something she'd been doing all day, even though it now felt raw and swollen. Her father didn't make excuses, but what good did that do? The years they'd been a thousand miles apart weighed on her mind. No matter how much he'd tried, he couldn't make it seem like he was there for them. Thank God they'd had the last year and a half to really get close again. Being nearby had made all the difference. It was clear he was a good man who'd screwed up once and had paid a dear price. Through it all he'd never said a bad word about her mother. That said a lot about his character.

"I'd like to move out before she gets home. I know I'll never get the straight story out of her."

"Do you really know that?"

She shrugged, looking away from his pointed gaze. "I dunno. I thought I knew when she was lying. I didn't."

"You've invested over a year of your life with her. Spending a few hours hearing her out doesn't sound like too big a commitment, does it?"

Reluctantly, she said, "No, I suppose not. But it makes me sick to think of looking into her lying eyes."

"But you don't mind her sleeping with other women…"

He trailed off when she gave him a sharp look. How could she explain this? There was a big difference between sex and love. Marina needed extra sex. Case closed.

He tried again, phrasing the question differently. "Isn't this just another woman she's having sex with?"

"Technically, but it's different. It's very different. She lied, Dad. She cheated."

"By sleeping with another woman." His eyes narrowed in thought. "It's hard for me to see the difference. Besides, wouldn't you hate to move out of this place?" He picked up his hands and gestured around the apartment. "This is the nicest place I've been to in Dallas."

"It is nice, but it's awfully expensive. I wanted to move some place more in my comfort level, but Marina was already here..."

Jeff stood up and gently patted his daughter on the shoulder. "You'll figure this out, Chicklet. You always do. You've been an adult even when the adults in your life were acting like kids."

She stood up and embraced him, relishing the strong, warm comfort of his hug. "Thanks, Dad, and try to erase everything I told you from your memory bank."

"I'll do a core dump." He kissed her on the cheek. "I'll call to check up on you. But if you need to talk before then, call me. Promise?" He looked into her eyes, and the concern and caring that showed in them brought a lump to her throat. She hugged him tight, then walked him to the door.

After her dad left, Callie spent a long time staring at her computer screen. She started and stopped and started again, finally composing an e-mail to Marina. It didn't truly satisfy her, but it felt better to get some of her feelings out.

Marina,

I'm sorry for not taking your calls, but I can't talk to you right now. I'm not even sure I'll be here when you get home. This might be more than I can take.

I've been thinking about one of the talks we had when we got together. You told me that having an open relationship would keep us from ever being tempted to lie to each other about sex. I trusted that promise, and having you break it might kill our relationship. I wish you hadn't done something so hurtful, but you did, and I don't know if I can stay here and work through this.

Callie.

CHAPTER THREE

THE NEXT DAY Callie greeted the day more enthusiastically than she'd been able to the day before. Feeling relatively like herself, she spent the early afternoon trying to get some work done. She tinkered around, trying to come up with a design for a logo and a full professional stationery and business card setup for a local firm, but nothing was coalescing.

She was about to call it quits when someone buzzed from the lobby. She went to the video display by the front door and was dismayed to see Marina's mother Fawn, standing in the lobby, anxiously prancing like a child who had to use the bathroom.

Callie pressed the button. "Come on up."

It took a few minutes for Fawn to reach the fifteenth floor, but Callie didn't spend the time checking how she looked. She normally spent an anxious hour getting ready to spend time with the Boltons, but at this point she didn't give a damn what Fawn thought of her.

She opened the door to a brisk knock and stood aside to let Fawn enter in her normal grandiose fashion.

“Oh, I’m so glad you’re here. Marina is gonna be so relieved.” The cultured Dallas accent that Fawn usually effected was obliterated by her natural Arkansas twang.

Callie started to walk towards the living room, but remembered her manners and waited for Fawn to lead the way. “You could have just called. I would’ve taken your call.”

“Oh, I left early this morning and I didn’t want to wake you. Besides, this is too personal to talk about on the telephone.”

“You left…were you in Austin?”

“Yes. Parker and I are going to be in Austin until this legislative session is over. There are some very big bills that the legislature is going to consider, and he’s working harder than I’ve ever seen him.”

Privately, Callie didn’t think that having lunch, cocktails and dinner constituted real work, but Parker was a lobbyist for the pork producers and that was the nature of his profession.

“You didn’t have to drive this far, Fawn. This is something Marina and I have to work out on our own.”

“I know that, but I’m not sure you know how much you mean to her.”

Trying to keep the annoyance from her tone, Callie said, “That’s something I should know from her, isn’t it?”

“I know, I know.” Fawn’s hands fluttered like a baby bird learning to fly. “I’m just not sure how good she is at telling you how she feels. She’s a deeply emotional person, you know, but it’s hard for her to express herself.”

Marina could explain her way out of almost anything. She had a silver tongue that could get her whatever she wanted. But Fawn couldn’t see that since she was the one frequently talked out of substantial sums of money.

“That’s not how I see her. I think she’s really good at saying what she wants.”

"In some ways. But I don't think you see the real her. She's very needy."

That was crazy. Almost delusional. Marina was one of the least needy people in the world, but Fawn needed to be needed and Marina definitely liked being pampered. Callie had often thought that Marina would have been more well-adjusted if she hadn't been an only child. As it was, her mother and, to a lesser extent, her father, focused all of their hopes and demands and energies on her alone.

"I'm touched that you came this far just to talk to me. I really am. But…"

"Look, honey," she said bluntly. "I know all about your agreement, and you have to admit that this little dustup isn't very serious in the whole scheme of things."

Callie's mouth dropped open and she had a brief fear that it would stay that way. How could Marina reveal something so private? Then she recalled that she'd just told her father. That reminder set her mind reeling for a few moments and she had to compose herself enough to speak.

"I had no idea you knew about our…"

Fawn's hand flipped a few times, as though shooing flies. "She tells me everything. I know about her other girls too, sweetie, and if she cared one whit about this girl in Boston, I'd know about it."

"That may be, but she cheated on *me*, Fawn. She has all the freedom anyone would need, and she cheated."

Fawn leaned towards Callie and her voice grew softer and more earnest. "That's one way to look at it, honey, but another way is that this is like a country road, and Marina just went past the mailbox a little bit."

"That's not how I look at it. How would you like it if you found out that Parker was sleeping with another woman?"

To Callie's surprise, Fawn gave her a look that was almost sympathetic. "When I was just a little girl my grandmother told me that there were two kinds of women. One kind you married and one kind you didn't. I didn't really understand what she meant then, but I came to. Men have a drive. A drive that no respectable woman could meet. I'm surprised you didn't learn that before you met Marina, you being with men and all."

"I learned that a lot of people have strong sex drives, but part of what makes us human is our ability to control our urges. We're not solely driven by instinct."

"Of course not. But we're not very far away from barnyard animals. A bull might have sex three hundred times a year, but he sure as heck isn't with the same cow. I don't know what Parker does when he's away from home, and I will never, ever ask."

Stunned again, Callie said, "Really? You're not even curious?"

"Not at all," she said, making *all* sound like two syllables. "I think part of your problem is that you talk about these things too much." She reached out and touched Callie's hand, squeezing it gently. "Marina is very much like her daddy. If you let her have her head, she'll be wonderful when she's back in the paddock."

Callie wasn't sure what part of this barnyard discussion was making her head spin, but she'd had all of it she could take. She stood up. "I'm being a terrible hostess. What can I get you to drink?"

"Oh, nothing, sweetheart. I'm going to go by our house, fix myself up, and meet a friend for some shopping." She lowered her voice as though someone were listening. "There isn't a thing to buy in Austin."

Urging Fawn towards the front door, Callie put a hand on her shoulder. "I truly appreciate your coming by. I think it's great how much you care about Marina."

Fawn gave her a robust hug, enveloping her in a cloud of floral perfume. " I care about you too. You've probably never suspected this, but Parker and I had a hard time accepting some of Marina's choices."

Most of the Metroplex knew that the Boltons were devastated when Marina came out to them, but it wouldn't do any good to try to relieve Fawn of her delusions. Callie merely nodded.

"But both Parker and I love you. You're exactly the type of person that Marina needs. You're so much more understanding than the women she's been with before."

Understanding or a sucker? Being understanding wasn't a fault. Being a sucker was. Marina couldn't push her that far. Self-respect was something she'd never give up. For anyone. "I appreciate that," Callie said, making herself smile. "I'll certainly consider everything you've said."

Fawn patted her on the cheek and started for the door, turning one last time to say, "Don't forget about how they keep that bull happy."

"Oh, I can honestly say that I'll never forget that." *Even though I'll try.*

On Monday morning, Callie was sleeping peacefully when she was startled awake. The bedroom was dark, but there was just enough light to see a figure standing in the doorway. She was trying to find the breath to scream when she heard what sounded like a sob.

A rough, hoarse voice murmured, "It's me."

"Oh, dear God." She tried to convince her heart that it had nothing to fear, but it didn't believe her and continued to race. "I tried to scream and nothing came out."

Marina approached the bed tentatively. "I'm so happy you're here," she whispered. "I was sure you were going to be gone."

Callie sat up and pushed her hair from her eyes, confused by the darkness. "What time is it?"

"Uhm…six forty-five."

"There aren't any flights that get you in at this time of day. Where've you been?"

"I was scheduled to come home this morning, but I knew I'd never be able to sleep, so I caught the last flight to Los Angeles, then got the redeye that left LA at one a.m. For a change we were right on time."

Drily, Callie said, "Maybe that should be your new schedule." Part of her wanted to bash Marina's head in, but another part—a part she couldn't make sense of—was glad to see her. There was some kind of pull that Marina had over her, and she could no more resist it than she could explain it. Just being in the same room with her relieved some of the pain. There was a real connection between them. That was irrefutable.

Still looking very tentative, Marina said, "Can I get into bed with you? I can't even tell you how much I've missed you."

Feeling some of the barriers start to come down, she extended a hand which Marina took. "Sure."

With remarkable speed and even more remarkable disregard for her clothing, Marina stripped in moments and climbed into bed. She settled into Callie's embrace and began to cry. The tears seemed to flow unabated, which was surprising. Callie had only seen Marina cry a few times during their history and each time it had been out of frustration, not sorrow or pain. Seeing Marina allow herself to be vulnerable was touching in a way that a boatload of apologies never would have been. She tenderly rubbed Marina's back and let her cry until they finally fell asleep in each other's arms just as the sun began to peek into the window.

Late the next morning they sat in the bright, sunny kitchen, eating brunch. Three cups of coffee hadn't helped Callie wake up enough to go over Marina's sins. But Marina seemed fixated on making sure she explained what she'd been thinking when she'd slipped and how determined she was to never screw up again.

Something about Marina's explanation seemed forced, even rehearsed, and it dawned on Callie that she had probably written the points down and gone over her speech on the long flight. How could she get through to Marina? How could she show her the damage she'd done? The pain she'd caused? But it was so hard to reach that part of her. Did she have to take her as she was? Or could they both learn something from this? It was so tiring. Relationships were so damn much work.

She sat there, half listening to Marina prattle on. Marina seemed to be telling the truth. But she'd believed her before and was paying for it now. Her heart hurt. It felt physically bruised, as though she'd been kicked in the chest. Hearing Marina's version of what happened seemed a waste of time, and actually made the pain worse. Angela's name was an acid in her stomach every time she heard it. But no matter what Marina said, Angela was not the problem—Marina was. She wanted to cut to the chase and work out a plan of attack that would prevent Marina from getting into the same situation ever again. That was their only hope.

Since it was a lovely day, they went to the park next to their apartment and sat on a bench in the sun, people watching. They didn't speak much, and didn't talk about the cheating at all, silently agreeing to discuss that particular topic at home.

The wind picked up and Callie shivered against Marina who suggested they go get tacos.

"I didn't bring my wallet."

"My treat." She smiled that seductive smile and Callie found herself echoing it. They walked to one of their favorite restaurants and Callie ordered a frozen margarita, an appetizer and an entree, something she never did when she was paying. It was small recompense for what Marina had put her through, but it was something.

They got home around nine, and Marina started up again. "If you met her you'd be very surprised that I hooked up with her. She's not my type at all."

"I don't want to meet her. Ever. She's not the problem. You and I had the agreement, and you're the one who broke it. I want you to tell me how you're going to make sure you don't do it again."

"It was because of work," Marina insisted for the fifth time. "I thought she might turn against me if I refused."

"You're always going to have a job. What will you do next time?"

Marina's eyes lit up and Callie could almost see an idea pop into her head. "I'm going to steer clear of women. I don't ever want to sleep with a man again, so that should take care of it."

How could Marina be so dense? It wasn't possible to ignore women. What she had to ignore were the first signs of sexual attraction. Everyone felt them. Committed adults put a stop to them and avoided that person. But Marina didn't seem to see that at all. A fog of depression settled on Callie. It was enervating to have to explain something to a woman who had no idea what you were talking about. "I think we've beaten this topic to death. I don't know about you, but I'm worn out. Let's go to bed early. I think we'll both feel better when we get some rest."

When Callie came out of her bathroom, she saw Marina waiting, a bright-eyed look of anticipation on her face. She recognized what that look meant, but lovemaking wasn't going to happen. Marina had a lot of work to do to make her feel safe again. And until she had some confidence that Marina would honor their agreement, she wasn't going to be intimate with her. Not again. But rather than refuse an overture, something she'd never done, she made clear what she needed. Snuggling up to Marina's side she draped both an arm and a leg across her body. "I missed you. I missed having you hold me and feeling your warmth when I wake up in the middle of the night. Can we start there and work our way back into being intimate?"

"Okay," Marina said without hesitation. "Sure. I'll do anything you want to get back to where we were."

Callie tilted her head and kissed Marina, making sure the kiss was devoid of sexual suggestion. "Maybe we can do even better than that."

If they couldn't, there wasn't much point in continuing.

The next afternoon Callie returned a phone call from her dad. "Hi, Dad. Thanks for calling to check up on me."

"I've been worried about you, Chicklet. What's going on?"

"Well, Marina came back from her trip and I guess we're gonna try to start over. She seems very contrite, so we'll see."

"Hmm, you don't sound very upbeat. Are you sure you want to give her another chance?"

"Yeah, I guess so." She paused a moment, then added with a short laugh, "That didn't sound too emphatic, did it."

"No, it didn't." He sounded tentative when he asked, "Is Marina pressuring you?"

"Yeah, I suppose so. But not in a bad way. She's been very remorseful. Much more than I thought she'd be. That's been the key."

"Well, as a guy who's been in her position, I'm glad you're giving her another chance. I'd have given anything to get one."

"I know that," Callie said quietly. "And, even though I know Mom had every right to do what she did, that's been in the back of my mind."

"Now, don't try to compare apples and oranges here. To be honest, what I did was worse."

"Worse? You've gotta be kidding."

"I wish I was. But the way I see it, Marina just stepped out of line. I broke out of line and ran, knowing I could lose everything if I got caught. I think that's a hell of a lot worse."

Callie didn't reply for a few moments. She considered the accuracy of her dad's statement. He had been playing with four lives when he cheated, and the repercussions had sent shock waves that still reverberated. When compared with that, Marina really hadn't done anything very serious. All they had to do was wipe the slate clean and get back to a position of trust. Maybe her dad was right. All Marina had done was have sex with someone she shouldn't have. There were worse things a person could do.

CHAPTER FOUR

MARINA WAS IN Dallas for the entire week, and by the end of it she and Callie were, at least on the surface, back to normal. They still hadn't made love, but Callie knew that Marina would be receptive if she gave her any indication that she was ready.

Callie was on the phone with her friend Pam when Marina walked in the door that night. She stopped mid-sentence when she saw Marina's face, and quickly made an excuse to hang up. "What's wrong? You look like you've seen a ghost." She rushed to get to her quickly.

"I think I did." Marina dropped her briefcase and let Callie ease her coat off. By the time Callie hung it up Marina was sitting on the sofa, leaning forward with her hands hanging loosely between her knees, her lapis lazuli ring perfectly matching the blue slacks she wore. Glancing down she saw that Marina was still wearing her heels, something she never did on the off-white carpet.

"Tell me what's wrong." Callie sat down but didn't touch her, clearly able to read the hands-off message that Marina's affect was transmitting.

"Angela called me when I was driving home."

Callie tensed at the mere mention of the name, but somehow knew this wasn't about Angela.

"She told her girlfriend about what happened and now they're going to break up."

Starting to relax, Callie spent a moment trying to figure out why this was such bad news. Then it hit her. "Are you worried she'll want to be with you again?"

A quick look of supreme annoyance flashed across Marina's features. "That's ridiculous. I'm worried that Angela will blame me. And if she blames me, she's not going to want to have me sitting in the same room when they have their weekly regional managers meeting."

Following the tangent rather than the main point, Callie said, "You'd have to go to Boston every week if you get promoted?"

Clearly more annoyed, Marina got up as though she needed to distance herself from such stupidity. "No. They do the meetings by teleconference. I was referring to the fact that she won't vote in my favor when my promotion comes up. And her vote is worth twice anyone else's. She's the big cheese's favorite." She went to the antique wooden cabinet that she used for a bar. Opening the door, she pulled out a bottle of single malt and poured a dram or two. She stood there, posture erect, looking like she was ready to take over the world. One hand pushed her jacket back to rest on her hip, the other held the glass in a loose grasp, her heavy silver watch dangling from her thin wrist.

Callie found her incredibly attractive when she stood like this. She looked like she was thinking of something complex—and that she was capable of figuring out whatever the problem was. Marina had always been in sales, but her posture often let Callie fantasize that she was in some branch of the military or law enforcement. She loved to imagine her in a crisp uniform, making some life or death decision without showing even a spark of fear.

Marina's gaze was fixed on the middle distance, her eyes slightly narrowed, making them look even more intelligent and cunning. Her golden brown hair sparkled with highlights as the setting sun painted it with light. For the first time all week, Callie felt a spark of sexual interest, but she tamped it down, knowing it was her libido talking. That primal pull that Marina exerted was in full force, but Callie wasn't going to be dragged along with it. Not until she felt safe.

Her instinct was to offer sympathy and hugs, but that never worked with Marina. So she tried to think like Marina would and get to the problem, not the emotion. "What can you do?"

"That's the question, isn't it?"

Callie had obviously shown that she understood the severity of the issue, because Marina walked back to the sofa and sat down. She placed herself into her seat so gracefully that Callie felt her vulva tingle. She fantasized momentarily of taking the Scotch from Marina's hand, putting it on the table and falling on top of her. But, even if she felt safe doing that, Marina would never respond to such an obvious overture. Making the first move was her job alone. Focusing, Callie said, "I'm sure you have some ideas. What are they?"

Marina settled down more deeply into the cushion. She tossed her head from side to side, sending her hair cascading across her shoulder. Just a hint of her perfume floated over to tickle Callie's nose, making her heart beat a little faster. She reminded herself that her vulva didn't control her actions. Desire didn't have to result in sex. A lesson Marina had yet to learn.

Marina set her glass down and ticked off options on her recently manicured fingertips. "One—I can try to convince Angela that she's better off without such a controlling girlfriend."

Callie didn't think that was the best idea, knowing that being opposed to cheating wasn't overly controlling in the real world. But she didn't comment, knowing Marina was on a roll.

"Two—I can try to switch to group sales. They need a regional manager in the Southeast."

She didn't care for that option, either. Marina would want to move to Florida, but she wasn't a fan of heat or humidity.

"Three—I can try to get Angela to let me talk to the girlfriend. I might be able to convince her that it was all my fault."

"Would you really do that?"

Marina gave her a look that ranked in severity between angry parent and sentencing judge. "I'd do anything to make sure my stupidity doesn't ruin my career."

"Let me talk to her."

Marina's head turned quickly, her interest registering in her eyes. "What's your thinking?"

"My thinking is that you're the last person I'd want to hear from if you were cheating with my girlfriend. I'd be much more interested in hearing from someone who was more in my position."

"But you're not in her position. Angela was supposed to be one hundred percent monogamous."

"I assumed that. That *is* the norm, you know."

Marina shrugged, then waved a hand in the air as she often did when she was being dismissive. "It shouldn't be. It doesn't work for hardly anyone."

"That's open for debate," Callie said, not interested in bringing up the oft discussed topic. "I wouldn't lead with that fact. I'd try to get her to tell me how she was feeling and I'd tell her that I was very confident you and Angela won't be seeing each other again."

"That's true, you know. I'm thinking of getting a tattoo on my upper thigh that says 'don't shit where you eat.'" She showed her first smile of the evening.

"Classy." Callie reached over and squeezed her knee.

"I'd use a really nice font. You've showed me how design can make a huge difference in a message."

"If you're going to do it, do it in Latin. I'm sure the Romans had an equivalent expression. So, what do you think of my offer?"

"I'm going to go to the gym and spend an hour on the rowing machine. If I still think it's a good idea when I'm finished, I'll propose it."

"Then I'm going to call Pam and go out for a few drinks."

"I'll pay for a guest pass if you want to go with me." There was an unusual tone in her voice. If Callie hadn't known better, she would have thought that Marina didn't want to be alone.

"You know the only indoor exercise I like is bending my arm."

Marina smiled fondly and tweaked Callie's cheek. "You and your beer."

"I like beer, and I like bars, and I like playing pool. I should have known I was a lesbian years ago." Marina held up her hand and Callie slapped it. Somehow they'd gotten onto the same team. They were working through a problem together. Something that was always empowering. This was what lovers did.

"I'll see you when you get home. Say hi to Pam for me."

"Will do," Callie said, even though she was fairly sure they'd never met.

Saturday morning found Callie rehearsing what she was going to say to Angela's girlfriend, Regan. She'd told Marina the points she wanted to cover, and now they were hashing them out. For a change she bristled at Marina's micromanaging. "You can go to the gym or into your office or go run around the block, but you can't be near me when I call."

"Come on!" Marina leapt to her feet, her face showing her outrage. "I won't interfere."

"I don't think that's a promise you can keep. I won't sound natural if you're listening to me, and I think it's important that I try to make some form of connection with this woman. She won't listen to me if it sounds like I'm reading a list of talking points."

Marina stood there for a moment, looking like she'd explode. But her eyes darted around the room for a few moments, her intelligence showing in their depths. "I'm not happy," she said, "but I'll walk around the block. Just promise to call me the second you hang up."

"I will. Now get going so I can concentrate." That had felt good. She had to take charge more often. Marina could rule the bedroom, but she had to push back in the rest of their lives. Maybe there was a glimmer of hope that she could make lemonade out of these lemons. She waited until the front door opened and closed, then she dialed the number. On the third ring a pleasant, business-like voice answered, "Scituate Inn."

"Hi, I'm looking for Regan Manning."

"Yes?"

"This is Callie Emerson, Marina Bolton's girlfriend. I think Angela mentioned I was going to call?"

There was long silence on the other end, then Callie heard a door close. "Yeah. Hi. This is Regan."

Callie cringed a little when she heard her pronounce her name. She pronounced it with a long *e*. Ree-gan, rather than Ray-gun, as Callie had said it. "Is this a good time to talk?"

"It's not bad. I'm at work, but there aren't many people here this morning. I should have some privacy."

"Just let me know if you need to go and I can call you back at a better time."

"I will."

Now that Callie had the floor she felt tongue-tied. "How've you been?"

After another pause, Regan said, "I've been better. This is the first time anyone's cheated on me."

"That you know of." Callie was amazed that sentence had come out of her mouth. A lot of people believed monogamy was possible, and it didn't seem right to throw reality into their faces.

Regan seemed to share the sentiment. Her voice turned very frosty. "If it happened before I never learned about it."

"That was a stupid thing for me to say. I guess my cynicism about people comes through sometimes."

"I'm not very cynical, and I don't want to be. I need to trust my friends and lovers, and when I can't trust them anymore I don't forgive easily…if at all."

Callie laughed softly. "I used to be like that myself, but I changed. Now I tend to assume that people will screw up, and I'm more likely to forgive them."

"I don't really want to change, thank you."

Callie could hear Regan shuffling papers or moving something around, and was fairly sure she was losing her. She found herself revealing more than she'd planned. Her voice was soft and thoughtful when she said, "I didn't plan on changing, but…over time I realized that most people can't be monogamous. It just made sense to change the rules. If you can't beat 'em…"

It was Regan's turn to talk but there was nothing but silence.. Finally, Regan said, "So you assume your girlfriend will cheat and it's not an issue if she does?"

"No, it's not like that. Marina and I worked out a way to have some freedom. We're lovers. Partners. The other stuff is just sex." She was surprised to hear herself call Marina her partner. That was a term she never used. Were they partners? That sounded awfully—permanent.

Regan's voice was as cold as ice. Each word was crisply enunciated and cut short. "Angela and I don't have an agreement. I'm not interested in that kind of agreement. I'm interested in being with someone who makes a promise and keeps it."

Callie started to talk just as Regan made some of those "I'm finished" kinds of noises. Undaunted, Callie continued, "If that works for both of you, that's great."

"It works for *me*. Obviously Angela's not as committed to the idea as I am."

"Maybe she just made a mistake. I'm not sure what went down between them, and frankly I don't want to know, but I'm confident that Marina doesn't want it to continue."

There was just a glimmer of hesitation when Regan said, "Angela says the same thing." Some of the frost left her voice and Callie could tell that her mind wasn't completely made up.

"I don't want to talk smack about my own girlfriend, but Marina can be pretty persuasive. She said they'd both had too much to drink, and she probably made the first move." That was the exact opposite of what Marina said had happened, but she didn't feel that she was lying by making that conjecture. It was entirely unbelievable that Marina would let someone seduce her if she didn't want to be seduced. Being exploited wasn't in her nature.

Sounding just short of incredulous, Regan said, "It doesn't bother you that your girlfriend screws around like that? Doesn't that just make you some other girl she has sex with?"

How dare she! She didn't have to take this from a stranger. Hotly, she said, "No. That's not how it is. We have an agreement." She took a breath. "Actually, we have a list. You can't have sex with someone if her name isn't on the list."

Regan sounded like she wanted to reach through the phone and punch Callie. "I would have liked to know that Angela's name was on your damn list. Then I could have kicked her out *before* she humiliated me."

"No! No! Angela wasn't on the list. She's exactly the kind of person I never would have allowed Marina to sleep with."

"What the fuck is wrong with Angela?" Regan demanded. Then she muttered a soft, "What in the hell?"

"There's nothing wrong with Angela. But I'd never allow Marina to put somebody on her list who wasn't single or in an open relationship. And people from work are always off limits. That's just stupid."

Regan sounded hurt and very fragile when she tentatively said, "So does it hurt less for you?"

"Yeah, maybe. Oh, I don't know." Her head started to throb. It was hard enough talking to Marina about this. Now she had to tell Regan about it? When Regan didn't say another word she realized she had to suck it up and get to it. "A few years ago my lover did something pretty tame in comparison and it hurt a lot more. I guess I've gotten less sensitive to sexual things. When Marina's with me, she's mine alone and that's worked for us."

"I want Angela to be mine whether I'm watching her or not."

That stung a little, but Callie didn't acknowledge the slight. Their agreement was obviously too out of the norm for most people to understand. "I guess that's the ideal, but it's hard to get. I've decided it's more realistic to allow for some flexibility."

"Yeah, it sounds like that worked out great." Regan's sarcasm was ill disguised.

"Obviously it didn't work out very well this time. But I'm committed to making this work. That's a promise *I* made and having Marina break a promise to me doesn't give me an excuse to break one to her."

Regan was quiet for quite a while. "It was nice of you to call."

"I might not be where you are now, but I was there a few years ago. I really do know what it feels like to have the person you love most break your heart."

Regan sounded like she might be sniffling away tears. "Yeah. Thanks. I've got to go." And with that, she broke the connection.

Callie sat perfectly still for a few seconds, the phone still in her hand. She and Regan had been talking about exactly the same betrayal, but there was a fierceness, a raw hurt that Regan obviously felt. Callie couldn't summon that same degree of outrage, and wondered why this had affected Regan so much more profoundly. Regan was probably younger and hadn't suffered as many blows. Once she'd been through it a few times, it wouldn't hurt nearly as much.

Marina answered her cell phone on the first ring. "What happened?"

"I think you'd better review your other options because the phone call didn't turn out very well."

Anxiety permeated Marina's voice. "Tell me everything."

"Why don't you come upstairs, honey?"

"Don't want to waste time. What happened?"

"It wasn't a horrible conversation, but she didn't seem very willing to give Angela another chance."

"Tell me more! You were on the phone for hours."

"I was on for about four minutes. She didn't seem very interested in talking to me and she seemed really pissed off. Obviously, I don't know her at all, but if I had to bet, I'd bet that she was finished. She said she felt humiliated."

"Over a harmless fuck? What is *wrong* with people?"

Callie didn't comment. To have Marina ask that question indicated a complete lack of understanding of human nature.

CHAPTER FIVE

THE TENSION IN the apartment over the next few days was just short of unbearable. Marina was short-tempered and edgy, and for the first time, Callie felt nothing but relief when Marina had to leave for San Antonio early on Thursday morning.

After Marina kissed her goodbye, Callie gave in to her urges and stayed in bed. She had some phone calls to make and she was working on finishing a book cover for a local publishing company, but she always did better work when she was under the gun. Just having Marina out of the house made her feel better than she had in days, and she found that her libido was just as happy as the rest of her. She spent almost an hour fantasizing about random women while she touched herself from her shoulders to her knees, relishing the sensation of her own body. Afterwards, while she was showering, it occurred to her that she hadn't had one image of Marina in her fantasy film reel. That was odd for her, very odd. Thinking of Marina was always part of pleasuring herself. And when had she ever been glad to get her out of the house? This wasn't good news. If she didn't want Marina at home and she was afraid to have sex with her…there wasn't much left.

At ten o'clock that night Marina called and Callie could tell that she had good news just by the way she said hello. "They're not breaking up!"

"You talked to Angela?"

"Yeah, of course I did. The girlfriend sure isn't going to call me."

"Right. Stupid question. Did Angela say what happened?"

"Not really, and I didn't ask. All she said was that they were going to try to make it work."

"I'm glad. Now maybe you can relax a little bit."

"I'm the one who's glad. I think your phone call made a difference. You're very persuasive when you want to be."

"Maybe she just loves her."

"I hope so, and I hope if they ever do break up it's not because of this. I think I've dodged a bullet."

"Do you…" Callie was afraid to ask the question, but she had to. She had to know. "Do you talk to her much?"

Marina answered very quickly. "No. We have to talk about work, of course, but that's it."

That was a lie. It had to be. She knew just how it had gone. Marina had been subtly persistent, calling Angela several times, never about work. Marina wasn't the kind of person to let the chips fall where they may. And she never let chips fall when she could manipulate them in some way.

Callie went into her office and tried to concentrate on that book cover that was almost due. Thinking about this mess wasn't helping. It just made her doubt Marina more, and that wasn't the direction she wanted to go in.

Callie was in the kitchen making dinner the next night when Marina arrived home from her trip. As soon as she opened the door she called out happily, "Sweetheart? Where are you?"

Callie went to the doorway and gave Marina a frankly puzzled look. "I'm right here."

Without even taking her coat off, Marina dashed across the living room and gathered Callie up in her arms. " I missed you," she said, kissing all over her face.

Callie giggled while pulling away. "That tickles!"

Marina released her and patted her on the butt as she walked away. "Let's go out to dinner and celebrate."

"But I'm making your favorite enchiladas."

"They're just as good the next day. Come on. We'll go someplace really nice. I feel like this is a new beginning."

Callie looked at her and saw the longing in her eyes. She had a very difficult time saying no to Marina under the best of circumstances, but when she could tell that something was truly meaningful to her, it was impossible. She considered her finances and decided that she could delay the scheduled maintenance on her car for another couple of weeks. "You call and get us reservations and I'll get ready." As she passed her, Marina snuck an arm around her waist, held her still and kissed her deeply. Callie tried to respond as she normally would, but it felt forced and she went into their room trying to ignore the dread she felt in the pit of her gut. When one of those forceful kisses didn't make her tingle—something was very wrong.

The next day was rainy and cool, but Marina's parents were in town and she wanted to go meet them and play golf. Callie knew how to play and was, in fact, better at the game than Marina was, but she didn't enjoy playing with the Boltons. The family acted like each shot was vital. Because it seemed more like work than play for her, she opted out. But Marina was so disappointed that she made an offer she knew would please her.

"I think I'll stay home and get your new computer set up. I know you hate doing things like that."

Marina grinned happily. "It's not so much that I hate it as that I'm terrible at it. You're the only techie in this family."

Callie gave her a quick hug. "I hope your clients don't know how little you know about technology."

"I'm a sales person, not a programmer. I have people who can talk tech…thank God." She went into her office and came back with two laptops. "Just take everything from the old one and throw it onto the new one. You can do that, right?"

Callie smiled. "Yeah, I can do that. It'll take some time, but it's not hard. I can work on my own stuff while yours is crunching away."

"Hey, could you put the contacts from my old phone onto the new computer?"

"Sure. Your old phone had a chip, right?"

"Uhm, a chip is…?"

"Let me see it, honey."

Marina went to get it, returning a few moments later. "Sorry I don't pay attention to things like this."

"It's fine. This is my field."

"Are you sure you don't mind?"

"I don't mind a bit. Make sure you dress warmly. They're predicting this might turn to ice."

"Excellent. If the weather's bad enough we'll have the course to ourselves."

"That's one way to look at it," Callie said wryly.

She wasn't a snoop. Callie had quite a few qualities she was less than proud of, but she wasn't a snoop. Hacking into Marina's old phone was something she never would have done before. But she couldn't let go of her suspicions, and having them made staying untenable. She didn't want to know what Angela and Marina talked about. If she'd had the transcripts in front of her she wouldn't have read them. But she was almost certain that Marina was lying about the length of her relationship with Angela and she wanted…needed to know the truth. She actually felt that snooping might help their relationship because if she found out Marina was telling the truth, she could finally let this all go.

She pulled the chip out of the phone and used a device she'd bought years earlier when she was working in IT that let her pull off all the instant messages stored on the phone. Even the ones that had been erased.

It didn't take long to find what she was looking for. She went back almost two years to what looked like the beginnings of their flirtation. Her stomach was sour and there was a bitter taste in her mouth as she read random sentences from those early interactions.

She supposed there were business reasons to text someone's personal phone, but those seemed rare. You texted with a business colleague if you wanted to become her friend, or her lover.

It looked like things stayed at the flirtation stage for a long time, probably six months. But it was clear they had slept together a year and a half ago. A year and a half ago. Right when she'd moved to Dallas. Marina started having an affair…a real affair…not just sex…just after they'd agreed on their rules.

Her heart pounded and she wondered if she might actually pass out. Colors swirled behind her tightly closed eyes, and she bent over putting her head between her knees.

Getting up, she held onto the desk for a few minutes to steady herself, then went into the kitchen and opened a beer. The tiny bubbles tickled her throat, and the sensation of the ice cold liquid distracted her for a few seconds.

She chugged the entire bottle, wishing briefly that she could tolerate Scotch. Once her nerves settled down, she steeled herself to go back into the office and finish her grim task.

She saw quite a few entreaties from Angela begging Marina to be discreet. She also saw a piece of a frantic interaction where Marina was trying to convince Angela that their affair wasn't going to harm her relationship with Regan. Marina had been the one pushing it. This was all coming from her. Lying, cheating, scum Marina.

Her brain was racing. What to do? Leave now and be gone when she got home? Or stay and talk? The mere thought of that made her stomach turn. Putting her mind on hold was what she needed. Getting into project mode, she went about finishing the routine task of transferring information from one computer to the other by rote. It took her a few hours, and she spent much of that time trying to decide what to do, even though she was desperate to stop the mental clamor. She was so confused, so buffeted by images of Marina's lying face that she knew she needed some time before she did anything permanent. Rash decisions were never good ones, so she packed up her computer and a few days worth of clothes, then left a brief note for Marina saying she had to go home to deal with a family matter.

Once she was out of the apartment, Callie felt a little better. The air seemed cooler and fresher, and her head cleared somewhat. While she sat in her car, she used her phone to check prices and availability of flights to Phoenix. Because it was last-minute, prices were very high, but she didn't want to drive for fifteen hours. She made a reservation and hoped she wouldn't be at the airport all night long because of the rain and wind. Nonetheless, the airport was a better place than her home because Marina wasn't at the airport.

CHAPTER SIX

CALLIE WAITED UNTIL she was assured a seat on the last flight of the day to Phoenix before she made a call. She could have chosen her mom or either of her sisters, but she called Terri. They'd known each other for almost twenty years, and there was no one who understood her better, or judged her less. And from where she stood, nothing was more important.

⁂

At midnight, Terri was faithfully waiting at the arrivals level of the Phoenix airport. She reached across the car and flung the door open as Callie approached. As soon as Callie slid into the car, Terri said, "Do you want to talk about it now, or wait until we get home?"

"I guess now," Callie said quietly. "There's a lot I haven't told you."

"I figured as much." Terri gave her a fond smile. "I know you like to keep problems to yourself until you figure them out."

"I do. But I can't figure this one out alone."

⁂

Because of her frequently changing schedule, Terri had settled into being a night owl, so she was wide awake and ready to listen. They went to the first all-night diner they saw, and Callie ordered a burger, hoping that it would sit well in her somersaulting stomach.

While they ate, Callie went through all of the highlights and the lowlights of the past few weeks, appreciating the sympathetic comments Terri made along the way.

"What do you think you're going to do?" Terri asked.

"I don't see that I have any choice." Pushing her coffee cup away, she stacked her fists on the table and rested her head on them. "How can I maintain any sense of self-respect if I let her lie to me over and over like this?"

Terri reached over and gently rubbed Callie's back. "Why is this a deal breaker for you?"

Callie turned her head enough to be able to make eye contact. "Lying and cheating isn't enough?"

"It would be for me, but it surprises me that it is for you."

"I do have a little self-respect left." Callie's cheeks colored and her eyes showed a rare fire.

"That's not what I meant, and you know it. I meant that it makes sense to me that Marina lied. She was just covering her ass and trying to make it sound like less of a big deal than it was. In a way, she was trying to make it easier for you."

Callie sat up and looked at her friend suspiciously. "I've never heard you defend anything that Marina has done."

"I'm not sure I'm defending her now. I'm just surprised that this is what makes you want to throw in the towel. This all seems like it's part and parcel of the same crime; and if you forgive her for the crime this seems like it goes along with it."

"But she lied, Terri."

"She lied by cheating too. To me, that's a much bigger issue. But that's how I look at the world. Monogamy is the only thing that works for me."

Callie smiled at her fondly. "I know two of your former girlfriends who'd agree that's your rule."

"Women are dogs," Terri said, shaking her head. "I don't know why you ever got mixed up with one."

"Men are dogs too. Maybe I should just get a dog." She tossed her head back and ran her fingers through her hair a few times. "I don't think a dog would have me given how I must look."

Terri reached over and pinched her cheek. "You look adorable as always. Now let's get out of here and get some sleep. We can cut Marina up tomorrow."

The next morning, Callie woke and had to spend a few moments figuring out where she was. She turned and saw Terri also just starting to wake up. "Thanks for letting me sleep with you," she said, yawning.

"I didn't want to make you sleep on the couch, and I sure as hell wasn't going to."

"You're a good friend. And as much as I dislike Phoenix, I'm moving back here if Marina and I break up. I like you more than I dislike my hometown."

Terri put her hands behind her head and lay there contemplatively for a few moments. "How do you decide who's on the approved list?"

"You really want to know? You've always expressed a real disinterest in how we set things up."

Turning on her side, Terri gazed at Callie in sober reflection. "I'm interested. I always have been. But you didn't ask me for advice when you were first getting together and I didn't want to pry."

Callie reached across the space that separated them and ruffled Terri's dark hair. "Why do you want to pry now?"

"I don't want to, and if I am, tell me to butt out."

"You're not. I'm just curious why you want to know."

"I think I could understand better if I knew why that skanky slut wouldn't have been on the list."

"I don't think Angela's a skanky slut. If I'm really being honest, it was probably Marina's fault."

Terri turned and lay on her back again. "That's kind of an amazing thing to hear you say." She paused a few seconds then added, "I wish you felt you deserved better."

"Knock it off! I know you care about me, but I'm not with Marina because I'm desperate."

"I didn't..."

"Yes, you did." Callie sat up and poked a finger into Terri's side. "I deserve a great relationship, and it's been great up until now."

"It has? Great?"

Terri looked so unconvinced that she scrambled for examples of how great things had been. When she couldn't think of any immediately, she shifted to what seemed more important. "I'm really into her. I'm not sure why, but I am. She turns me on more than anybody I've ever been with, and having good sex is very important to me." That sounded weak. Terri would never buy it.

But Terri held her hands up in surrender. "Sorry. Sorry. I don't mean to judge you.

Callie softened her hand and absently patted Terri. "It's okay. I can see why you might think I'm settling. But I don't think I am."

Terri smirked. "So tell me how a person who goes ballistic over some pretty minor unfaithfulness with a guy winds up with a woman who refuses to be faithful—while not settling."

Callie flopped onto her back. "It was different when Rob cheated on me. It was much worse, even though what he did wasn't as bad."

"I was there. You were truly brokenhearted."

"Yeah, I was. For a long time."

"It was a very long time. Maybe you should think about why it was so hurtful to have Rob step out of line."

"I have thought about it. All that makes sense is that I trusted him more. I was so much more invested."

"Really?" She peered at Callie curiously. "I thought you were invested in Marina."

"I am. In some ways. But with her it's more…" She knew there was a way to explain this without sounding like a user, but she wasn't sure she had the knack. Where was Marina when she needed her—she could pull it off. "It's more about the possibility of having something deeper. We don't have it yet. Our relationship is really a work in progress."

"But it's been worth it, right?"

"Yeah. Of course. Being with Marina helped me get over Rob. She helped…put things in perspective."

"Like how?"

"I know you don't understand this, but it took some of the pressure off not to have monogamy be the major focus."

"You were very successful." Terri had an angelic look on her face that remained even when Callie pinched her.

"Wise guy."

"Tell me about your perspective. All you've said so far is that you decided not to care when Marina slept around."

"It wasn't like that." Letting out a sigh, Callie said, "We worked everything out ahead of time. After we met she went back to Dallas, but we talked on the phone twice a day. She came to visit a week later and we had a great time in bed. When she showed how much she wanted me, I could forget about Rob looking at those sluts on the internet."

"Damn, Cal, I didn't know it was that bad." She reached over and snuck an arm around Callie and hugged her close. "You should have told me."

Callie shook her head. "I was embarrassed. I felt so unattractive, Terri, and Marina helped a lot. She might have a lot of faults, but having someone want you like she wants me makes me feel sexy. Hot, as a matter of fact."

"You are hot. Damn, you never had trouble finding guys and my lesbian friends were always checking you out." She bumped her with her shoulder. "You know that."

"That's just talk. Marina showed me. She's still all over me when we're together. Somehow that matters to me. A lot."

"Okay. Whatever works. So how did she convince you to have an open relationship?"

"When we were apart she romanced me." An attractive blush slowly climbed up her cheeks. "She's very, very good at getting what she wants, and she wanted me."

"She must be good at it. I've never been more surprised than I was when you told me you weren't going to be monogamous with her."

"Yeah, it must have sounded weird. But I stood up for myself and insisted that we have limits."

"She wanted what? To be able to do anything anytime?"

"Basically. But that was a nonstarter. So we worked out the details over time and we were both pretty happy with it. Well, I was happier with it than she was, but I think she was happy enough."

"So? Do I have to lie here all day to hear the details?"

"Number one was that our relationship had to come first. No exceptions."

"That sounds like a good starting point, but how do you do that?"

"We decided that we'd never sleep with anyone who lived anywhere near Dallas. We were monogamous in the Metroplex."

"Huh. Great for Marina, but not you. You don't go anywhere."

Callie brushed off the comment. "We also agreed that we'd only sleep with people who were either single or in a similar relationship."

"Isn't that hard to find?"

"That's an odd question. There are tons of single women in the world."

"No, no. Women in similar relationships. Are there a lot?"

"I have no idea. I don't know any."

"Huh."

Terri was quiet after making that sole utterance. When it was clear she had no follow-up, Callie continued. "The biggest issue for us, and one that Marina hated the most was that we'd tell each other about someone we were interested in *before* we slept with her."

"Why didn't Marina like that one?"

Callie laughed. "For the obvious reason. In her previous relationship she could sleep with anybody."

"Anybody?"

"Yeah. She and her ex agreed they'd do what they wanted and never talk about it."

"Wow. I can't see why you'd bother being in a relationship if you could just screw anyone you met."

Her patience fraying, Callie said, "There's a difference between sex and love. Marina and I are trying to build a relationship. She just has casual sex once in a while when she's on the road. It doesn't have to affect me at all if I don't let it. I'm in control of my reaction."

It was so hard to put all of it together to make sense of what she did. The familiar pangs of sadness still hurt when she thought of her dad and Rob. "That's something Rob kept telling me, but I was too hurt to listen. My dad said the same thing. I should have listened to both of them. My mom should have given my dad one pass and I should have forgiven Rob. I was stupid. He was a very good guy, and I cut him loose too fast."

"He hurt you, Cal. You said you couldn't trust him anymore."

"I know, but I was harsh. That was the dumb part."

"Rob was a good guy, but it was his fault too. He could have fought for you."

"Yeah. I guess he let me go easily too." She shrugged. "Marina's really trying to convince me to stay, and that matters a lot."

"Sounds like she made sacrifices to get you in the first place."

"She did. She really had to scale back to get me to buy in."

"And up until now you really believed she was being honest?"

"I'd like to believe she's honest about most things."

"Isn't that kinda…hard?"

Laughing at herself, Callie said, "At this point? You have no idea."

"Let's say she usually *is* honest. Why do you think she screwed up?"

"Arghh! I think she did it—purposefully—to improve her chances for a promotion."

"Wow."

"I know…it sounds horrible, but she doesn't pretend to be anyone she's not. She's very honest in that way."

"Then why not tell you the whole truth? Like *before* she slept with her."

"I assume she lied because I wouldn't have agreed. Sleeping with a coworker is dangerous, and Angela was in a committed relationship. That's two strikes."

"But…"

"Marina's not used to hearing 'no.' If she really wants something she's pretty likely to go ahead and take it if she can."

"Even if it hurts you."

Callie had to think about that one for a while. "In my heart, I believe that she was confident I wouldn't get hurt. I believe she does care for me; she's just very, very willful."

"She sounds like a handful."

"Oh, she is, but I knew what I was getting into when I signed on. I have no one to blame but myself."

Terri got up to take a shower and make coffee, while Callie lay in bed and tried to stop the persistent thoughts that rumbled through her brain—the ones that kept asking why she'd put up with Marina for as long as she had. It was bad enough when tendrils of doubt crept in, but to have to enunciate all of her lover's faults to Terri…that had been like a slap in the face.

Marina was manipulative and willful…and deceitful if she had to be. Her needs were primary. Always. Over time Callie had trained herself to be some sort of empath—always testing to see if she could touch her or kiss her or even speak. So why had she stayed? That was the imperative question, and she had to be able to answer it before she went home.

Marina called at nine a.m. on the button. "Are you okay? I've been worried sick about you."

"Yeah, I'm fine. Something came up and I felt like I needed to be in Phoenix for a couple of days. I'm sorry I didn't give you more notice."

"You don't sound right."

"Well, I'm not alone…"

"Call me back as soon as you can. I'm worried about you, honey. Do you want me to come and be with you?"

"No, I'm fine. But it's going to be hard for me to get much free time. I promise I'll call you if I need anything."

"That's the best you can do?"

"Yeah, I'm afraid that's the best I can do. I need a few days at home to sort some things out. I'll call when I can."

"I love you, Callie. Promise you'll call me if you need anything. I'm going to be home until Tuesday and then I have to go to Acapulco until Sunday. Hey, do you want to go with me? My treat? It's a boring conference, but I'll have some free time."

"I don't think so. I'm not sure how long I'm going to have to be here, so I'm afraid to make any plans. But that's very sweet of you to offer."

"I love you," she said with even more feeling. "You sound really tense and I thought a few days by the ocean would make you feel better."

Callie had to force herself not to say what she was thinking. A couple of months ago she would have jumped at the chance. But now she just wanted some distance.

They lay around Terri's apartment for most of the day, drinking coffee and watching TV. They both loved to watch with the sound down and make up dialogue that always had them in stitches. It was the kind of thing that Marina wouldn't have enjoyed a bit, but it was a long-standing tradition for Callie and Terri, and they always had a good time doing it.

They'd just eviscerated a home improvement show, riffing on the idea that the couples who were decorating each other's homes were going to switch wives at the end, when Terri asked, "How'd you feel the first time Marina slept with someone else?"

"Ugh! Don't remind me," Callie moaned, holding onto her stomach as though she were about to vomit. "It was like being beaten with a rubber hose. It took me weeks, maybe months to get over feeling like she was cheating."

"I never knew that. We talk almost every day and I never had a suspicion."

"I wasn't very proud of it."

"You? Why would you be ashamed of that?"

"Not of that. But I wasn't proud of myself for being in an open relationship and then having such a hard time getting comfortable with it. I didn't want anyone to know how I was struggling."

"You totally had me fooled. But…" Terri sat up in her chair, gazing at Callie with a look she couldn't quite decipher. "How'd it feel the first time *you* slept with someone else?"

"I'll…I'll let you know."

"What?" Terri sat up even straighter. "Are you saying you've never done it?"

"Yeah, that's what I'm saying." It was horrible having to admit this.

"Holy God! Why not?"

"'Cause I haven't wanted to."

"Haven't wanted to! You went through this whole negotiating thing. You've got permission!"

"I have to want to, Terri." She smiled and batted her eyes. "I've had offers, but I've never wanted to."

"Is Marina putting pressure on you to stay monogamous?"

"Ha! She's told me to sleep with people in Dallas since I don't travel. She doesn't mind if I sleep with a neighbor or a friend. Heck, she wouldn't care if I slept with her mother. She's fearless. She says jealousy's for people who don't have self-esteem."

"She's probably fearless because she knows you don't want to," Terri grumbled.

"She doesn't know." Callie said softly.

"What?"

"She doesn't know. I lie to her."

"That's very, very strange. You're in an open relationship, but you don't want to use it. She lies about not sleeping with people and you lie the other way. Who's on your list?"

"People I made up. Stop looking at me like that! Don't worry. I've never said I sleep with you."

"I'm not worried… Okay, that's not true. I don't want to be involved. I'd feel weird if she thought we slept together."

"She doesn't think that. But she's told me that I could. She actually wonders why we don't."

"You'd be a big improvement over my last few mistakes, but I've never felt sexual towards you. You're more like a sister."

"Exactly. But Marina doesn't understand that. I don't think she likes people she isn't attracted to."

"That must be exhausting." Terri sat there for a few moments, her gaze traveling past Callie's head. "She must have an ego the size of Texas to urge you to sleep with your close friends."

"She's very, very confident. If I found someone I liked better, she'd be fine. She's never had a lick of trouble finding someone new."

"Obviously. But you've set this up so your girlfriend can sleep around. What's in it for you?"

"Other than embarrassment?"

"Aww, shoot, I don't mean to embarrass you." Terri moved from her chair to sit on the edge of the couch where Callie lay sprawled out. "I just worry about you."

Callie took her hands and hugged them against her body. "I know that." She placed a kiss on Terri's hand. "I can't explain why it's worked, but it has up until now. I like having time alone and she likes traveling. We don't share enough interests to be together all of the time, and to be honest, she wants too much sex too often for me. Having some other women carry the load has been good."

"How much does she want? I know you've got a very good appetite."

"I shouldn't tell you everything," Callie teased, gently biting Terri's hand.

"Too late to back out now. What's she good for?"

"Every day. Sometimes twice. And that'd be okay, but she wants full-out, sheet-drenching sex. No quick orgasms before you fall asleep kinda sex."

"Amazing." Terri shook her head. "How many other women has she been with?"

"That I know of?" she asked dryly. "Not many. Four or five—besides Angela. Every time she does it, though, it calms her down for a while. She needs that escape valve. And so do I."

"Do you think she's a sex addict?"

"Maybe. I'm not sure that's a real addiction, but if it is she probably has it. To get a night off, sometimes I'll stay out late playing pool so I know she'll be asleep when I get home."

Terri leaned on Callie and moaned, "Why do you get too much and I don't get any?"

"I could lend you Marina."

"No, thanks. You're much more my type, sis."

Callie pulled Terri onto her and kissed every part of her face and neck that she could reach, peppering the giggling, thrashing woman with kisses. She finally stopped and they stayed just like that for a few minutes, holding each other as their racing hearts calmed. This was it. Having someone you could be yourself with. Someone you could trust your heart to. Someone you knew would never hurt you on purpose. Someone who loved you as much as you loved yourself. That was something Marina could never do. It was silly to hope for.

Terri had been invited to a big party, and after debating for a while, they decided to go. They got to the house fairly early, just after the snacks had been put out. Terri laughed when Callie moved a pair of chairs just behind the folding table that held cheese and crackers and corn chips and salsa and various dips.

"Come on, don't make me look like I'm the only one eating," Callie insisted, shoving another dip-laden cracker into her mouth.

"You *are* the only one who's eating." Terri took a chip and bit into a corner.

"You're the only person I know who takes six bites to eat a corn chip."

"That's why I'm the same size I was in college." She tilted her head back, looking down her nose. "If you don't stop stuffing your face, you won't be able the wear the jeans you wore yesterday."

"You know I eat when I'm upset."

"I know." Terri leaned over and kissed her on the temple. "I wish you weren't so conflicted."

Callie purposefully piled three pieces of cheese onto a cracker. Biting into it, she shook her head. "I'm not."

"Huh?"

"I'm not conflicted. I'm determined."

"To do what? Other than eat all of their food."

"To kick Marina to the curb."

"What? Why do you seem so calm?"

"I was half out when I found out about Angela. Finding out Marina lied about it almost got me out the door." She leaned over and kissed Terri's cheek. "Talking to you convinced me."

"Me?" Terri pointed to herself. Her face bore every sign of complete amazement. "What did I do? Hell, I told you what she did wasn't so bad."

"I know. But when you asked what had been great about our relationship and I couldn't come up with a list"—she formed her hand into a semblance of a gun and acted like she was firing it against her temple—"that was death."

"Damn." Terri shook her head, still looking dumbfounded. "Are you…upset? Sad? Anything? I can't tell."

"Yeah, sure I'm sad. But I've really been inching out ever since it first happened—so I've had time to get used to it."

"What are you going to do?"

"Damned if I know. I can't decide if I should go home and pack up while she's still gone or make up my mind about things and go later."

Terri took her hand and gave her a pleading look. "Move back here. Please, please, please."

"I might. But I can't think about that now. I've gotta get out first." She started to make up another cracker. "Can we go out for tacos or something? I'm still gonna be hungry. This isn't nearly enough food."

After Terri left for work, Callie took a run around the neighborhood. A day or two at her mother's house seemed like the right move. Then she could make up her mind about whether to move back to Phoenix or stay in Dallas. The thought of a little mothering was too tempting to resist.

Her phone rang as she was heading for the shower. When she saw the text that showed on the display, her heart started to beat wildly. It was Regan. What to tell her? Damn, there were too many decisions to make and too little time to make them.

"Hi Regan."

"How did you know it was me?"

"When I called you, I made a contact entry for you. It's incomplete because I just put down your first name. I didn't know your last."

"It's Manning."

"M...a...n...n...i...n...g?"

"Yeah."

"Okay. I've got it. I like to be organized, if that wasn't obvious." She waited for a couple of seconds to see if Regan would say why she'd called, but she was greeted with silence. "What's up?"

"I...I probably shouldn't have called, but I haven't told anybody about what happened with Angela and I'm..."

"Oh, wow. I don't think I could do that. I just spent seven hundred dollars that I couldn't afford to come visit my best friend and spend a couple of days feeling sorry for myself."

Regan's low, gentle laugh echoed across the miles. "I've been doing that since the day I found out. Feeling sorry for myself, that is. But I haven't talked to anybody."

"No one at all?"

"No. Nobody. I learned my lesson years ago. My first girlfriend and I had a big fight, and I told anyone who'd listen. We made up almost immediately, but a lot of my friends never liked her again."

"So you're keeping this all inside yourself just for Angela's sake?"

She sighed, and the ragged exhaled breath showed Callie that she was on the verge of tears. "I guess."

Sensing that Regan was struggling for control, Callie took up the slack. "I think that's very kind of you. If you told your friends that Angela cheated on you, they'd hate her." She wasn't sure what to say next, but Regan didn't seem anxious to jump in. "Are you and Angela talking about this much?"

"No, not really. Angela's more of a doer than a talker."

"Sounds like Marina. Maybe that's what makes them good salespeople."

"Maybe."

Callie was thinking that Regan wasn't much of a talker either. "I'm usually the one who wants to talk, but not this time. For some reason, I just want to try to forget about it." *Oh, damn. Tell her now or hold off until things are settled.*

"Oh, shit. Here I am bringing up something you don't want to talk —"

Act like nothing's changed. That's not a terrible lie. "No, like I said, I'm in Phoenix visiting my friend Terri. We've been talking about it nonstop. I just don't want to talk to Marina about it. This is the first time I can ever remember her trying to get me to open up about something and me not wanting to."

"How long have you been together?"

"Just over a year. No, wait, a year and a half. How about you?"

"We had our third anniversary in September. I thought it was supposed to take seven years to get the urge to cheat."

"That must be the average," Callie said, chuckling at Regan's dry humor. "Probably takes some people fourteen years, and some jerks cheat on their honeymoons." *Jerks like Marina.*

"I guess it could be worse, huh? I'm sure this is Angela's first time."

"I wish it hadn't ever happened. And I'm sorry my girlfriend was involved. That makes me feel responsible somehow."

"No more than I am. I just don't know what I'm supposed to do now. Do you know what I mean?"

"I know exactly what you mean. I thought I'd leave immediately, but I hung on like I was waiting for something else to happen. Good or bad. Just something." *Like finding out Marina's been with your girlfriend since we got together.*

"You know, that's how it feels for me too. Like I need another piece of information."

"Yeah, that's it. Marina's been really nice, but that hasn't helped. She actually offered to take me to Acapulco this weekend and I refused. This the first time she ever offered to pay for me to go anywhere cool, but I didn't want to be with her."

Regan's voice grew even softer. "Angela's coming home from Acapulco tonight."

"You know, I tried not to think about that, but it makes sense she'd be at a national sales conference. I'm surprised that Marina wanted me to go."

"Angela offered to take me, too. Do you think they both wanted some protection?"

"Maybe." Even though it was like pulling teeth, she liked talking to this woman. It was nice to have someone who really understood how it felt. The important thing was making Regan aware of Marina's history so she could protect herself. "Uhm…I'm not sure how to do this elegantly, but you should be using protection."

"Protection? What kinda protection?"

"Uhm…protection from STDs. Marina claims she's always practiced safe sex, but I can't guarantee that's true."

"Oh, fuck." She took in an audible breath. "Have you done that?"

"We haven't had sex since this happened, but we always have. She's ready to get back to business, but I guess I've been too hurt. I tell her the vibes are off."

"There aren't any vibes at all in our house."

"That makes sense. She has to regain your trust."

"No, that's not it. Our troubles go back a long way."

"But you've only been together for three years."

"Yeah, I know. I think part of the reason Angela cheated was because of our problems. And that sucks," she said emphatically.

"Wanna talk about it?

She waited a beat. "Aren't we?"

Even though Callie couldn't see her, she was sure Regan was smiling. Her voice had changed just a little bit, gotten a little lighter. "Yes, I guess we are. Do you want to add anything? Or should I just guess?"

"You can probably guess and hit it right on the head. It's the all-too-common, lesbian bed death."

"I don't know a lot about that, but three years sounds awfully fast for death."

"Try less than one year," Regan said, clearly disgusted. "And the thing that makes me the maddest is that she's been telling me there's nothing wrong. It's always because she's tired or she has to go on a trip or she just got back from a trip or she has PMS or somebody next door has PMS, or someone down the block just got back from a trip…"

"Uhm, if this isn't too rude, why are you still with her?"

"Because I made a promise to her. I didn't want another casual girlfriend. I wanted somebody to build a life with, and I thought Angela was that woman. There are so many things about her I respect and admire, but when it comes to sex, she seems completely incapable of discussing it and working through our problems."

"You know, Marina's a bit like that too, but about other things. I guess I'm lucky that we get along really well sexually."

"You are, but I think every couple has something that doesn't work. I was very willing to hang in and work this out. But having Angela cheat on me made me doubt everything I believed about her." She took a big breath and once again it sounded ragged. "She broke my heart, and I don't know how it'll ever heal."

"Oh, Regan, I feel so bad for you. I wish I could help you heal faster."

"I'm sorry I'm such an emotional mess. I'm not sleeping, and when I do fall asleep, I wake up with nightmares. I don't normally cry much, but I guess being exhausted makes me more emotional."

"Anybody would cry from this."

"Do you?"

"Uhm…to be honest…not a lot. Maybe that's something to think about, huh?"

"It might be. I don't know how you normally handle things."

"I can get pretty emotional. I've tried to figure out why this hasn't impacted me the way it has you, but I've struck out."

"Well, having your agreement probably makes it less of a shock." Callie didn't respond immediately and Regan quickly said, "I hope that didn't sound judgmental. I can't imagine being in an open relationship, but it's not fair of me to think that being cheated on isn't painful no matter how it comes about."

"Thanks. What you said did hurt a little bit."

"See? That's what adults do. They apologize when they say or do something hurtful, and then they get over it. How do I make Angela be like me?" She laughed again, clearly teasing.

"I don't want Marina to be like me, luckily. Pigs will fly before that would happen.

"Well, I'm not sure how long I'm going to be able to hang in, but I don't think I'm ready to give up yet."

"I don't know what your schedule's usually like, but I work from home, and I can make time to talk to you any time you feel like it. Promise me you'll call."

"Thanks, Callie. I will. It's helped a lot to talk to you."

"I'm being honest, Regan. Call anytime."

Callie thought she'd heard her sniffle one last time when she said, "I will."

CHAPTER SEVEN

CALLIE TOOK HER time getting her bag packed, planning on easing into her mother's orbit. They got along great for short time periods, but with tensions as high as they were, it might be risky. But emotional comfort won out, and she called a cab to take her across town.

On the way, she thought about her father's cheating as she almost always did when she was at the family home. Given how young she'd been, it had taken a while—three or four years—to finally understand what her father had done. Gretchen had helped out with that. She'd not only explained what sex was, she'd made it clear that's what Dad had done with the woman from his office. That accounted for weeks and weeks of nightmares. Thinking of Dad putting his penis into a spot she didn't know women had was a major freak out. But it had slowly started to make sense why Mom was so upset. That seemed like something you'd have to do with someone you were married to. It also seemed gross beyond belief.

What didn't make sense over the years was Mom allowing the betrayal to color every part of her life. Being bitter was at least partially a choice. No one liked being with a depressed, angry woman. That would not happen to her. Marina was not going to leave a scar. A bad scrape, maybe. But that would heal.

Pulling up in front of the house, she breathed a sigh of relief noticing her mother's little gray car was gone. She went up to the door, and paused to look around. She hadn't been home since she left for Dallas and things had changed. The neighborhood had gotten a little more upscale. Some of the younger homeowners had done the intelligent thing and planted desert friendly plants in their small yards. But Callie's mom, Patricia, still had a lawn and a pair of orange trees fighting for every drop of water they could get.

Standing there in front of the only home they'd ever had made everything clear—she could never come back. She'd worked hard in the past year and a half to build a graphic design business, and even though much of it wasn't local, some of it was, and she knew she'd been hired because of her proximity.

Plus, she'd made a nice group of friends in Dallas. Terri was, without question, her closest friend, but with her schedule, she wasn't available very often. Callie considered that she probably talked to her more from Dallas than she had when she lived locally. Plus, as much she loved her mother, and her sisters, they were best when taken in small doses. Staying home just long enough to get her bearings seemed like the best idea.

Callie used the key that she'd kept, opening the door to the remarkably evocative smells of her youth. It brought back so many memories, both good and bad, that just being in the building made her tired. She went into the guest room, Gretchen's old room, stripped off her clothes, and crawled into the single bed. The mattress was probably thirty years old, but it felt strangely comforting to let the sheets, worn smooth from use and age, caress her body and, to some extent, her psyche.

At three o'clock she called her mom at work and give her a little while to digest the news. "Hi mom, it's Callie."

"What's wrong?"

Slightly annoyed that she couldn't ever talk to her mother without her assuming something cataclysmic had happened, she said, "Nothing. Well, I guess that's not true. Marina and I are breaking up and I wanted to get away for a while."

"Come home!" It was more a demand than an offer, but Callie was glad to get it.

"I am home. I got here a little while ago. Want me to make dinner?"

"No, of course not. I'll make dinner. Now take a nap or go for a walk or something. I'll be home soon and you can tell me all about it."

Even though she knew she should insist on doing something productive, Callie was quite pleased to get a little maternal pampering. She knew she was in desperate need of it, so she decided to relax and enjoy it.

Surprisingly, Patricia showed up with pizza. She hustled in through the side door, carrying her purse, a briefcase and a big box that she was trying to keep horizontal.

Callie heard her and dashed into the kitchen, taking the box from her hands. As she put it down on the table, her mother's arms were around her and, unexpectedly, she started to cry, something she couldn't recall doing in front of her mother in her adult life.

"Oh, my poor girl. Tell me what happened."

She gently pulled away and scanned the kitchen for a box of Kleenex which she found on the counter. She took a few and blew her nose. "Why don't you go change clothes and I'll get dinner ready." Patricia looked like she wanted to argue, but she gave her daughter a quick kiss and went towards the bedroom.

By the time Patricia returned, Callie had set out plates and napkins and utensils and there were two pieces of pizza on each plate. "This looks great, Mom."

"Emily told me about this place and it's so good I find myself stopping there at least once a week on the way home. I knew you'd like it too."

"That was nice of you. Pizza is comfort food for me." She took a bite and smiled in satisfaction. "This is fantastic. This alone was worth the trip."

The pleasant atmosphere lasted for just another few seconds. "Marina didn't cheat on you, did she?"

Callie had sworn she was not going to get into details, but the look on her face must have given her away.

Patricia slapped her hand onto the table in outrage. "A woman! A woman did this to you! How can that be?"

"Women are jerks too, Mom."

"Oh, Callie, I was so happy when you told me you'd fallen in love with a woman. I was sure a woman would be able to keep it in her pants."

"Marina couldn't."

"Then good riddance! Thank God you found out before you had children."

"We didn't even share a checking account. We were a long way from having children."

"Well, I'm glad to see you had the sense to leave. I just can't believe a woman did this to you," she muttered, looking completely perplexed. "But I'm proud of you for throwing her out."

"I threw myself out. It's her apartment."

"Nonetheless"—Patricia looked into her eyes—"I know how hard it is to break up with someone you love. It takes a lot of guts to have a moral code you stick to, even when it's hard." She took Callie's hand in hers and chafed it lovingly. "It was hard, wasn't it, baby?"

"Yes." Callie broke down in tears, ashamed that she'd given Marina so many chances, but a little glimmer of pride burned in her chest at having finally stood up for herself.

She could hold out for only three days. Her mom was solicitous and sympathetic, but thinking about Marina and their unfinished business kept her awake at night. She finally made a reservation and went back to Dallas, getting there while Marina was at work.

Even though it was expensive, she went to a packing supplies place and bought proper boxes for her things. It was somehow less humiliating than cadging them from the grocery store. She'd lost track of time and started when she heard Marina's key in the door. Her heart was racing and her stomach turned when Marina burst into the room, arms extended. "I've missed you!"

Callie blocked her hug with her forearms. Marina almost stumbled, catching herself by sticking an arm out and using the wall for support. "Why'd you do that?" She looked hurt. Very hurt.

"I did that because I know the truth about Angela." Again, her stomach threatened a revolt. "I know you've been with her almost since we got together."

Marina blanched, and that alone made Callie feel empowered. Now she'd know how it felt to be kicked with no warning.

Marina backed up and slowly kicked off her heels, then removed her jacket. She looked strangely contemplative, thoughtful. When she turned back, she swallowed noticeably. "Okay. I can't argue with the truth. How did you find out?"

"Immaterial. It's the truth and you just admitted it." She grabbed another box and put her printer in it, wadding up newsprint to cushion it.

Marina extended a hand, but Callie swatted it away. "It's over. You don't get to touch me anymore."

"Oh, Callie. Come on." She sat down on the desk chair, her legs spread apart in a very ungainly, uncharacteristic way. She looked nothing like a powerful businesswoman today. "Give me a chance."

"I did. I gave you a chance when I first learned about her. If you'd told me the truth then…"

"Shit." She leaned over and rested her head on her folded arms.

She looked so defeated, Callie felt a momentary pull on her heartstrings, but she fought that off. "Yeah. That's just what I said when I found out."

"But look at the context. That's what matters." She swiveled out to the side and put her arms on her thighs, gazing at Callie with new determination.

"Nonsense. There's no context for lying."

"Sure there is. This was just about business. If you hadn't found out this would never have come up." Confidence radiated from her face. "Was I less interested in you because of her? No! Did you ever want to have sex and I turned you down? Of course not. I was always there for you when I was home. How does what I did away from home affect you?"

Continuing to slap tape onto the next box, Callie scoffed, "Stupid question. Really stupid."

"It's not!"

She stopped and stared at her. "It is, Marina. Lying is bad for relationships. Especially when the lies started before I'd unpacked. How could you do that?" *Don't cry. Don't you dare cry. She doesn't deserve your tears.*

"Here's the context." Her voice had taken on the slow, calm manner she had when she'd practiced a client presentation. Clear, concise and full of shit. "We were at some offsite conference, and we'd both had too much to drink. We were in…" She appeared to think for a few seconds. "Las Vegas. Of course, it was Las Vegas. We'd been out with some vendors, and they took us to see a show. They were mortified when the show had a dozen mostly naked women in it and kept apologizing. On the way back to our rooms, Angela let something slip about how hot the women were. I took a chance and said none of them were my type." She smiled in memory, the simple act making Callie want to bean her. "I said I preferred a woman in a great fitting suit."

"Which Angela was wearing."

"Yeah, of course."

Of course. Like you'd ever give a compliment that didn't buy you something.

"So she admitted she was gay and we…you know." Marina almost looked contrite.

"That's all it took," Callie said flatly. "Just a willing lesbian."

"No, not at all. I'd been interested in her for over a year. I just didn't think it was smart to start something up with someone who was farther up the chain. She made it feel safe."

It was a guess, but it was probably right. It could be sold with conviction. "You and I were already together. Didn't that enter into your thought process?"

"Sure. Of course it did."

What a scummy excuse for a girlfriend. What had I been smoking to put up with this? Am I blind in every area of my life? "Tell me how. I dare you."

"Look." Marina stood up and started pacing, hand on hip. "I figured she was kinda…grandfathered in. I'd been interested in her long before I even met you. And, frankly, I thought it could help my career. When I get promoted to vice president, it will be great for us, Callie. I'll be making serious money."

"Money?" Her cheeks felt scalding hot. "How does your money affect me?"

"Well, once I start making serious money, I can pay for more things. I asked you to come to Acapulco. I was gonna pay for the whole thing."

"Right." She went back to her box-building.

"I would have been more generous. I really would have."

"Doesn't matter."

"Yes, it does." She plunked down on the floor right beside the new box. "We've been together long enough that I feel more secure with you. More like this is permanent."

"I don't feel that way." She whipped the box away and moved it to her other side. "I'm packing my things and taking off."

"Come on." Marina got to her knees and scrambled around Callie. "Don't shut me out. Listen to me."

"You're free to talk. No one's stopping you."

"After we slept together I realized it was a mistake."

"Nice timing. So you kept at it for eighteen months to make it right?"

"No. Once we did it, I had to let her decide when to end it." She made a face. "She sucked in bed. She said her girlfriend was the one who wasn't any good, but I think it was her."

She could be killed, dismembered and packed in the new boxes. No one would miss her. The thought made a spark of pleasure roll down Callie's back. She took a long breath, trying to keep her voice calm. "I don't want to hear how she justified it. That's irrelevant."

"No, it's not. She was starved for sex. She said her girlfriend was a complete dud and that she didn't get off on her at all. But she wanted to stay because she loved her in every other way." She sat back on her heels, blinking. "Why you'd want to stay with someone who wasn't good in bed is beyond me, but that's what she said. So she wanted to keep me around to blow off some steam. That's why I had to keep doing it. I swear, I didn't like it!"

Callie sat down so they were eye to eye. "The fact that you don't understand why that makes you a user is part of the problem." With the flat of her hand she smacked Marina's temple. "Your head is empty of morals!"

"It is not." She scooted back, just out of Callie's reach. She was almost sulking. "You're the one who tried to get me to agree to things that made no sense."

"Like honesty and being true to your word?"

"No. I tried to be honest. I told you how hard it would be for me to get permission before I had sex with someone. You were warned."

"And you told me you'd do it."

"I tried. It just wasn't possible. What was I supposed to do? Meet a woman at O'Hare and tell her I had to call home before I could go to her hotel? That's ridiculous."

"How many others?" There had clearly been others. But acting upset about it would make her clam up.

"Not that many." Marina had that look on her face. The I'm-lying look. It was always the same. Too earnest. Too sincere.

"So you lied since the first day and haven't stopped."

"It's not a lie if it doesn't hurt anyone. Being honest was the problem. Hiding it let me have what I wanted and you have what you wanted—some control over my libido."

"Yeah, that was some control."

"You wanted security. Lying gave that to you." She gazed up at Callie with what looked like complete confidence in her claim.

"You're a pathological liar, and I regret the day we met."

Marina started crawling across the floor on her knees again. "Please don't say that."

Callie got up and stuck her foot into Marina's chest, stopping her in her tracks. "Keep your distance. We're done. Finished. Forever. You can bank on *my* promises, and that's one I'll never renege on."

CHAPTER EIGHT

TEMPORARILY ENSCONCED AT her friend Pam's house, Callie waited a couple of days to call Regan. Telling her the whole truth wasn't an option. If it was true that Angela had learned her lesson, Regan's finding out about the duration of the affair would screw things up. Regan was taking things slowly, being very careful not to forgive too easily. She'd find out soon enough if Angela was as full of it as Marina was.

Regan was just getting home when Callie reached her. "Hi, it's Callie."

"Hey, how are you?" She sounded a little better. A little lighter.

"I'm pretty good. I wanted to tell you something."

The sound of a chair scraping across a floor echoed in the background. "What is it?"

"I…decided to break up with Marina."

"Oh, Callie, I'm sorry." After a beat she asked sharply, "Did something else happen?"

She had to give her something. But she had to focus on Marina. "Yes, I found out that Marina's been cheating with other women too.

But the worst thing is that she honestly doesn't see that what she did was hurtful. That's more than I could take."

"God." Regan took in an audible breath. "I really feel bad for you. That must hurt so bad."

Her voice was so full of compassion that Callie almost started crying. It was so soothing to have another woman get it—in every way. "Yeah, it really does. It makes me feel foolish, which isn't any party either."

"You're not foolish. You trusted someone who didn't deserve your trust. She's the bad guy in this. Being trusting is a good thing."

"Maybe. I'll have to think about that. Getting burned two times in a row might make me demand a weekly lie detector test."

"Don't let it affect how you feel about yourself. This was Marina's fault. She's the one who should be ashamed of herself."

"Don't bother telling her that. You'd be wasting your breath."

Over the next couple of weeks, Callie and Regan chatted nearly every day. Regan was solicitous and very gentle, always willing to listen. They'd gotten to the point where they were talking about other facets of their lives, but the betrayal kept coming up.

"Did you know that Marina is coming to Boston this week?" Regan asked one afternoon.

"No. I had no idea. How'd you find out?"

"I looked at Angela's calendar. She keeps it on the computer in her office and I've started to check it. It said there's a general sales manager's meeting starting tomorrow. I don't like spying, but she's made me doubt everything she tells me."

"You'll get over that. I'm sure of it."

"I'm not."

"That's a pretty dramatic statement. I haven't heard you that adamant since the first time we talked. Are you gonna give me a little more?"

"It's finally gotten clear in my head. I don't trust her anymore. I've started to assume that everything she tells me is a lie, and that's killing me. "

"I understand. I really do. I'm right there with you."

"I wish I could believe that it was just one slip-up. If I was sure they'd only been together that one time…"

"You think that—" Callie caught the incredulity in her voice and tried to back pedal. "You think that would help?" she finished weakly.

"How many times was it?"

Regan's voice was so firm and demanding that Callie didn't even consider lying. "It was more than once. I thought…I thought you knew that."

"Tell me everything you know."

"Look, I could tell you what Marina said, but she lies about everything. I don't want to screw things up for you. Ask Angela. She's the one who matters."

"Tell me!"

"They were together more than once. I know that's true. Other than that…I'm not sure what to believe."

"That's it," she said briskly. "It's over. I can't deal with this another minute."

"Wait. Wait. Don't jump off a cliff because of that. Angela was probably afraid to tell you. She should have been afraid, right?"

"Yes!"

"She was probably trying to hold onto you, Regan. Making it sound like a one-time thing helped."

"Then how in the hell am I ever supposed to believe her again?" She let out a long breath and said, "I'm going to follow her tomorrow."

"Follow her? You can't do that!"

"Yes, I can. I'm going to figure out a way to tell if they're still doing it."

"But how will you know? They have to see each other for business."

"True. But if they see each other for anything other than business, I'll have my answer, and I can walk away from this without second-guessing myself."

"I don't know how you're going to do this, but I'll help in any way I can."

"I know you will. I'll figure out how to give her enough rope to hang herself with. If she's still standing tomorrow night, I'll give her more time. If not—she's dead to me."

Relief flooded over Callie. Regan was clearly no sucker. She couldn't afford to be when she was mixed up with liars like Marina, and it had become more and more obvious that Angela was just as bad.

The next day Callie couldn't get a moment's work done. She was tempted to fly to Boston just to be there for Regan, but she couldn't afford the expense of a last-minute airfare. She called in the morning

"Regan, do you have a friend who could be with you tonight?"

"Yeah. Sure. But I'd rather be alone."

The thought of Regan sitting there alone, waiting to know if she was being betrayed was almost too much to stand. She wanted to support her in any way she needed. They were sisters in some strange way, and she hated the thought of her sister struggling through this alone.

"Are you sure I can't talk you out of your plans? You could come down here the next time Angela has to be in Dallas. That would be the same, right?"

"No. I've made up my mind, and everyone knows I'm the hardheaded one of the family."

"Everyone knows I'm the one who hates turmoil."

"You don't have to be in on this. Really, you don't."

"Yes, I do. I have to be there for you. That's more important than my need to keep everything calm."

~

When Callie's phone rang later that night, she jumped as though she'd been stung. She was wearing her earphones, so all she had to do was press a switch to hear Regan's voice.

"I don't think I'd be very good at police work."

Even though she was tense, Callie found herself smiling. "Where are you?"

"I'm at a coffee shop across the street from the restaurant. I actually went inside and asked for the group from Cambridge Software, and some guy tried to lead me there. I'm sure they thought I was crazy when I said I was just checking."

"What are you going to do? Just sit there?"

"Well, I could go wait in the lobby of the hotel. It's just down the street from the restaurant."

"Which hotel?"

"The York. That's where Cambridge puts everyone up."

"Not Marina. She only stays at the Sheffield. She says it's for the points, but it's probably so she can have a parade of women striding through the lobby and not have any co-workers know."

"Not what I wanted to hear tonight," Regan said softly.

"Damn! I'm sorry. I'm making things worse, aren't I."

"You're not. It's really helping to have you to talk to. Can you look up the Sheffield? I don't know the address."

"Yeah, of course." As she searched she asked, "Aren't you afraid of being spotted in the hotel?"

Quietly, Regan said, "Marina doesn't know what I look like."

Letting out a breath, Callie said, "Right. Right. But you don't know what she looks like either."

"Yes, I do. I googled her. Plus, there's a picture of her on the company website. She's pretty."

"Okay—so you know what she looks like and when she goes into the hotel alone, I hope you can go home and try to make up with Angela."

"I hope so too. I really do. If Marina goes into that hotel alone I'm going to wipe this from my mind and throw myself into making a fresh start with Angela." She paused for a moment. "After I tell her I know she was lying about how many times they were together. A relationship has to be based on trust. I'll find out the truth or it's a waste of my time."

Callie had to wait almost two hours to hear from Regan again. She spent the time trying to do some work but hadn't been able to concentrate for ten minutes straight. Even though it was dark out, she was considering going for a run when the phone rang. She pressed the switch and knew, without a word being spoken, that something very bad had happened. "Regan? Are you there?"

"Yes." Harsh, ragged breaths filled the line. It sounded like she was on the verge of sobbing. "They went into the hotel together, and I decided to give them a few minutes just in case they were exchanging files or documents or whatever the fuck they do."

With her heart thudding in her chest, Callie asked, "How long ago was that?"

"Thirty or forty minutes. I don't know what to do. Do I go up there? Do I accost her and make a scene in the lobby when she comes back down? Do I go home?"

She sounded so remarkably sad, so disconsolate, that Callie desperately wanted to be there for her. She wished she could magically appear in Boston and hug Regan so she knew she had a friend—

someone she could trust who knew how it felt. "What do you think would make you feel better?"

"I'd like to go home…to my parents' home. I want to tell my mom what happened and have her make it all go away."

"How far is that?"

"I don't know," she said, sounding confused. "Maybe a half hour? But…" She took in a shaky breath. "My mom's in Florida now. I forgot."

"Do you know anyone who lives closer? Anyone you trust?"

"My sister is about ten minutes away."

"Do you think she's home?"

"Probably. Or she's just getting home. She usually leaves work by eleven."

"Think about it for a minute. Will she listen to you? Will she be on your side?"

Regan barked out a short laugh. "She acts like she likes Angela, but she doesn't. She'd like nothing more than for me to break up with her."

"She sounds like the right person to be with. Call her before you go, so you don't waste a trip, and don't leave before you're sure you can drive safely." A thought occurred to her and she added, "Take a cab. I'm worried enough about you as it is."

"Thanks," Regan said, sounding a little more in control. "I just don't want to see her."

"Then get out of there. Go to the hotel bar or to another place nearby. Don't put yourself in a position you don't want to be in." She could hear Regan moving around, then she heard some street noise.

"I'm going to go to my car, if I don't freeze to death first. Then I can call my sister and make some plans."

"Okay. It sounds like you have things under control. But promise to call me when you get where you're going. I'm worried about you."

Regan's footsteps echoed noisily and Callie could tell she was in a parking garage. She heard a car door open and when it closed the background noise was greatly reduced.

"Thanks. I'm not thinking clearly."

"That makes perfect sense. Don't forget to call me back."

"I won't. Thanks for being there for me. I could tell how tense this whole thing made you."

"You'd do the same for me." That was undeniable. You could rely on people with morals.

CHAPTER NINE

DURING REGAN'S MOVE back to her parents' house and the difficult weeks that followed, she called Callie almost daily for support.

"My mom and dad are in town for my nephew's birthday, and they're making noises about having me committed," Regan said one afternoon.

"Committed? Are you joking?"

"Yeah. Kinda. But they're both hovering over me so bad that I'm about to lose my mind. Then they'll really have reason to have me locked up."

"Doesn't sound like fun in the Manning house. It must be hard on your parents too."

"Yeah, it probably is. But my mom knows I can't take much supervision. We have a long history," she added, chuckling.

"So you're still really sad?"

"Yeah. Moody, too. And the smallest thing makes me cry…at work! I've never done that. That's what makes them think I'm bonkers."

"Are they pissed at Angela? My mom wants to have Marina neutered."

"Nah. I didn't tell them why we broke up. I don't want them to dislike her." She sighed. "It took me so-o-o long to get everyone to even act like they liked her. All for nothin'."

"You've mentioned something like that before. Why's she so hard to like?"

"She's not. She's actually really charming. But she's a lot older than I am."

"Really? Hey! I have no idea how old you are. Or how old Angela is, for that matter."

"I was twenty-seven when we got together and she'd just turned forty."

"Ooo, my mom would have been suspicious of that too. Was your age difference a problem?"

"Not for us."

"Really? I'd think it would be hard to combine friends."

"We didn't do much of that. We made new friends from our neighborhood. We live…lived on a really nice block in Cambridge. We had barbecues and Christmas parties and all sorts of things. I'm gonna miss those guys," she said, sniffling.

"You can still see them."

"Nah. Wouldn't work. It was a neighborhood thing. Usually pretty extemporaneous, you know? You'd see someone out and you'd ask them over for a beer. That kinda stuff. We babysat a lot and walked dogs when our neighbors were on vacation."

"Sounds nice," Callie said wistfully.

"It was. We had a great house."

"We had a great apartment. High floor, great views, nice pool. We were right in the middle of all of the action in Dallas. I could go running in a park that was really close."

"I could run along the Charles."

"You run?"

"Yeah. I have since high school."

"Me, too. I ran cross-country."

"I ran the four hundred and the eight hundred when the coach was desperate."

"Oh, I bet you were great."

"You'd lose that bet," Regan said. "I was only decent, but I loved being on a team."

"I always wanted to run cross-country in an area like you live in... you know, where they have hills and streams and forests. We usually ran on flat golf courses."

"Really? I don't know much about the West. I've never been further west than New York."

"You're not missing a thing in my humble opinion. Phoenix is a good place to generate solar energy. Other than that..."

"I like where I am. But I can't afford to stay in Cambridge by myself, so I've got to look for a place. I used to complain a little about driving to Scituate every morning, but I should have kept my big mouth shut."

"Is Cambridge nice?"

Regan sounded like she was going to cry again. "It was perfect. Something about it was perfect for me. It was so vibrant and alive. Having all of the students around probably helped. But it's got such great history too. You'd love it."

"I've never been east of New York, but I love history."

"What is it with New York? Why stop there?"

"The buildings are so tall you can't get over them. At least they looked tall to me when I was there. I was just a kid though, so everything might actually be five or six stories."

Chuckling, Regan said, "Why were you in New York?"

"My dad took me on a business trip with him when I was young. My sisters were so jealous. It was wonderful."

"You have sisters? So do I. I'm the middle of three."

"No kidding? So am I. That's pretty funny. Do you have brothers, too?"

"No, just girls. You?"

"Us too. That's quite a coincidence, isn't it?"

"Yeah, it is."

Callie's laugh had an evil edge to it. "Don't you sometimes wish you were an only child?"

Regan laughed as well. "Not very often now, but all the time when I was little. Are you and your sisters close?"

"Yeah. They both live in Phoenix, so I don't see them very often. How about you?"

"I see mine more than I'd like to some days. We all work together."

"Oh, my God! We couldn't do that in a million years."

Regan laughed. "Sure you could. You just have to get into the habit early on. My parents have owned a restaurant since we were born, and we always were either hanging out or working. It seems completely natural now. I can't imagine working with strangers."

"That's really cool. What kind of restaurant is it?"

"It's actually a restaurant and a banquet hall. Most of our business is from weddings. The restaurant side is small; we only seat thirty-two. But we can accommodate up to two hundred fifty for a party."

"Do you have a website?"

"Sure. It's not great, though. I should make it a lot better, but I can't do it myself, and I haven't taken the time to find anyone to help."

"I know this isn't the ideal way to find business contacts, but you found me."

"You do websites?"

"Yeah. I'm a graphic artist now, but I started out as a programmer. I've been designing almost exclusively, but I can still throw code with the best of them."

"We'll have to talk about that. But I should get back to work now. Whatever work I'm allowed to do. My mother's basically taken over my job until I'm 'myself,' whatever that is."

"I've been pretty productive. I feel better when I get into my work and really get lost in it."

"Are you comfortable staying with your friend?"

"Yeah, I am. Pam's a sweetheart. She's even suggested we alternate nights on the sofa. But I can't take advantage of her any more than I already am."

"Hey, my mom keeps telling me to take some time off. I think I might."

"You can come visit me. I'm sure Pam would love to have another person on her couch. There's a little space the cats haven't claimed."

"Sounds nice, but I've been dreaming about going somewhere warm. It was nine degrees this morning and we've got this dirty snow everywhere that looks disgusting after the dogs pee on it."

"Gosh, Boston does sound nice."

"It is. Trust me on that. But doesn't the Bahamas have a nice ring to it?"

"Hell to the yes! But I couldn't manage it right now. I'm going to have to find an apartment and—"

"My treat. I don't want to go alone, so you'd be doing me a favor."

"Regan! That's ridiculous! I can't let you pay for me."

"Sure you can. I use a credit card for every possible business purchase, so I get zillions of miles. I get a voucher every month or so to fly anywhere our regional discount carrier goes. We all use them whenever we fly, but we've got a couple that are going to expire soon. So the airfare wouldn't cost me a thing."

"The hotel would!"

"Yeah, it would, but no more than it would if I went alone."

"They're a fairly pale green. But a lot of people say they look blue depending on what I'm wearing."

"Wear something that makes them look green so my job's easier."

"Now tell me what you look like."

"Ooo, wish I could but my sister and her kids just came over. It's gonna be a riot in here when the kids find me." Callie could hear a pair of voices yelling out Regan's name. "They found me," she said. "Gotta go. See you tomorrow. Can't wait!"

CHAPTER TEN

WHEN CALLIE LOOKED out the window of the plane and saw the lush, green island they were heading for, she practically squealed. She liked nothing more than greenery, but the ocean was a close second. She'd never seen the Atlantic, save for a quick view of it from the Hudson River when she visited New York, but her parents had to forcibly wrestle her back into the car when they'd visited Los Angeles when she was a child—she'd been mesmerized by the Pacific.

She was grinning from ear to ear when a tall, lean, lovely woman approached her and said with complete confidence, "If a thousand women in Dallas look like you, I'm moving."

"Regan!" She wrapped her arms around her and hugged her for a full minute. When she pulled away, she held onto her waist and looked her over. "Why didn't you tell me how gorgeous you are?"

"I was going to, but the boys interrupted me." She pulled Callie into a desperate hug. "It's so good to see you."

When they broke apart, Callie kept an arm around Regan's waist while they waited for her bag. Since they were so close together Callie couldn't do what she itched to do—get a better look at Regan. It was strange. She'd had a very clear view in her mind of what Regan would looked like. In fact, when she was scanning the crowd she was looking for her imagined image. But this woman was nothing—absolutely nothing like she'd imagined. It was like the woman she had her arm around was an impostor, and it was going to take a while to convince her brain this was the same person she'd been talking to on the phone. "You seem a little shaky. Are you okay?"

"Yeah, I guess. I probably should have chosen a different country. Angela brought me here a few months after we fell in love. I have great memories." Her voice was almost too quiet to hear.

"Then we'll have a terrible time and replace those good memories with awful ones." Callie squeezed her tightly.

Regan hugged her back, saying, "You're the one person in the world who I actually want to be with. Thanks so much for coming."

"Thank you! I'm so happy to be here I could wet myself." The bag cruised by and Regan reached out and grabbed it.

They started to walk towards a long line of taxis. "I was a little worried that you'd be as depressed as I am, and we'd just sit in silence and think about ending it all."

Callie stopped abruptly, turned and grasped Regan by her biceps. "Are you…"

"Kidding. I'm not that depressed. I promise."

Nodding, Callie started to walk again. "I assumed I'd be able to tell if you were. You seem like a normally happy person who's had her heart broken, not someone who's clinically depressed."

"That's about right. I'm normally pretty lighthearted. I think that's why my family's concerned. I shrugged off my girlfriend troubles in the past."

"But this time it's bigger than that."

"Yeah," Regan said solemnly. "This time I was really in love."

Now that she'd listened to her voice for a couple of minutes Callie's brain had started to accept the dissonance. When they got into the taxi,

Callie sat as far away from her friend as she could, just so she could take more of her in. By the time they got to the hotel it was as if Regan had always been a tall, lean brunette, and the conjured image of her had been the illusion.

They entered their modest room in a decent, but by no means luxurious, hotel on the beach.

Looking slightly abashed, Regan stood by the door and said, "I assumed we'd share a room, but I didn't ask first. Is this okay?"

"Absolutely. When I went to stay with my friend Terri, I slept in her bed so I'm clearly very flexible. I hate to waste money on hotels."

"Angela would say that's something you stop doing when you're an adult."

"Angela can kiss my ass. We don't have to listen to those two anymore."

"I didn't mind listening to Angela." She walked over to the bed and started to unpack. "She wasn't a snob. But she'd been traveling for business for twenty years. She was long past the 'bunk with a pal' thing."

"I share rooms with my sisters, my mom, anybody I can convince to pay for half. I'll never be past sharing with a pal."

"I think I'm at the midpoint between you and Angela. I will *never* share a room with my parents." She laughed as she started to put her clothing into one of the dressers.

Callie didn't follow suit. She went to the window and stared out at the beach, filling her lungs repeatedly with the fresh, moist air. "I'm moving here. Actually, that's not true. I already live here. I'll just send for my things. I already checked and there's no surcharge to use my phone, so I could work from here easily."

"I'd come visit you every winter."

"Then we're decided. I'll just troll the beach looking for someone to support me until I get on my feet."

"Let's put our suits on and start looking."

~

When Regan came out of the bathroom, Callie exclaimed, "I'm not going to the beach with you looking like that! Nobody's going to look at me, and I'm the one searching for a sugar momma...or daddy. I'm really not picky at this point."

Regan actually blushed from the praise. "You look adorable. You're very, very cute."

"Well, you look hot and hot always trumps cute." Callie said cute the same way she'd say *vomit.*

"The only good thing about this breakup is that I've lost weight." She patted her flat belly, nothing but skin moving when she did.

"Don't lose another ounce. Everything's right where it should be." She smiled as she looked Regan over again. "Honestly, you are a fantastic-looking woman. In my mind, you weren't nearly this pretty."

"Well, you don't look anything like I pictured you. Nothing at all. How *did* you picture me?"

"Mmm, I thought you'd be shorter than me, with light brown hair, brown eyes. You looked kinda like...Kelly Adams."

"Who's that?"

"A girl I went to college with." Callie's eyes crinkled up when she smiled. "She had light brown hair and she was shorter than I am. You look nothing like her, by the way. Your hair is much better than Kelly's, and your eyes are gorgeous. I'm a sucker for blue eyes."

With a half smirk, Regan said, "Angela used to teasingly call me a pale-eyed devil."

"Your skin's fairer than I thought it would be."

"I'm Irish. We're all pale."

"Does everyone in your family have that beautiful dark hair?"

Regan grasped a hank of her hair and let it fall from her fingers. “My dad and I have the darkest, but he’s turning gray. My sisters are more brunette, like my mom. I never envisioned you as a redhead, but your hair is beautiful, as advertised. But you can’t look at me with those adorable dimples and tell me not to say you’re cute.”

“I guess there are worse things to be, but I’d rather be hot. I think you dark-haired girls achieve hot easier than us redheads.”

It was clear that Regan was a little embarrassed by the compliments. She put on a pair of running shorts and a tank top, then put sunblock and a magazine into a bag. “Ready?”

“Yep. I’ve got a new sunblock that guarantees ‘no more freckles.’”

“Do you want me to count the ones you have now so you can get your money back if it doesn’t work?”

“No, I don’t mind them. At least I don’t have them all across my nose like Gretchen has.” She chuckled evilly.

~

Regan was undergoing her own travails in fitting Callie into her mental view. In her mind Callie was trashy looking. She’d looked like the kind of girl who was still hanging around the bar at two a.m., trying to outshine the competition. In fact, Callie was adorable. Fresh faced, bright-eyed, and energetic. Those dimples made her look impish and… adorable. There was no other word that she could think of, and that was as big a surprise as if she’d been missing a few teeth and had two inches of dark roots showing from platinum blonde hair.

~

Each quickly adjusted to the reality of the other. Callie was irrepressible. She had almost boundless energy and was childlike in her enthusiasm. As soon as they found a place for their towels, she ran into the ocean, shouting for joy. “This is phenomenal!” She splashed the clear, clean water around with her hands, making big sweeping motions. “I’ve never been in the Atlantic. It’s now my favorite ocean.”

"You're easily convinced." Regan ran in, splashing around a little less riotously. "You've been here for two seconds." She picked up her feet and treaded water with just her arms.

"But I'm in love. L. O. V. E." Callie dunked her head into the water, blinking rapidly when she pulled her head out. "I can see for miles!"

"You can rent a mask if you'd like to have that be a little less painful." Callie couldn't have been any cuter. Marina would have had to have the sex drive of a goat to keep up with her and have energy left to screw around.

After spending two solid hours frolicking in the water like a pair of children, they finally lay on their beach towels, both nearly exhausted.

But Callie still chattered away. "I wonder if it's less expensive to ship all of my electronics here or if I should have my sugar momma buy it all new."

"Don't think I didn't notice you saying you'd take a sugar daddy. Is that true?"

"I'm clearly not very good at picking sugar anything. I couldn't get Marina to buy me a pack of gum."

"Really? You didn't share your money?"

"Nope. Nada. What's hers was hers and what's mine was credit card statements. She made a lot more than I did, and she didn't share the wealth."

Regan took a minute to process Callie's situation. Had she and Marina even *been* partners? What kind of partner would let you struggle financially when she could help?

Callie tilted her baseball cap, keeping her eyes shaded. "When I left the corporate IT world to start my own business, I really took a hit."

"Did you do that when you moved to Dallas?"

"Yeah. I wanted to be with Marina and I didn't want to waste another year in IT. I should have waited until I had a cushion but"—she puckered her lips in an air kiss—"love pushed me."

"Regrets?"

Callie rolled over onto her stomach. "Can you move the umbrella just a little? I don't want to burn my feet."

Regan leaned over and adjusted it carefully. "How's that?"

"Excellent. It's nice to have a beach buddy. It's harder than I thought it'd be to set up an umbrella for maximum coverage."

Callie hadn't answered the question. How could she not have regrets? It sounded like all she got from Marina was the ability to sleep with other women. But she had that when she was single. Why bother being in a relationship at all? "Glad to help. Now back to the sugar daddy issue. Are you…flexible?"

"Fairly. I was thirty-three the first time I experienced the love of a bad woman, so lesbianism isn't a lifelong habit."

"Thirty-three?" Regan exclaimed. "How old are you?" She scrambled to take the bite out of the comment. "That didn't come out right. You don't look like you're even thirty. I thought you were my age, or younger."

"Good save. I was just gonna kick sand in your face. My mother and sisters and I just had a fun-filled thirty-fifth birthday party last week."

"But you were with Marina for a year and a half."

"She was my first." She put her hand over her heart and made it pat rapidly.

"Freaky. I don't mean that judgmentally. I'm just surprised." Flabbergasted was the better word. Callie'd gone from never being with a woman to being with anyone who walked by? What in the hell…?

"I always knew I was attracted to women, but I was in two long-term relationships with guys and all of a sudden I was thirty-three. It catches up with you."

"You liked being with men?"

"Yeah, I did." She gave Regan a puzzled look and said, "I didn't sleep with men to punish myself. Why do you act like it's odd? That's the majority position, you know."

Regan slapped a hand over her face and left it there for a second. "I'm not being very smooth today. I think I'm trying to say that I don't know any women who switched once they'd been in the game for a while."

"Now you do," Callie said, wrinkling her nose. "I think I'll stick with women, even though being in a relationship with a woman wasn't as different as my friends said it would be. But women smell a lot better and they're generally less gross. Not having to use birth control is a big plus too." She smiled broadly.

Being with a woman *was* just like being with a guy when you set up your relationship in a way most guys would kill for. She probably could have slept with men too. Or would that have crossed Marina's boundaries? Did she even have any? Their entire relationship was beyond comprehension.

Regan gazed at Callie, and once again that nearly angelic face made her doubt her gut reaction. "You know, you have two completely different smiles. When you smile really wide your dimples don't show and the corners of your mouth curl up. But your other smile is more like a grin and both dimples show. It's fascinating."

"I'm glad I can entertain you with just my face."

"I don't know anybody with dimples. That's probably why I'm trying to figure them out."

"All three of us have them. You should have come to my birthday party last week."

"I would have if you'd told me about it." She tossed a bit of sand at Callie. "I'm buying your dinner tonight as a belated present."

"When's your birthday?"

"May 28th. It's usually Memorial Day weekend."

"Great. We'll spend Memorial Day together and I'll reciprocate. What birthday is this?"

"Mine." She grinned impishly.

"What's the number? You said you thought I was your age."

"Twenty-nine. Again."

"Come on. How old are you?"

"If I live that long, I'll be thirty. I'm really looking forward to spending my thirtieth birthday living in my old bedroom. Maybe my parents' will take me out for ice cream."

"They'll have to fight me for the pleasure." She put both hands up like a boxer.

"You win. I know just where we'll go."

"I like people who can make quick decisions."

"Then you'll love me. I make 'em all day long."

After another bout of splashing and playing in the gentle waves they lay on their towels again, enjoying the encroaching sunset. "How old were you when your parents got divorced?" Regan asked.

"Mmm, I was in second grade, so that's what…about eight?"

"Was it hard?"

"Whew!" Callie whistled. "Hard isn't the word. My dad had an affair, and my mom threw him out and salted the earth that he'd walked on."

"Ooo, that sounds horrible."

"It was…it really was. We went from being on the edge of upper middle class to lower middle in a weekend. And the worst part was that we became pawns in their arguments that continue to this day."

As she spoke her voice started to shake and tears filled her eyes. She seemed to try to stop them, making a determined face, but it did no good. The tears would not stop. She looked so sad, but it was clear she didn't want to show it. Callie'd probably looked just like this when she was a little girl trying to be brave. "Poor thing," Regan said softly. She felt a knot in her throat, and realized she was on the verge of crying herself.

"I hardly shed a tear over Marina, but I can bawl like a baby talking about my parents' divorce. Funny, huh?" She wiped her eyes with the corner of her towel.

"No, it's not funny at all. It must have been horrible."

"It was. Gretchen was on my mom's side and Emily and I were caught in the middle. I was always daddy's girl, so I was really stuck. I felt bad for my dad, but I was also mad at him for doing something so stupid and harmful." She sighed. "This was before I even knew what sex was, so that made it worse. I just knew that one day my mom hated my dad and he was moving out."

Regan grew quiet, just watching the rhythmic ebb and flow of the waves. The divorce must have set the course for this strange path. Having your parents split when you were so young must have been world-shattering. Maybe it made her more casual—less invested in a relationship. A few minutes passed and when Regan spoke again, it visibly startled Callie. "I'm surprised you're not more upset about Marina and Angela. I'd think cheating would be a big deal for you."

"Ask my last boyfriend how big a deal it was," she replied, rolling her eyes. "He had the fires of hell rain down on him."

"Damn! Your boyfriend cheated, too?" Okay, this was starting to make sense. She's been burned and burned again.

"Kinda. Sorta." She shrugged. "Not technically."

"Thanks for clearing that up."

"Oh, fine. You give me that ridiculously charming smile and I can't ignore you." She took a breath so deep her chest perceptively rose and fell. "He was using the internet to go to chat rooms. I caught him when I was fixing his computer and found a cache of porn." She made a face. "Disgusting."

Looking at women was disgusting? How did that make sense? Marina was having sex with real people, not images on the internet. There had to be more. A lot more. "What about the chat rooms?"

"Having virtual sex." She scowled. "Like that makes it all right."

"With strangers? Or women he knew?"

Callie blinked, as though the question was a ridiculous one. "Strangers. He never would have done that with women he knew."

So he had talked dirty with strangers. And that was enough to throw him out. But Marina could have real sex with real women and that was perfectly fine. Maybe it was a question of honesty. "Did he confess?"

"Yeah. He told me when I said I'd seen the porn. I've got to hand it to him. He confessed to everything. I didn't have to browbeat him like I did Marina."

"Was it horrible porn?"

"What's horrible porn?"

"I don't know…like bestiality or something?"

"No! It was regular porn. Dozens of clips of women having sex." She paused, her eyes narrowing. "A lot of it was stuff we didn't do, now that I think of it. I guess he liked looking at things that were…different."

"You broke up with him immediately?"

"Yeah, pretty much." She looked up at the sky, which had turned a beautiful shade of lilac. "I make it sound like I tore him limb from limb, but I really just cried for a week. I wouldn't let him come near me, so he left to stay with a friend." She sighed heavily. "He never came back."

"Your choice?"

"Yeah. I shouldn't have been so harsh. He never touched another woman, and he was always ready to have sex when I was. So I wasn't really harmed by his 'hobby.' But he was so insensitive about it. He wouldn't admit he'd done anything wrong and I couldn't forgive him when he wouldn't."

"You were hurt."

"Heck, yes! I was really hurt. If he would have at least acknowledged that I was justified in being hurt I might have forgiven him. But, in his defense, he was usually very sensitive. I think he was embarrassed, and he got hardheaded when he looked foolish. We should have worked harder to reconcile, but…we didn't. I'm not sure why."

"How long were you together?"

"Six years. We were thinking about having a baby." She sniffled, wiping her eyes quickly. "He got married this year to someone not nearly as cool as I am." She lowered her eyes and showed just a hint of a teasing smile.

"You poor thing."

"Yeah, he really broke my heart." She sat up and squared her shoulders, looking like she was taking her first view of a new day. "But that made me rethink my views on fidelity. When Marina happened along a few months later, I decided that it made sense to try something different."

That could explain a few things. Keeping your lover at a distance. Letting her do the things you fear so you don't get hurt when she does them. "How'd that work? Generally, I mean? I know it didn't work so well in one case."

"It worked well. Until…you know. She told me from the beginning that she didn't do monogamy, so it felt more honest."

"Uhm, I guess that's one way to think of it. For me that would be like saying, 'I'm gonna hit you every once in a while, so you'd better learn how to duck.'"

Callie laughed, showing her dimples. "It's not for everyone. And it took me a long time, probably close to a year, to get even vaguely comfortable with it. I was just hitting my stride."

Regan's vivid blue eyes darted back and forth for a few seconds before she revealed, "I decided to give Angela another chance when she told me about your and Marina's relationship."

"Really?"

"Yeah. I figured she got seduced by you she-devils." She laughed, almost guffawing. "But now that I know you, I can't even conjure up the evil home-wrecker image I had of you. You're a very kind person."

"I try to be. I told Marina I could only consider it if we would only have sex with people who were single or had the same kind of relationship we did. I never wanted an innocent woman to be involved." She reached over and grasped Regan's arm, squeezing it. "I'm so sorry you got hurt. If I hadn't agreed to it…"

That was a huge relief. At least Callie had tried to protect other women. Knowing she'd tried to keep the damage of being in that kind of relationship to just herself and Marina was admirable. "No way. Marina was a cheater, pure and simple. She was a bigger cheater than Angela, in some ways. She could have had hundreds of other women, but she chose my Angela."

"I don't know if I believe her, but she says she did it to ingratiate herself so she'd get promoted to Angela's level."

Regan stared at her for a very long time. Then she said, in a low, dangerous sounding tone, "If that's true, I'd better never meet her. I think I'd kill her."

CHAPTER ELEVEN

THEY HAD A nice belated birthday dinner for Callie at a restaurant not far from their hotel. Even though it was fun, Callie could tell that Regan was still bothered by their talk at the beach.

After dinner they went back down to the water, took off their shoes and walked along the low, quiet surf. "You seem kinda…down," Callie said after they'd walked a long time in silence.

"Yeah. I am." She walked along, not speaking for a while, then she said, "It doesn't seem to bother you much that Marina was trying to screw her way to the top. That bothers me. A lot." Her voice was cold and dangerously low.

Callie reached out and took her hand, slowing her to a stop. "No, no, that's not true. I…I think I have to tell you the whole thing."

"What?" Regan's eyes looked dark and hard in the moonlight.

"We talked a couple of times after I left. I think I got the full story out of her." She paused, took a breath and said, "Do you want to hear it? It's…not good."

"Yeah, I do. I need to know the truth, no matter how bad it is."

They started to walk again, with Callie finding it easier to talk when she wasn't looking into Regan's innocent face.

"They started working together a year before Marina and I met. She said she was attracted to Angela from the beginning but she didn't know she was gay."

"Probably true. Angela isn't out at work, even though I know she could be."

"Neither is Marina. Which irritated the heck out of me. She wouldn't even consider taking me to events at work, even though two of her salesmen are openly gay."

"Same for Angela. It would have had to change for us to get married." She nodded her head slowly when Callie stopped and stared at her. "Yeah, we were thinking of getting married. We wanted to start a family."

Callie put an arm around her and they wound up standing in the warm water, holding each other for a few minutes while each shed some tears for their fractured plans.

"I'm so sorry," Callie said again.

"Me, too." They started to walk again, with Regan holding Callie's hand as a child would an older sister.

"So Marina was attracted to Angela, but they never acknowledged it. Until one night, about a year and a half ago…" Regan gasped and Callie squeezed her hand. "I told you it was bad."

"A fucking year and a half ago," she muttered. "Asshole! Bitch! Whore!" Her voice had risen until she shouted the last word. "The God damned bitch!"

"I know, I know," Callie said, trying to soothe her. "It's bad."

"How could she talk about having children with me? How could she?" She started to cry in earnest, with Callie holding her and rubbing her shaking back.

"I don't know how she could do it, but she's an idiot for losing you. Especially for someone like Marina. She's not one tenth the woman you are."

Sniffling away the last of her tears, Regan stood up tall and took some deep breaths. "I'll try to keep it together. I really do want to hear the rest." A second passed and Regan grasped Callie by the shoulders, her grip so intense it could have left bruises. "A year and a half? That's how long you were together!"

"I know." She put her head down and took in a breath. "They started up just when I moved to Dallas. I didn't get to have her to myself for even a week."

Regan threw her head back and screamed. "Filthy bitch!" Shaking, she wrapped Callie in a hug so fierce her feet left the ground. "I'll strangle her if I ever meet her. For both of us."

They stood there crying for a few minutes, the sound of their tears drowned out by the gentle lapping of the waves. Finally, they started walking again, arms interlocked as though each was trying to hold the other up against a hurricane-force wind. "Do you want to hear the rest?" Callie asked.

"Yeah. Give it to me."

"They were at a conference in Las Vegas and they came out to each other. I guess there had been some kind of veiled flirtation because they hooked up right then."

"A year and a half ago."

"Yeah."

"Marina didn't have an explanation for why it happened?"

"She's just a slut." Regan didn't ever need to learn the truth. Angela's excuse was so damn cold. How could she tell Marina that Regan was lousy in bed? That was such a betrayal of someone she'd claimed to love. Regan was precious. Even more precious than she'd seemed when they'd talked on the phone. No matter what, she was going to take Angela's insult to the grave. Torture couldn't have gotten it out of her.

"So how did this help Marina's career?"

"Well, if she's being honest, she said Angela wanted the affair to continue, even though she didn't."

"Great."

"Marina claims she knew she'd made a mistake by doing it that first time, but she thought it was harmless. She knew she was in trouble when Angela wanted her to arrange to travel to Boston more often. That's when she started to worry Angela would veto her promotion if she turned her down."

"So it was all Angela's fault, huh?" She sounded bitter and sarcastic, but that wasn't who Regan really was. Callie could only hope that Regan didn't allow herself to let this sour her and make her jaded. She was too nice a woman for that.

"No, she didn't claim that. She admitted Angela would never have been on the list of people I'd approve, but since she'd been attracted to her since before we got together, she saw her as kinda grandfathered in."

"What do you think?" Regan's voice carried over the warm, moist wind.

She sounded so hopeful, like she was depending on Callie to reassure her. Unable to resist the unspoken request, Callie stopped and pulled Regan close, trying to let the moon illuminate her face. "I think she's a user."

"At least."

"And I think she's a person without a real conscience. Even though she claimed to be so contrite about sleeping with Angela, she admitted that they didn't click at all. And, to be honest, I think that's the main reason she didn't want to continue to have sex with her." She took a deep breath. "I'm an idiot for letting her into my life, much less my heart."

Regan nodded slowly. "Okay. Then we can be friends."

They walked back to the hotel in silence. But Callie's brain wouldn't slow down a bit. If Marina had screwed up the friendship she was starting to rely on, she would have killed her. Regan was the kind of person she needed in her life. Someone with morals that didn't change with the weather

They were both quiet on the long walk back to the hotel. They weren't holding hands or touching any longer, and Regan still felt like punching someone. How could Callie have stayed? How could she have given Marina a second chance? There had to be some sick secrets behind that sweet facade. Where were they hiding?

After they got ready for bed, they turned out the lights and each lay in her respective bed, neither one ready for sleep.

"I don't think Marina told me the whole truth," Callie said quietly.

"About what?"

"About how easy it was to convince Angela to sleep with her."

"Why?" Damn. That had sounded way too sharp. But Callie would get a fist in the face if she had any more bad news to deliver piece by piece. Enough was enough.

"I know Marina. When she wants something, she figures out how to get it. I think she wanted Angela, and the fact that she was off limits in many ways made her more fixated on her."

"What do you mean, 'many ways'?" Regan asked, unable to keep the rancor from her voice.

"Well, she was in a relationship, she wasn't pre-approved, and she was a colleague. I never would have approved someone like Angela."

"And what does that mean?"

"She was someone on a higher level who had a vote about Marina's future. What else?"

"Sorry. I'm just a little sensitive about her. I always suspect a racial angle, even where there isn't one. Angela always said I had too much oppressor's guilt."

"Angela is…what? Black? Latina?"

"Black." Regan turned on the light and blinked towards Callie. "You didn't know that?"

"No. How would I? I've never seen her."

How could she not know? A computer geek who didn't search the internet for a picture of the other woman? Maybe there were so many other women that the details didn't matter anymore. This was so screwed up. Regan got up and rooted around in her purse, finally finding what she was looking for. She handed Callie her keychain which had a heart-shaped locket on it. Callie opened it and studied the tiny picture. "She's beautiful."

"Yeah, she is." Regan flopped back into her bed and drew the sheet over herself. "You really didn't know?"

"No idea. But, knowing Marina, that was part of her allure. Being black would make Angela just a little bit more…"

"What?" It was impossible to keep from snapping at her.

"Marina wanted whatever she wasn't supposed to have, and being partnered, being in a position of authority, and being black would be a trifecta for her." With a quick look at Regan, she added, "Her parents are socially and politically prominent conservatives. They had a very hard time with her being gay. Her having a black lover would truly freak them out."

"Typical racists?"

"No," Callie said, after a few seconds. "It would be more that it's outside the norm in their social circle. Once her parents got comfortable with her being gay, she started sleeping with guys for the first time in her life. She just wants to tweak them any way she can."

"She sounds like a teenager."

"Yeah, in a way. But she still does just what they want her to in most things. She's seriously screwed up. I wish to God I could have seen how screwed up she was long before now."

"I don't mean to be rude, but it's hard to believe you didn't see it." Blind people could have seen it from a hundred yards. Callie didn't seem that oblivious.

She looked down, seemingly chagrined. "I guess love is blind. In her defense, she's smart and fun and sometimes playful. She's really good at her job, and she has a lot of long-term friends. So she has her good points. I should have paid more attention to how she treated her parents. That's a sure sign of character."

"But you can have idiots for parents and still be a good person."

"True. But Marina's too tied up with them, and that's voluntary. They're really, really involved in her life, and they try to control her with money."

"They bail her out a lot?"

"A whole lot. And for their generosity Marina loves to surreptitiously screw with them. Never to their faces…except for being gay. But even then they caught her in the act. I don't think she would have ever voluntarily come out to them." She put the keychain on the bedside table. "What a miserable person she is."

"Then why did you give her another chance? Why did you try to convince me to give Angela another chance?" *Listen to yourself! You knew she was evil, and you stayed with her. For what?*

"Stupidity. Blindness. I don't know." Callie turned off the lights and lay down again. "I really regret that. I hope you can forgive me one day."

"Don't worry about that. I'm interested in *why* you did it. Not because of me, but because of *you*. Why did you think you had to settle for someone like her?"

"I don't know," she murmured. "My friend Terri has been asking me that for over a year and I've been telling her that I wasn't settling. I'm gonna have to spend some time thinking about that."

Regan was sure she could truncate the thought process. Callie had not only been settling, she'd been participating in a dangerous game that had blown shrapnel all the way across the country. But she was obviously blind to that. Maybe hopelessly blind. "I hope you can. Before you get into another relationship."

"I think I might choose to be like my mom. Bitter and lonely. At least I'll only hurt myself that way."

Regan didn't respond, and eventually Callie fell asleep, her rhythmic breathing filling the quiet room.

The next morning Callie opened her eyes to the bright sun streaming in through the open window. The air held the scent of the jasmine plants that ringed their balcony and just a touch of the sea. She opened her eyes and turned to see Regan lying on her side, her head propped up on her hand, looking at her.

"That's not true, you know."

"What's not true?"

"If you become bitter it affects a lot more people than you. You can't tell me it doesn't hurt you to see how your mom is."

"Of course it does. I think I was just grousing. I'm not the bitter type."

"I hope not, because I want you as a friend and bitter people don't appeal to me."

"Okay, I'll be cheerful just for you." She got up and patted Regan's dark head.

Regan called after her as she went into bathroom, "Good enough. Reality doesn't have to intrude on my fantasy world. As long as you seem happy, I'm happy." That wasn't true. Not a word of it. But it was nice to dream.

Their flights for home left around noon, and Callie was up early, putting on her running clothes when Regan woke. "Hey, where are you going?"

"To run on the beach. I've been slacking."

"Slacking? You've been working nonstop on my site."

"But I haven't been running. I've got to make up for that today. I'm gonna do ten miles."

"Ten miles?" Regan sat up and scowled. "Wait for me. You'll probably kill me, but I'll try to keep up."

Callie held a hand out and pulled Regan to her feet. "With those long legs you'll leave me in the dust. How tall are you, anyway?"

"Five eleven or so. Mostly legs," she said, grinning.

"If you ran middle distance you're probably faster than me anyway. Maybe I should start now and have you catch up."

"No way. You wait right here. I'll just be a sec."

Callie sat down and opened her computer, using the few minutes to try to load some images before the other guests started using the Wi-Fi. She was going to finish the web site no matter what. Regan was going to get her money's worth.

When they got to the beach Callie pulled off her shoes. "I've never run on sand. Wanna try it?"

"Mmm, I'm faster on an even surface."

"No. Really?" Callie gave her a smirk. "Who would have guessed that?"

"Oh, all right. I can keep up with your cross-country nonsense." She started to pull off her shoes. "You people and your uneven terrain."

They started off slowly, and within a half mile had settled into a nice, moderate pace. Callie could tell that Regan wasn't extending herself, probably trying to make sure her footing was safe. Callie could use her normal stride, which was a little shorter than a track runner's would have been, and that let her easily keep up with Regan's longer limbs.

"This is fun," Regan said after a while. "I haven't run with anyone in ages."

"I haven't either. I should get back into running with a group. It helps motivate me."

"We have so many runners in Cambridge that it gets crowded." Regan's face fell as she corrected, "We had. I have to learn how to use the past tense."

"You can find some buddies in Scituate."

"If that's where I end up. I'm itching to move out of my parents' house. I've got to get my own place."

"Me too. Here's to our new adventure." She said this with such false enthusiasm that Regan couldn't help but react with a smile. There was something about Callie that was impossible not to like. And she truly needed someone to help her see where she'd gone wrong. If she could see that, she might turn her life around. There was a good person in there who'd simply lost her way.

CHAPTER TWELVE

AS SOON AS Callie returned from the Bahamas, she started to search for an apartment. Her only goal was to decrease her monthly expenses. It didn't matter where the apartment was or what shape it was in. Only money mattered. She'd spent so much keeping up with Marina that she hadn't been able to save a dime—one more lasting effect of wasting a year and a half of her life.

Within a week she had a short list of potential apartments and was ready to dive in. It only took two days, and by Friday she had signed a lease.

Regan phoned when Callie was packing the few things she'd used for her stay at Pam's. She'd come to rely on the calls, feeling better talking to Regan than to most of her Dallas friends. Regan not only understood what she'd been through, she was interested in talking about it. Her other friends listened, but she could tell they wished she'd get over it.

"Are you all set for moving day?"

"Is anyone ever ready to move? I'm going to get my moving truck at eight and I've got four friends to help. I'm sure I'll be the only one ready at eight, but they'll all show up eventually."

"I wish I could be there to help you."

"Liar. No one wants to help anyone move. Even professional movers don't want to."

"Okay, so I'm lying, but I still wish I could help you."

"That's just because you're nice."

"Yeah, I am, but you're fun to be with and I'd like to see Dallas."

"You should have come when I was still living with Marina. Now that was a nice apartment. It was almost worth the airfare."

"I'd rather visit you in a refrigerator box than visit Marina at the nicest apartment in Dallas."

"That's a very good answer. You might regret saying that after you see my new place, but I appreciate that you feel that way."

"Have fun tomorrow." Regan used the same fake enthusiasm that Callie sometimes adopted.

"That was a dreadful attempt. You have to work on that."

Her voice was even more full of glee when she said, "I'll work on it this weekend while you're having fun!"

On Sunday evening Callie called Regan and reached her when she was out running. "It's eight o'clock here. What are you doing out running at this time of night?"

"I was really busy all weekend and this is the only time I had. Delaney had some function with her husband's family, so I had to take over for her and oversee a huge twenty-fifth anniversary party."

"Older sister pulling rank?"

"Yeah, she does that occasionally. But that's cool. She takes over for me, too."

"Are you in charge of parties very often? You haven't mentioned it before."

"No, not very. It's not my thing. I much prefer dealing with suppliers and purveyors and doing the business side. I like being around people, but I don't like being around people who are having a party. Don't tell anyone I told you this, but our banquet clients are huge pains in the ass."

Callie could imagine Regan's face quirking into the charming grin that graced her face when she was saying something she knew she shouldn't say. It was a very lovable trait, and she felt herself missing Regan—even though they'd just gotten back from vacation.

"I can imagine. But I bet you do a great job."

"I'm certainly not going to try to wrestle the job away from Delaney, that's for sure. So how did the move go?"

"It was okay. I had to give away boxes and boxes of stuff to fit into the new place, but I'm glad I finished. I'm not *finished*-finished, of course. There are a zillion things I haven't put away, but my roommate, doesn't have much of anything so I was able to bring more than I thought I'd be able to."

"It sounds like you just moved boxes. Don't you have furniture?"

It was an embarrassing admission, but there was no reason to withhold the truth from Regan. "I sold all my furniture when I moved to Dallas. None of it was up to Marina's standards."

"What a jerk! I'm liking her less every time we talk about her, and I didn't think that was possible."

"She never said that in so many words. But her apartment was fully furnished when I moved in, so all I brought were my electronics, which were considerable. Marina wasn't the kind to say rude things. She just manipulated you into doing what she wanted."

"I'd rather be around someone who said rude things. At least then you know where you stand."

"That's probably true." But being manipulated into selling your stuff for pennies on the dollar wasn't anything to boast of.

"Is your roommate a nice guy?"

"He seems to be. He's in his last year of med school and he swears he's hardly ever home. I don't think we'll wind up being best friends or anything, but that's fine with me."

"Do you have to buy a bed?"

"No, I'm using his. He's going to sleep on the sleeper sofa in the living room."

Somewhat hesitantly, Regan said, "Are you sure you've thought this through?"

"Yeah. I want to save money and this place is only going to cost me five hundred dollars a month. He's the one who's getting the bad end of the deal, but he's cheaper than I am, so he's giving up his bedroom and I'm paying a hundred more than he is."

"Are you sure you can be happy living like that?"

"No, not in the long term. But it should be fine for a year or so. If I work hard and keep an eagle eye on my expenses, I'll have some money in the bank and I'll feel much better."

"You really took a hit when you went into graphic design, didn't you?"

"I took a fifty percent pay cut, but I'd do it again. Business was good, but I was paying seventeen hundred a month to live with Marina. That was way too rich for me."

"That's a lot!"

"Don't I know it? She had an expensive mortgage and the common charges were really high because they had two pools and some tennis courts."

"Did she make you pay half?"

"Not quite. She accounted for the tax break she got, then we split the difference."

"That's still not fair. She's building equity."

"Not in this market," Callie laughed. "She lost everything…or I should say her parents lost everything they put down. She's going to have to get a new girlfriend pretty quickly to keep up the payments because she sure can't sell it."

"I hope they put her in debtor's prison."

"Bitter, bitter. I'm the one living with a guy I don't know who's ten years younger than I am and sleeping on his crummy old mattress. I'm the one who should be bitter."

"But you're not, because you're a good person and you know things are going to improve."

"Things will improve in an hour or so after I scrub this disgusting bathroom. Living with a man will cement my decision to be a lesbian. At least we know how to pee *inside* the toilet."

"On that disgusting note, I will finish my run, my friend. Don't inhale toxic fumes when you're cleaning."

Callie was still trying to adjust to her new living situation when Regan called a few weeks later. "Hi! Guess what I think I'm going to do?"

"Uhm…that's a tough one. Give me a hint."

"You don't need a hint. Just guess!"

"You've found a new girlfriend."

"Oh, yeah, that's it." Regan let out a sharp laugh. "I'm still crying over the one I just lost."

"Well, some people like to jump right back in."

"Not me. It's gonna be a good long time before I'm ready to get back out there. But I am doing something that I should have done years ago."

"Getting a dog?"

"Oh, you're not even close. I'm thinking of buying a house…or an apartment, to be more precise."

"You're kidding! I had no idea you were thinking of that."

"I wasn't. But I was looking for apartments and saw that I could buy for not much more than rent per month."

"What are you thinking of?"

"I saw a place I liked today. A townhouse. I think it'd be just right for me."

"You're not going to buy the first place you see, are you?"

"Yeah, I might." She laughed softly. "I know what I like and my parents know what things should cost. If I can get this place for what my dad says is a steal…I'll do it."

"Wow. You don't screw around!"

"No, I like to make decisions quickly. I've always wanted to live by the water, so this place should be fine. This will make me feel like an adult. No girlfriend paying the bills."

"How many girlfriends have you had?"

"Three serious ones." She paused for a second. "Hey. It just dawned on me that each one lasted about three years. What am I doing wrong?"

"Nothing from my vantage point. You'd still be in your last one if it wasn't for my stinking ex."

"Surely you can think of worse terms for her. And if you can't—I can."

Just two weeks later, Regan called Callie with good news. "We finally reached an agreement. I'm a homeowner."

"Awesome! When do you move in?"

"April thirtieth is the closing date, so I guess I get the keys then. I've never done this before, but that seems logical, doesn't it?"

"I've never done it either, but I'm getting a lot of pleasure from watching you do it. Thanks for sending me pictures."

"I went to see it so many times the seller must have thought I was nuts. The last time I took about fifty pictures. My real estate agent was sick of me too."

"I was surprised you kept going back. I actually thought you'd made up your mind the first time you saw it."

"I had. But he was being really hard-assed about price. I thought if I kept going back he'd get the message that I really wanted it."

"Yeah?" Callie said, not catching on. "How does that help lower the price?"

"I wasn't sure it would. But I wasn't going to pay more than I thought it was worth. I hoped that my coming back to see it again and again and then barely increasing my offer would show him that I wanted it, but I couldn't or wouldn't pay much more."

"Cool. I never would have thought of that."

"I dicker over prices every day. I've gotten a lot better at it over the years."

"Should I come help you move or do you still want me to visit over your birthday?"

"Hmm, that would normally be a tough choice, but I don't have a whole lot to move so I don't really need help. I'd rather have you come for my birthday. Can you stay for a week?"

"A week! You'll be sick of me in half that time. No one should ever visit for a week."

"No, I won't. Besides, I have lots of plans. We'll go to P'town for a long weekend, then we'll hang around here for a few days. It's like two separate vacations."

"P'town?"

"Yeah, yeah. Provincetown. You've never heard of it?"

"It sounds kinda familiar..."

"It's at the end of Cape Cod and it's mostly gay. We're gonna go for Women's Weekend. You'll love it. I guarantee it."

"Gay...women...how can I argue? I'm not ready to jump into the dating pool yet, but it couldn't hurt to look."

"I don't think I'm even ready to look, but I love being around a big group of women. It's nice to feel like we're the majority."

"We are," Callie said, chuckling.

"Lesbian women, not women in general. It's nice to be around hundreds and hundreds of lesbians."

"I don't think I've ever been around hundreds. Well, I went to a WNBA game once…"

"Very funny. You're gonna love it. And you can meet my family and see the restaurant. I'll have to work when we're here, but you can do some sightseeing during the day. There's a lot to see around here."

"I looked Scituate up on the net. There's a whole lot of history around you. I'm really excited."

"Your mom teaches history, right?"

"Yeah. American history. She made all of us fans."

"Is there a…lot of American history in Phoenix?"

"Sure." Callie waited a second then blew a raspberry. "No! There's a lot of Native American history, but I'm into Jefferson and Franklin and those guys."

"Then you're gonna love New England. We're lousy with history."

"I'm counting the days."

"Me, too. I found a nice B&B for us in P'town. Is that okay?"

"Sure. I'm doing well on finances, so I can pay up to $100 a night. Will that cover it?"

"No problem. This place is tiny but it's only seventy-five dollars a night."

"Really?"

"Yeah. You don't mind sharing a room, right?"

"I'd prefer it. Heck, I'll sleep on the floor if you can find a third."

"Two's enough for me. How about a bed? They say they'll try to give us twins, but they might only be able to manage a queen."

"No problem. I'd always rather save a few bucks. Just tell me when to arrive and I'll make my reservations."

"Come on Thursday before Memorial Day. We'll drive to P'town on Friday and come back on Monday afternoon. Then we'll hang out around here." She paused for a second. "Stay through the next weekend. Then I'll be able to take you into Boston and show you around. It's silly to come here and not see the city."

"I don't want you to get tired of me. I'm being serious. You probably like having some time to yourself."

"No, I'm not like that. I like being around people. Actually…even though I'm looking forward to it…I'm kinda worried about living alone."

"Really?"

"Yeah. It's good for me to try it, but I don't think I'm gonna like it. After a month of being alone, I know I'll love having you around, and since I'll have a fast internet connection, you can't claim you have to be home to work."

"I'd love to stay for a while. But only if you're one hundred percent positive you won't get tired of me."

"One hundred percent. I'm absolutely positive I won't want you to leave even if you stay a month. Now, go make that reservation and start your list of things you want to see."

"Will do. Congratulations, Regan. I can't wait to see you and your new house.

Callie had two months to plan her trip, but as the day approached, she still felt like she hadn't done nearly enough research.

On the day she left she spent the morning packing up the last of her things while her father watched, teasing her unrelentingly. "I thought you were going on a vacation for pleasure, not for research. Are you writing a travel guide?"

"You never know." She smirked at him while she found a place for the binder she'd made of the "must see" places she'd discovered. "You know I like to be prepared."

"I'm surprised you've never been to Boston. Actually, I'm surprised your mother never took you there."

Callie glanced at him, always puzzled by his inability to understand how little money the family had after he left. A week-long trip to Boston for the four of them with hotels and meals would have cost more than her mother made in a month; it was a trip they would have never considered. But her father had a blind spot about money, seeming to think he was the one who suffered the most financially from the divorce. Once in a while she had the guilty pleasure of fantasizing about telling him about the things they did without—about never having what the other kids had, about how jealous she'd been when her friends went to Disneyland, about her mother's having to tutor the rich kids all summer just to make ends meet. But she never would have told him those things. He wouldn't have understood, and it was too late to fix it now.

She banished the dismal thoughts, "We all love history. Mom was great at making it come alive for us. I've read so many books on the colonists and New England that I feel like I've been there. I just hope I don't have my expectations set too high."

He played with the big orange tag on her bag, asking casually, "What do you expect from Regan?"

"What do you mean?" She blinked, puzzled.

"You know..." He looked at her and tilted his head back and forth. "Are you dating?"

"Me and Regan?" She shook her head dismissively. "She's my pal. I'd be a wreck if it hadn't be for her. We've really been able to boost each other up when we've needed it."

"And that's all?"

"Yeah." She stopped and looked him in the eye. "Why do you ask?"

"I just wondered. It's been a while since you broke up with Marina and I assumed you were…moving on."

"I'm not ready. I'm sure of that. Besides, I've never even thought of Regan in that way, and I've never gotten any indication that she's into me, either. We're friends…like Terri and I are."

"I don't know why you'd want to just be friends if you could have more. I still don't think I understand this whole lesbian thing." His expression was so befuddled that she had to laugh.

"I'm not sure I understand it either, Dad, but I'm sure I'll learn the tricks eventually."

"I thought maybe you'd give men another try."

"I guess that could happen." She sat on her suitcase so she could zip it closed. "I'm not that concerned with the sex of who I date. At this point I only care about how honest they are. That's more important to me than genitals."

"I prefer genitals." His single dimple showed when he flashed his youthful smile.

CHAPTER THIRTEEN

CALLIE'S PLANE LANDED more or less on time, and as soon as they allowed it she called Regan. "I'm here!" Her voice with filled with excitement and was half an octave higher than usual.

"Good deal. It'll take about a half hour to get your luggage, so I'll swing by the pickup area at eight thirty. If you're not there, I'll keep circling, okay?"

"Great. See you soon. I'm excited!" She switched off and said more quietly to the man in front of her who had turned to glare at her. "Sorry. I'm excited."

Callie walked outside just as Regan drove by the first time. A remarkably small, bright red car pulled up and Regan called out, "It doesn't look like it, but I promise everything will fit." She put it into park and jumped out, running around to the curb to hug Callie. They embraced quickly, then Regan started trying to get the big bag into the small car. "I had to do this every time Angela went anywhere for more than a few days. I got pretty good at it." When it was snugly secured in the tiny trunk, she ran around and jumped in, turning to smile relievedly. "It's great to see you."

"Same here." Callie reached over and grasped Regan's arm, squeezing it tightly. "I've been looking forward to this like you wouldn't believe."

"Cool. Very cool." Regan checked her mirrors and started off. "Sorry about the tiny car, but I got it when I moved to Cambridge. Parking was unreal there and the less you had the better it was."

"I like your car. It suits you. But I'm not sure where those long legs are."

"Check and see how much further back my seat is. Yours is at the normal person position."

Callie put her hands in the air and shook them. "I'm jittery. I hardly slept a wink last night, but I feel like I've had ten cups of coffee."

"Then let's not make plans for the morning. We'll leave for P'town whenever. You'll probably want to sleep in."

"No, I'm fine. I can keep up. I don't need a lot of sleep if I'm doing something fun."

"Then I hope you don't need much sleep this week," Regan said, flashing a warm smile.

They left the house the next morning at ten a.m., after stopping at a diner in town for a breakfast of coffee and cheese omelets, which Callie pronounced one of the best she'd ever had. They'd only traveled a few miles when Callie said, "I've decided. This is much nicer than the Bahamas."

"It is nice, isn't it? I haven't traveled much, but I can't imagine too many places better than New England. We've got everything. Skiing, fishing, hiking, great bike trails. Small towns, big cities." She took in a breath of the clean, moist air. "But in my humble opinion you can't beat the Irish Riviera."

"Hmm, I thought the Riviera was in France. I swear, you can't trust a thing you learn in school."

"That's what we call the towns along the shore down here. You can't throw a rock and not hit an O'Malley or a McShane."

"I like it. A lot. Especially this salty air. I've been dying for moisture in the air my whole life. I've had enough of having my lungs scarred by dust and sand."

"Is Phoenix really that bad?" Regan shot her a quick glance. "I've never been anywhere that's real dry."

"No, it's not bad. A lot of people love it. Both sets of my grandparents moved to the desert from the Midwest. Voluntarily," she added, chuckling. "We had a chance to get out. My dad had a job offer from IBM when I was real little, but he didn't want to live in New York."

"Oh, right. I forget your dad's in the computer business."

"Yep. I think that influenced me in choosing my major." She smiled a sickly sweet grin. "Daddy's little girl."

"That's kinda nice."

"Yeah, it's nice to be able to speak the same language. I wanted to go to school to learn design, but the best schools are all private. So I went to Arizona and figured I'd have a real trade."

"So, is there anything good about the desert?"

"Sure. It can be beautiful, especially at sunset and sunrise. But we didn't live where you could see the mountains or the real desert, for that matter. We just lived in a nondescript neighborhood where it got a hundred and twenty degrees in the summer. To me, that's the worst of both worlds."

"You've really never liked where you live?"

"No, I can honestly say I've never liked it. A fair-skinned, redheaded girl is not the ideal desert dweller. I spent my youth covering myself with sunblock and looking for shade. I'd probably feel different if I lived in a house facing the Superstition Mountains or if I could see the desert blooming in the spring. But all I remember is being hot in the spring and summer and fall and being cold from the dry, cold wind in the winter. I just wasn't made for Phoenix."

"But Dallas is better, right?"

"Yeah, it's better in lots of ways. But it doesn't have an ocean," she said, dreamily, looking past Regan to see the vast expanse of blue, with whitecaps peaking every few feet. "I've always dreamed of living near the ocean." She smiled, a hint of sadness showing in her expression. "I guess I've always been a fish out of water."

As they motored down the Cape, Callie entertained Regan, calling out every time she saw a fish shack or a place advertising fresh lobster. "You really like to eat, don't you?" Regan asked, after a while.

"I lo-o-o-ove seafood. When I was a kid we never had it, so I didn't know what I was missing. "

"*What?* You never had seafood? Any kind of seafood?"

"Just fish-sticks at school."

"Amazing."

"I didn't really start to eat it until I went to college. There was a place we went that had shrimp by the bucket and my friends used to have to fight me to get any. I've never met a fish I didn't like."

"We were raised on fish." She pursed her lips. "Other than a good burger or a hot dog once in a while, I hardly eat meat."

"I eat a lot of chicken, but I'd go for seafood all the time if I had a good place to buy it where it didn't cost twenty dollars a pound."

Regan smiled at her. "It sounds like you can eat two pounds by yourself, so you'd have to shop for bargains."

"If I lived here I'd learn how to fish."

"Don't tell my dad that," Regan said, eyes wide. "None of us likes to fish, to his great disappointment. He'd recruit you in a second."

"You say that like I'd object."

"You know…I think you need to stay longer than a week. You've got a lot to accomplish."

By eleven Regan's stomach couldn't resist Callie's near constant discussion of seafood. "Okay. It's awfully early, but I think we'll stop for lunch."

"Oh, boy. There's nothing better than going on car trips with people who eat at least four meals a day."

"I don't think I'm going to have any trouble gaining back the weight I lost. I might gain it all back this week."

"Where are we going to go? If you can't decide we can go to two places. I can easily eat two lunches."

"Have you ever had Ipswich clams?"

"No, but I want to. Right now, please."

"I like traveling with people who are willing to try new things."

"Then we're gonna be very good travel friends."

Callie raved about the Ipswich clams and pronounced her crab cakes "world altering." When she took a bite of Regan's lobster roll, she said they'd have to come back for dinner even though Regan assured her that the roll only rated a B. They headed off again and now Callie could focus on the scenery, which she continued to rave about.

They arrived at twelve thirty, with Callie so excited that Regan feared for her blood pressure.

"This is so cute! I knew it would look just like this. Of course, I also spent about thirty hours looking at pictures on various photo-sharing sites."

"I think it's great that you spent so much time getting ready for this trip. There's nothing blasé about you."

"I can be blasé, but not about things that really interest me. And I could hardly be more interested than I am now."

"It's cool for me because almost everyone I know is from the area. I don't get to see New England through an outsider's eyes very often."

"I'm a rank outsider, but I hope that doesn't last long."

Regan parked her car in a sliver of a spot in front of a saltbox-style home, painted one shade darker than the crisp blue sky.

"Is this it?" At Regan's nod, Callie said "This is the cutest house I've ever seen."

Regan stood still for a moment, a puzzled look on her face as she gazed at the simple building. "Really? These kinda houses are a dime a dozen."

"I've never seen one until today." She tilted her chin, clearly thinking. "Nope never. It's really cute."

"Yeah, I guess it is. They've put on some little touches that make it nice."

"These kinds of houses are probably like adobe-style houses in Phoenix. You get used to them and stop noticing."

"I'll try to pay more attention." Regan put an arm around Callie's shoulders. It wasn't possible to resist her charms. And she was the kind of person who liked to touch a lot. That was nice. She made you feel kinda warm inside. Like family. "You're helping me see things that I'd normally miss. I like it."

They got checked in and spent a little time putting their things away. It was almost three o'clock when Regan said, "Ready for a tour?"

"Definitely."

"Let's go for a running tour. Lace 'em up."

First they went all the way down Commercial Street, the main business street. They stopped whenever the mood struck Callie, which was often. When they had exhausted all of the stores, they went on a long run on the firm sand of the harbor-side beach. Callie kept taking exaggeratedly huge breaths of air and letting them out through her nose. "It's so wonderful to breathe air that's moist. At this time of the year in Phoenix I'd have to run just after dawn or at sunset and even then it would be too hot to enjoy it."

"Well, it's just getting nice here. It's too early in the season to go in the water, but it might be warm enough to lie on the sand tomorrow. Cross your fingers."

"I don't care if we can do that or not. It's so nice to see you again that I'm just happy to talk…and eat."

That evening, the air was cool but not brisk, and it was very pleasant to stroll down Commercial Street while Callie marveled at how many women were there.

"There are more women during Women's Week in October. This weekend's primarily for singles. The one in the fall has more couples.

"I guess we've come to the right one." Callie said giving Regan a smirk.

"I hardly notice attractive women. My normal instincts are all screwed up."

"I don't know how you could ignore this many women. I haven't been looking at home, but this is paradise."

Regan smiled and patted her on the shoulder. "Feel free. You have my cell phone number. Just call me before Monday at noon and I'll find you."

"I think I'll stick with you. Besides, I don't think I'm ready to hook up again. Sometimes women are more trouble than they're worth."

They decided to go to a dance at one of the bigger venues. It was crowded and very loud, but they found places to sit next to the bar in a little nook that allowed them to shout into each other's ear. Callie had playfully attached her own and Regan's orange sticker to her shirt, showing she was doubly single. "So, you're impervious to women these days?" Callie asked.

A frown furrowed Regan's brow. Why didn't Callie understand this? She must be ready to find a woman or she wouldn't ask that question. "Yeah, I suppose I am. Maybe seeing all of these women dance will shock my system back into working order."

"You'll dance with me, won't you?"

She took Regan's hand and tried to pull her towards the dance floor. There was something awfully nice about having a woman as pretty as Callie give off that sultry look. No wonder she'd found a girlfriend the minute she'd decided to give one a try. "You don't need me. Every woman who's walked by has given you a second look."

"Really?" A huge smile settled on Callie's face. "Maybe they can tell I've been on a starvation diet."

When a particularly cute woman gave her a questioning glance three times, Regan pointed to Callie, pointed to the woman and then touched her fingers together—then she put her hand on Callie's back and propelled her toward the woman.

"Your friend's trying to get rid of you," the stranger said when Callie bumped into her.

Callie turned and saw Regan's grin. She stuck her tongue out at her, then turned back to the woman. "No, she just wants me to have fun."

The woman's dark eyes glinted with interest. "Then let's start. I'm Tracy."

As they moved away Regan watched them avidly. Callie batted her eyes as if she was just playing, but Tracy looked smitten already. Who could blame her? Callie was the best looking woman there…when you took into account how much fun she was, she didn't have a bit of competition. You could see the energy in her eyes, even if she hadn't been dancing like she'd had twenty cups of coffee. Yeah, she was a prize. And if she wanted to be faithful, she'd make a damn nice girlfriend for some lucky woman. If not, you'd be better off alone.

Over an hour after she'd left her seat, Callie fought her way through the crowd to find Regan. It was as though she were spit out when the crowd disgorged her and banged her into Regan's knees. "Sorry!" she said, having to put her mouth almost against Regan's ear to be heard. She noticed a pretty dark-haired woman who was obviously talking to Regan. The stranger was looking at Callie as though she wanted her to get lost.

"Having fun?" Callie asked.

"Yeah. I'm good. Hang out if you want."

"Want me to stay?"

"You can, but you don't need to. I'm fine."

Callie was dancing in place, while leaning over to speak into the ear furthest from the woman who was clearly set on making something happen with Regan. "Wanna dance?"

"No, I'm fine right here. I just got a drink." She inclined her head towards the woman next to her. "Want to meet my friend?"

"I don't want to intrude. Have fun!"

Callie turned back towards the crowd. A woman swooped by and took her by the hand, grinning as she started to dance. Callie joined her and in a few seconds put her hands over her head and started to jump up and down in a happy cry of freedom as she sang along with the hit tune, "Now that you're gone, I can be who I wanna be…"

At midnight Regan said her good-byes to the woman she'd been talking with. She was from Quincy and they'd known each other briefly in junior college. They had a few friends in common and had gone down the list, chatting about who was where and with whom. The music had gotten even louder and Regan was starting to lose her voice, so she decided to pack it in. She'd seen Callie dancing with at least six different people and when she finally found her at the other end of the club, she stopped and stared in surprise. Callie was sitting on a woman's lap kissing her with malicious intent.

She stood there, transfixed for a few seconds, then moved far enough away so Callie couldn't see her. Her heart was thudding in her chest and she puzzled over that for a moment. Maybe the thud came from the music, but the beat wasn't the same. She was amazed to find herself looking at Callie just like the woman whose lap she sat on. Callie was so damn alluring. She had a way of staring into that woman's eyes like she was the most interesting thing on earth. Like every word out of her mouth should be written down.

Then Callie held the woman's head, kissing her fiercely as she shifted and straddled her lap. No wonder Marina was so into her. Callie was as hot as they came. Her hands were shaking when she took out her wallet, found a scrap of paper and borrowed a pen to write a quick note telling Callie the address of the house and asking her to call if she wasn't going to come home. Then she went back and placed it daintily on the table and started to walk away.

"Regan! Wait!"

She stopped and turned to find Callie goofily grinning at her. "Ready to go?"

"Yeah, but you don't have to."

"I came with you, I leave with you," she shouted. "This is Cheri." She turned and kissed her on the cheek.

"Are you sure?" Cheri said. "I could take you home. I have a car."

"That's sweet of you. But I'm here with my friend and I'll go home with her." Callie disentangled herself, then attempted to stand as Cheri held onto her waistband and tried to pull her back down. Callie deftly removed her hand, leaned down and gave her a quick kiss. "Maybe I'll see you tomorrow on the beach." She waved, then took Regan's arm as they headed for the door.

When they got outside, Regan spent a moment trying to dispel the image of Callie eating that woman alive. "I couldn't tell if you were ready to leave or if you were just being polite."

"Both." Callie grasped her arm and hugged it. "I can do two things at once."

"You looked like you were having fun." A massive understatement.

"Yeah, I was. She was super cute, wasn't she?"

"Yeah. She looked like a lot of fun."

"Yep. She liked to kiss as much as I do. Kissing is the best, isn't it?"

"Yeah, sure. I just don't have that…drive anymore. It seems like something I used to do, but lost interest in."

"I felt the same this afternoon, but my drive started to wake up tonight." She shivered in the cool air. "Cheri woke it up but good!"

CHAPTER FOURTEEN

WHEN CALLIE BLINKED her eyes open the next morning, Regan looked at her guiltily as she slipped into a pair of jeans. "Sorry," she whispered, "I didn't mean to wake you up."

The sun was shining brightly and Callie rolled over and looked out the window. "What time is it?"

"It's around eight. I'm starving. I thought I'd head down for breakfast."

"Do you want to go alone?" Callie tossed her head back and forced the hair from her eyes.

"No. Not a bit. I thought you'd like to sleep longer."

Callie threw the covers off, stood up and stretched. "It's a beautiful day and I'm in a beautiful place. Why would I waste such a nice day lying in bed?"

"Are you always a morning person?"

"Yeah, comparatively speaking. Marina always got up before I did and she made me feel like a lazy bum."

"And she was such a role model of behavior."

"Screw her. I'm sorry I brought her up. If you'll give me five minutes, I'll go with you."

"If you can really get ready in five minutes you might be the ideal woman."

Callie smiled at her and tousled her hair as she walked by. "I'm not saying I'll look good, just that I'll be ready."

She hadn't looked bad yet, in two countries and three cities. That wasn't exactly true. She'd looked wonderful. Simply wonderful.

After breakfast they strolled down Commercial to see what was going on. Callie saw a sign advertising a touch football game that was set to start in a short while. "Let's play!"

"Really?"

When Regan looked extremely skeptical, Callie said, "I can keep up. I might be old but I'm energetic."

"You're certainly not old by any means. I don't think *I* can keep up. These girls get rough. It's flag football, but they play like it's tackle."

"Are you serious?" She took Regan by the hand and started to lead her down the street. "You're too young to be tentative."

"I'm not tentative," Regan protested feebly, holding back a little as Callie practically dragged her along. "My track coach always warned us to stay away from any kind of contact sports to make sure we didn't hurt our knees."

"You're out of high school now, and no one will know," she whispered loudly. "It'll be our secret. And if you blow a knee out, I'll tell everyone you were helping an old lady across the street when a truck hit you."

They were put on different teams and every time they faced each other at the line of scrimmage, Callie put on a fierce expression and glowered at Regan, who was completely unable to keep a straight face. But she got into the game when their quarterback saw how quick Regan was. She kept trying to throw to her downfield, but she had a tough time throwing with anything close to accuracy. Time and again Regan was wide-open, but she never had a ball thrown within two feet of her.

Callie did better when she showed that she was fairly fearless and was able to jump over a fallen teammate or defender. She took a handoff and streaked along the sideline scoring a touchdown right before Regan caught up with her and pulled the flag from her pants.

Callie performed an exaggerated touchdown dance, then bent over and hiked the football between her legs to a surprised Regan who caught it defensively right before it hit her in the head. "You are fearless!" Regan said, clearly surprised.

"No, I'm not. I just love to win." She dashed away, singing, "I love to win. I love to win..."

The cool morning had turned into a lovely spring afternoon. They went to a coffee shop for drinks to go, then sat on a bench in front of the library and watched the parade of passersby.

The warm afternoon sun made Callie's hair glow in a copper radiance. Regan shielded her eyes and gazed at Callie for a moment. "I don't think a minute has gone by without somebody checking you out. Your hair is impossible to ignore."

Callie smiled mischievously and tossed her red hair over her shoulder. "I bet they were looking at you."

"No. They look at you, then they look again, then they take a quick glance at me to make sure I'm not going to mind."

Callie slapped her leg playfully. "You're good for my ego."

"Seriously, do you always get this kind of attention?"

"Attention?

"Don't play coy. I'm really interested."

Callie looked at her curiously and said "I'm not sure what you mean. Are you being serious when you say people are interested in me?"

Regan exaggeratedly rolled her eyes. She couldn't be dense enough not to see it. No one could ignore the kind of attention she got. "You're playing with me again."

"No, I'm not. I thought you were teasing."

"Come on. I was minimizing it if anything. When I'm ready to start dating again, you're the last person I'll hang out with. I'd get nothing but your rejects."

Callie looked around quickly as though she could catch someone in the act. "Now you're making me feel paranoid."

"Do you really not know? All those women talking to you at the football game weren't just being friendly."

Innocently, Callie batted her eyes. "They weren't?"

Regan pursed her lips and narrowed her eyes. "I can't tell if you're being straight with me or not. Do you know they're hitting on you?"

"I don't think they are. I think women are just friendlier than guys. They look a lot and make small talk, but that doesn't mean they want to jump on you. They're certainly not aggressive the way guys are."

"I don't know a lot about guys, but I think women are just as horny."

Callie patted Regan's leg as though she were a child. "Then you really don't know guys. Women aren't nearly as pushy as guys are. I danced with a bunch of women last night and none of them acted like they'd laid claim to me."

Every one of those women would have paid to sleep with her, and they would have claimed her if she hadn't danced away before any of them could catch her. How could she have slept around Dallas for more than a year and not have figured out how hot she was? Maybe it just didn't click for her. "You were too fast for them. I saw you slithering through that crowd." She placed her hands together and made them dart to and fro in tandem.

"It's different with women. Trust me. That's one of the reasons I don't see myself going back to men. If a guy wants you, it's hard to tell him to knock it off if you're not interested. It's much easier with women. Heck, if you just don't return the look very few of them would come back for a second try. It's much more polite. More civilized."

"Whatever you say. All I know is that you don't ever have to go home alone if you don't want to."

Grinning, Callie said, "Well, I didn't say you were wrong about that."

That grin was so confusing. Had she been teasing? There was a part of her that seemed wily. Like she knew exactly what she was doing. But then she seemed truly oblivious to how appealing she was. She was an absolute mass of contradictions.

For the next hour Callie played a little game where she tried to match which woman would look best with Regan. Regan seemed to enjoy Callie's interpretations, but after a while she said, "I'm just not feeling it. It's been six months and I'm not much more interested now than I was the day after we broke up."

Callie leaned over and gave her a gentle hug. With her arms still wrapped around her, she said quietly, "I know how hard this has been for you. I think Angela hurt you as deeply as it's possible to hurt someone."

When Regan pulled away, her eyes were bright with unshed tears. "It's so nice to know that you understand. Most people think I should be over this by now."

"I wish you were. I really do. But I know you have to just let it go at its own pace. When Rob and I broke up, I was a mess for a long time. The thought of being with another guy was repulsive."

Curiosity showing in her eyes, Regan said, "Do you think that's why you started dating Marina? The mere fact that she wasn't a man?"

"It's impossible to know. I was definitely open to being with a woman, but I wasn't determined to go gay. It just happened. She came along at the right, or maybe the wrong, time."

"I don't think I know anyone who seems truly bisexual. Most of the women I know who've been with men did it because of family pressure, or they were confused."

"I wasn't confused. That's for sure. I've always thought women were attractive, and I'm sure I would've dated a woman if I hadn't been with Rob for so long. I gave him my prime experimenting years."

"I'd think college was the prime time for that."

"Not for me. I spent my first two years partying, then the next one trying to get my GPA up. Then I met the coolest guy." She acted like she was on the verge of fainting, half falling into Regan's lap. "We were like a magnet and a steel bar. I was stuck to him for years. But he didn't ever get out of the frat boy thing and I had to move on."

"So just those two guys melted your heart?"

"Not hardly." She leaned her head back and laughed up into the sky. "I had boyfriends in junior high and high school too. I was into guys, Regan. *Really* into them."

"Well, I've got to say that once you decided to give women a try you did it in a big way. You went all in." Regan shook her head, looking both amused and amazed.

"Yeah, being with Marina probably wasn't the right choice for a beginner. But sometimes it's hard to see that when you're in the middle of it."

Somewhat tentatively, Regan asked, "If you had to do it over again would you change anything?"

"That's not a game I like to play. I made my choices the best I could. I just try to learn from them."

"What did you learn from Marina?"

Callie thought about the question for a long time. But image after image of Marina and Angela together assaulted her brain. It hurt like a punch to the gut, so she shut it off, refusing to invite that pain back in. "I'm not sure what I've learned. I thought I'd protected myself against being two-timed, but I got screwed over again." She knew she should have a better answer, but she wasn't interested in this game. Dredging up old hurts didn't make them go away, it just made the wound fresh again. There was nothing to learn from Marina, other than to stay away from anyone even remotely like her.

After breakfast on Monday morning they packed up to leave. Callie was full of energy and she took off for a run while Regan read the paper and chatted with the other guests. When Callie returned, she was carrying a large bouquet of flowers that she presented to Regan, proclaiming, "Happy Birthday!"

Regan blushed, but took the flowers and gave Callie a kiss on the cheek. "Thanks. I love getting flowers."

"My pleasure. I've never given a woman flowers. Oh, wait. Does my mom count?"

Their host, a friendly gay man of about fifty smiled at the pair. "You two make a cute pair. How long have you been together?"

"Oh, we're not together like that," Callie said. "We've just been friends for a few months, but we're united by a common goal." She grinned at Regan. "We're working to rid the world of cheating girlfriends."

"Good luck with that, girls. You've got your work cut out for you."

CHAPTER FIFTEEN

BECAUSE IT WAS the end of a three-day weekend, the traffic back down the Cape was very heavy, but neither woman seemed to mind. They'd both had a terrific time and neither was in a huge hurry to get back to Scituate.

They were about five miles from home when Regan's cell phone rang. Callie searched through their bags in the tiny car and found it just after it went to voicemail. She handed it to Regan. "My older sister. Probably calling to wish me a happy birthday." She opened the phone and hit a speed dial number, then put it on speakerphone. "Hi, Delaney. What's up?"

A voice that sounded quite a bit like Regan's but with a stronger Boston accent said, "You're gonna kill me, but I screwed something up on the computer. It's messed up all of the orders. I know it's your day off and I know it's your birthday. Happy birthday, by the way, but you've gotta get me the name of the guy who does repairs."

Regan sighed heavily. "He's not gonna make a call today. If you broke it, I can fix it. I'm not far from home. I'll come by."

"I hate to have you do that. Isn't there some twenty-four-hour place that I can call?"

"I'll be there in a half hour. Don't touch anything." She hung up without saying goodbye, then shot a quick glance at Callie. "I can drop you off at my house first."

"No, I'll go with you. Then I can meet your sister."

"Yeah, you probably should meet her before I kill her."

A half hour later they pulled into a very large parking lot, then went around the back of a series of buildings. They got out of the car with Regan still mumbling her unhappiness. "There's no reason for Delaney to be messing around with the main computer. I barely know what I'm doing, and I know ten times more than she does. She's always sticking her nose into my business."

To try to improve her mood Callie said, "I want to go in the front door, like a guest would. Then I can see how it would feel if someone was having an event here."

That seemed to pull Regan out of her funk. "I'm sorry. I know you were looking forward to seeing our place. Let's cut through the parking lot. When my parents bought this place only the original building was here, but there was a very big building next door that had some kind of woodworking shop in it. When they got a little money they bought that too, tore it down, and built the big reception room. They did it really smart though, by leaving a big empty space between the two buildings and landscaping that area really nicely. It's great for photos."

They got to the front and Regan's smile increased as they saw the entrance to the building. "The restaurant's here on the right and the entrance for a wedding or a big party is there on the left."

Both doors were beautifully carved and contained some lacy ironwork covering glass inserts. "It's lovely. Just beautiful."

"Wanna see the garden?"

"Absolutely."

They went in through the door to the reception facility and large glass doors looked out on a lovely garden, planted with leafy green plants and row upon row of annual flowers. A fountain spouted from a trio of large rocks, splashing water down the rock face and pooling in a small pond below.

"This is really, really nice. Anyone would be lucky to have a wedding here."

"This place is the result of a lot of years of very hard work, mostly by my parents. They should be coming up from Florida pretty soon; maybe by the end of next week. They're usually here by now, but they had some things to take care of before they took off for the summer."

They went back to the main entrance and Regan pushed open the door to the restaurant. As soon as they passed the entrance, a crowd of people yelled "Surprise!" and dozens and dozens of balloons descended from the ceiling. Regan slapped both of her hands over her face and shook her head, laughing. She looked around to find her older sister. "I was so ready to kick your ass!" She looked just a few feet away and saw her parents. "Mom! Dad!" She rushed over to them and they both wrapped her in a hug. She waved Callie over.

"Callie, I want you to meet my mom and dad." While Callie was shaking their hands, Regan reached out and clapped her arm around her sister's neck and pulled her over. "And this prankster is my sister, Delaney."

Callie was surprised at the family resemblance in all the Mannings. They were attractive people, but there was something special about Regan, some quality that made her shine no matter who she was standing by. A much younger-looking woman came up and introduced herself, "I'm Alana. You must be Callie."

Regan pulled her younger sister in for a hug. "This is the woman who made that delicious dinner for us the night you arrived. I know you'll be Callie's favorite because there's nothing she likes more than eating."

"That food was wonderful," Callie said. "If you were my sister and you fed me all the time, someone would have to stage an intervention."

"Well, I didn't cook today, but I think the food will still be good. Regan, introduce your friend around. Don't be such a lunk."

"I've been here two minutes," Regan said, with just a little bit of testiness showing in her voice. But she took Callie around and introduced her first to her grandparents, then to every cousin, aunt, uncle, friend and employee in the place. It was fairly crowded, with about forty people in attendance, and it took quite a while to make the entire circuit.

"Who are those people?" Callie asked, pointing at two men sitting at the bar.

"Customers. We're open today but don't have any parties scheduled because of the holiday. People tend to stay home on Memorial Day."

"You guys almost fill the place. " She looked around. "There isn't an empty table."

"We'll only have a few lonely guys like Johnny and Rich over there. They're the kinds of guys you don't want to make mad. They come here two or three times a week and they'd throw a fit if we shut them out."

"I guess you're always at the public's beck and call when you're in the restaurant business."

"That's an understatement. But this is the only job I've ever had, so I'm used to it."

They all ordered off the menu, but there was only one waitress on duty and she was inundated, so Delaney and Alana took the orders to the kitchen and helped serve the food. It was fairly chaotic, but it seemed what everyone was used to.

Callie had just about finished a truly delicious lobster salad club sandwich when Regan's father got to his feet and yelled in full voice, "Oh, no, you don't. You get out of my restaurant and you stay out!"

Callie looked toward the door but it took a few seconds for her eyes to adjust to the bright light. When they did, she was astounded to see Regan's father rushing towards a tall, elegantly dressed, beautiful black woman.

Regan leapt to her feet and reached the woman just as her father did. She wrapped an arm around him and pushed him aside as well as she could, saying something to him privately. Callie watched as Angela stood just inside the door, looking unsure of whether she should beat a hasty retreat or stand where she was. Regan was talking very animatedly, and her father at last nodded his head a few times. When she let him go, he approached Angela who, to Callie's respect, didn't flinch. He put out his hand and said, "I apologize. It's just that when my little girl gets her heart broken…"

"It's okay, George. I understand."

Regan's friend Sheila was sitting next to Callie. She said, "I think he should kick her ass."

Callie nodded. "That wouldn't be a bad idea."

Sheila leaned closer and whispered, "You know the whole truth, don't you?"

"Yeah. I know more than I wish I did."

"Regan's too good for that bitch. What kind of an asshole would cheat on her?"

Callie sat there and stared at the women who were now talking quietly to one another while the rest of the guests tried to act as though they weren't watching them. Regan had said Angela was beautiful, and she was much prettier in person than she appeared in the photo Regan carried. She was a little taller than Regan, but that could have been because of her shoes. Even on Memorial Day, she dressed like she was going to a conference in business-casual attire. What a dumb name. But that's how Marina dressed too. Women in power didn't seem to have jeans and T-shirts.

Angela's broad shoulders in a white linen blouse made her look imposing. She was the kind of woman who looked like she owned the place, even though she'd almost been thrown out. Marina had that too. The unflappable calm that let them look like they were in charge even when they weren't.

They were almost nose to nose and when Regan jerked back and forth as she made each point, her straight, dark ponytail bounced. She didn't have a two hundred dollar blouse on, or linen slacks that barely had a wrinkle in them. Her worn, white, golf shirt had shrunk so much it barely covered the waistband of her pale red shorts, and her battered deck shoes looked like she might have had them since high school. But none of that mattered. She was Angela's equal.

Something about Regan made you want to look at her, and her alone. Angela was beautiful and very compelling, and had probably spent a long time that day trying to look both elegant and casual, but Regan outshone her with almost no effort.

Maybe it was her height and the casual grace she showed when she moved—a fluid, athletic grace let her glide around more like a dancer than a runner.

But it was more than that. Somehow her maturity and her poise made her seem worldly and mature. Even though Angela was thirteen years older and had a very important position in the business world, Regan looked so comfortable standing next to her that she could have been her boss.

Regan's eyes flashed angrily, and she started to use her hand to gesture in Angela's direction a few times, finally pointing her finger and poking it into Angela's chest. As soon as she did that Angela put her hand on Regan's back, opened the door, and led her outside. When that happened everyone inside started talking louder and more excitedly. The entire group was talking about Angela and wondering how she got the nerve to show up at a big family party. But it made perfect sense when you thought about it for a minute. You just didn't let a woman like Regan get away without putting up a hell of a fight. If you had to show up someplace you weren't welcome—you sucked it up and did it. You had to fight for her. You'd be an idiot if you didn't.

Angela and Regan faced each other under the warm sun, the blacktop of the parking lot simmering under their feet. "I've never seen you look so angry," Angela said, her lush, full voice soft against the silence.

"I'm damned angry." Regan's eyes were dark and focused so intently they seemed like they could burn. "How do you have the nerve to waltz into my party? I haven't heard a peep from you since the day I moved out."

"Are you angry that I didn't call earlier or that I'm here now?"

"Both!" Regan saw her hands reach out to push Angela away, to knock the calm, self-assured look off her face. But some part of her body had the sense to back up and let her outstretched hands press against nothing but air. "Why couldn't you just leave me alone?" She felt her anger leave in a *whoosh*, replaced by an ache that seemed to blanket her heart. "I'm almost over you." That sounded like a complete lie and Angela would know it.

Reaching out with a tentative hand, Angela lightly touched Regan's shoulder. Her eyes were warm, her expression filled with empathy. "Don't get over me. Please." The last word was whispered, said so softly that Regan could only see it on Angela's lips. "I'll never be over you."

"You've been over me for months." Months! Not days. Not weeks. Not one word for months. It'd been like a death. A death that she had mourned. Now the corpse showed up and said it had been hiding.

"That's not true." Angela put her hand on Regan's shoulder once again and decisively led her to the entryway for the banquet room.

It was cool and quiet in the bright room, and both women stood for a moment, relishing the break from the heat. Angela kept guiding Regan, and they wound up sitting in the lovely garden, with the gentle, calming sounds of water cascading down the boulders. Regan took in a deep breath, smelling the sweet scents of jasmine and honeysuckle.

In her normal efficient style, Angela picked up right where she'd left off. "I didn't waste your time making excuses, and that's all I could have done at first. I know you. You're never interested in hearing promises. You want to see results."

Blankly, Regan asked, "Results? What results?"

"I've made some changes. Big changes."

"Like what?" Regan gazed at her warily. How could she look just the same? Hadn't this changed her forever? How could a dead woman keep talking like they'd just been apart because of a business trip?

"I found a very good therapist. I told her how I'd ruined a relationship I was devastated about, and she's helping me figure a lot of things out."

"Go on."

"I'm seeing her twice a week, and when I travel I call her and we have our session on the phone. I haven't missed one."

Therapy? For Angela? She'd rather have had her fingernails pulled out. She had to have changed a ton to let a stranger into her head. But how could anyone change that much? She was guarded with almost everyone. But she seemed sincere. More open.

"That's good. Therapy can really help you see your patterns."

"Right. That's a good way to put it. Carole has helped me see how so much of my behavior is harmful to a good relationship. She suggested I start taking a meditation class, and that's helped me relax at night. I'm sleeping better too, I don't have to read until I collapse."

That was impossible. Insomnia clung to Angela like her clothes. She'd be lying in bed, reading some journal, acting like it was vital to learn whatever was in it by morning. No one could function on as little sleep as she did. No one could put you off for 'just a few minutes' to finish an article like she did every time there was a hint of sexual energy in the room. But she could accomplish almost anything that she put her mind to. Maybe even learn how to sleep. "That's good. You must feel better."

"I do." She looked at Regan with her dark brown eyes, so full of warmth and caring. "But I miss you so, so much."

"I miss you too."

"You do?" Light glimmered in her eyes, and a small smile bloomed.

"Of course I do. I was going to be with you until I died, Angela. I was going to have a baby with you. How could I not miss you?"

Angela's head dropped, and Regan spent a moment looking at how her glossy hair shone in the late afternoon sun. Angela spent a lot of time and money getting her hair to look just like she wanted it. Now it looked marvelous. So soft and touchable. She had a desire to reach out and caress it, then slide her hand down to Angela's jaw and feel her swallow. Feel the warmth of her skin, her pulse point beating against her fingers. But that was over. She shook her head to dispel those dangerous thoughts and concentrate on the present.

"Carole's not an expert, so she's recommended a sex therapist. If you're willing—I'm ready to commit to going until we fix our problems."

Bitterly, Regan heard herself snap, "So you finally admit we had problems. Nice timing."

"It's awful timing. I know that. But we did have problems. Big ones. Actually," she said, taking a breath, "I'm the one with the problem. You were always ready to make love." Her head hung again, vulnerability radiating from her. Regan's hand lifted and hovered for just a second. But Angela lifted her head and squared her shoulders, in charge once again. "I'll fix whatever's broken. That's a promise."

"But how do you fix something like your sex drive?"

"I don't know. But if it can be fixed, I'll fix it. There's a solution to every problem. You just have to throw enough time and manpower into it."

"Manpower? I don't think that's the solution to this one."

"You know what I mean. I can overcome any obstacle if I work hard enough."

"I'm not sure that's true. You can't make me trust you again, and that's the biggest problem."

"Yes I can," she said with fervor. "I've talked to my pastor and my parents and most of my friends. I've told everyone what I've done to you. I've *shamed* myself, Regan. Uncovered my soul to all of the people I respect. They'll all be watching to make sure I've learned my lesson."

This was a revelation of the greatest magnitude. Angela's reputation was her most prized possession. She'd always been the model daughter, and admitting her failings to her parents had to be unfathomably painful. "Wow," Regan said quietly. "That must have been rough."

A sliver of a smile showed. "You have no idea. But I sinned against you and the only way to be forgiven is to throw light on my faults."

"Couldn't you just ask God to forgive you?"

Angela smiled, a gentle, patient expression that nearly melted Regan's heart. She had the most beautiful smile when she showed this side of herself. This was the lovable, almost irresistible woman she'd fallen for. From that first day they'd met, this was the open, kind smile that drew her in. "I sinned against you, not God. It's your forgiveness that I need."

"So why did you have to tell everyone what happened?"

"For insurance. I swear I'll never be unfaithful again, but I broke that promise once. Having all of the most important people in my life know will help keep me honest. Having secrets is bad for me. I realize that now." A flicker of a smile showed. "I came out at work."

"No!"

"Yeah, I did. No more secrets."

Unable to hold back, Regan gave her a quick, heartfelt hug. "I'm proud of you."

Grinning almost girlishly, Angela said, "I'm proud of myself. I've made a lot of positive changes in the last few months, but I've barely started." She gazed deeply into Regan's eyes. "I want you to come home. You can quit your job and concentrate on getting pregnant."

Regan's eyes grew wide. "Quit my job?"

"Sure. I got a huge bonus this year. It's not quite what your salary is, but it's close." Her whole face lit up with excitement. "We can start our family, Regan. It's what we both wanted."

"Wait!" Regan stood, staring down at Angela. "What the hell? You've been off doing all of this therapy but I'm still back at 'you broke my heart.'"

"But doing all of this shows you…shows you in concrete terms how much you mean to me."

Dropping back down onto the bench, Regan shook her head. "You're not listening to me. I still don't know why you slept with Marina."

Angela frowned, looking annoyed. "She's not involved in this. This is about you and me. We had problems that I ignored."

"Yeah, yeah, that's fine, but you destroyed us by sleeping with *her*. Not some anonymous stranger. Something about *her* attracted you. You'd better figure out what that was. It's a complete mystery to me."

Now Angela stood and started to slowly walk around in front of Regan. Her hands were balled into fists, and she bristled with nervous energy. "None of that matters. What I did was wrong. I admit that. What's important is how we move forward."

"Not to me," Regan said firmly. "I want to know why you did it."

"I told you. I was out of town, I'd had a few drinks and Marina made it clear she wanted to get together. I don't have any better explanation."

"You need one." Regan stood up and faced Angela. "You slept with her for a year and a half. If you were drunk every time, you've got another problem to tackle." A bolt of pleasure crawled up her spine when Angela's composed expression collapsed. How did it feel to have the rug pulled out from under her?

Angela sat there for a minute, eyes blinking in surprise. But then her outsized personality shut every weakness down. "Why does that matter? A sin is a sin if it was once or a hundred times."

"That's not true. You admitted you did it once. Why hide if it wasn't important to hide?" Let her figure out a way to slither out of that one.

"It was too embarrassing." She hung her head, looking ashamed. "I can't stand to admit how weak I was."

"You were very weak. And no matter what you claim, you'd damn well better understand what made you cheat and continue to lie about it until this very minute. That's the only way you'll ever be completely faithful."

"Are you saying you'll give me another chance if I can do that?" Her eyes were filled with hope, and she looked so expectant that Regan felt like she was plunging a knife into her when she spoke her truth.

"No. We're through."

When Regan walked back into the restaurant her cheeks were flushed and it was fairly clear that she'd been crying. She'd been outside for almost twenty minutes and Callie was desperate to know what had happened. But the first thing Regan did was point at her sister Alana, then walk into a room to the left of the kitchen that Callie assumed was her office.

Sheila let out a soft whistle. "Alana's in for a butt kicking."

"How's Alana involved?"

"She and Angela got to be pretty good friends. The only way Angela would have known to come here today was if someone had told her that we were having a party. Regan hates it when people get involved in her personal business, but that's never stopped Alana."

Alana and Regan were in the office for a long time, probably as long as Regan had been outside with Angela. When they finally emerged, they were both smiling, and Regan had her hand on her sister's shoulder. Everyone got fairly quiet and Regan stood on the step that led into the dining area so everyone could see her. "I'm sorry for all the drama, but everything's good. Now let's continue celebrating me." She flashed her warmest smile, and Callie felt her pulse pick up. She sat there for a second, trying to figure out why she felt flushed; then it hit her. It was Regan that was making her feel this way. There was something so attractive about her smile. Callie thought it was probably the most beautiful smile she had ever seen.

When Regan sat down, Callie felt almost tongue-tied; that had never happened to her before with Regan. She managed to ask, "Are you really okay?"

Regan barely moved her head up and down. "I'll tell you all about it later." She offered a less luminous version of the smile, one that showed her pain.

They arrived back at Regan's while it was still light. Regan suggested they go for a stroll by the harbor, so they set out for the short walk. "I've never been to a real harbor," Callie said, unable to keep the excitement out of her voice.

"This is a real one." It seemed like those few words had been very difficult to get out. It was obvious Regan was hurting, but being so close to the ocean was so cool that Callie had a hard time staying quiet.

The air was deliciously tangy with salt. The moisture from the ocean took the heat from the day and magically made it disappear. Faded gray shingled houses lined the shore and, as they approached, the noise of the waves slapping against huge rocks grew louder.

The bright white lighthouse was the biggest thing in sight, and the setting sun made it glow as if from within.

Muted bells clanged in the distance and gulls swept over their heads, cawing loudly, like the soundtrack of a movie set in a small New England town. A small building sat at the end of the pier. It was a burnished, weathered gray, with signs and notices, announcements of every sort covering its walls. A very early version of the local internet. It was magical. Simply magical. Like finding Brigadoon.

Unable to stay quiet, Callie tried to get a smile out of her friend. "This is where I live now. This is exactly what I've always wanted. Water close by, boats, fishing, good air, and a big city just twenty minutes away. I'd trade with you in a second. Just like that," she said, acting like a used-car salesman. "You'd have your own room with a view of the building next door and the trash bins. A very nice man sleeps in the next room, and he's almost a doctor. If you ever need CPR in the middle of the night, think of how convenient that would be."

Regan slung an arm around Callie's shoulders and gave her a quick hug. "I think you should stop fantasizing about moving and start making plans. I'd really love to have you…" She stopped and her composure started to fracture. "I need someone to talk to." She put her arms around Callie and collapsed against her body. It took all of Callie's strength to get her feet centered so she could hold her up, but Callie held onto her tightly and tried to soothe her as she cried.

"She's done everything I wanted her to do when we were together. She went to therapy, she's learning how to talk about what bothers her. Everything. But it's too late. It's just too late, and that breaks my heart all over again."

CHAPTER SIXTEEN

CALLIE WAS TRYING to figure out how to use the coffee maker when Regan stumbled out of her bedroom the next morning. "I've really got to get to work, but I'm dog tired. I don't think I slept ten minutes. Do I look as bad as I feel?"

Callie walked over and gave her a hug, then pulled back and moved Regan's dark hair around until it looked as neat as it always did. "You have the best hair. I've never known anyone with hair this straight. It falls right into place."

"Yeah, it does, as long as you don't mind it falling into the exact same place every single day."

"I think it's lovely. And you look just fine. Go take a shower and I'll have some coffee ready for you." She physically turned her and pushed her in the direction of her bedroom.

Regan came out about fifteen minutes later looking not much better. Her eyes were still bloodshot and red rimmed despite the shower. Callie handed her a cup of coffee. "What can I do for you today?"

"Nothing. I just wish I didn't look so bad. My sisters will be on me all day, and they won't buy my story when I tell them seeing Angela didn't bother me."

Callie plucked at a hank of Regan's hair, still wet from the shower. "Give me ten minutes and I can divert their attention."

A few minutes later, Regan was sitting on a stool in the kitchen, while Callie blew her hair dry. "You wanted to be a hair dresser?"

"It wasn't a driving need, but it was on my short list. I really like hair."

"Feels good." Regan leaned into her hand when Callie captured a fistful of strands and pulled them straight to let the air get to them all. "Helps my headache."

"I wish you could stay home."

"Me too. But I don't do that unless it's really necessary. I never get a mental health day. We've all agreed to only skip work when we're contagious, and I don't think they're as upset about Angela as I am."

Regan gave such a wan smile that Callie almost cried when she looked into her eyes, so filled with pain. She wanted to hold her, to stroke her back until she relaxed. Then take her back to bed and hold her until she felt better. But they didn't do that kind of thing. There were too many barriers to overcome. They were just friends. She tried to focus on their reality, putting all of her attention into styling Regan's hair. Using a comb, she pulled half of it back and held it. "I'm going to let the rest hang down." She put a band around the hair and then stood in front of her, arranging it just a little. "This looks really different, even though it's only a little change. You have such a great natural part that it works perfectly."

Regan got up and went into the bath, jutting her chin out as she moved her head a bit. "It does look good."

"I like it pulled straight back since your features are so strong. But change is good."

"You can do this any time you want. But if left to my own devices, it's going straight back. I'm lazy at heart."

"I'll get ready and take you to work, okay?"

"Yep. That's the plan."

Callie smiled and rubbed her hands together. "I've got my day all planned out. I'm going to go to the John Adams place in Quincy and a couple of other places around the area. Then I'll come home and get some work done."

"I like the way you say home. I just hope you mean it."

"I would really like to move here. I was very serious when we talked last night."

When Regan gave her a full smile, Callie's breath caught. It was impossible to look into those sky blue eyes and think of anything but being lost in them.

Regan brought dinner home from the restaurant and, after they ate, they went for a run around the harbor. Callie could tell that Regan didn't have much gas left in her tank, so they cut it short. When they got back to the townhouse Callie made what she hoped wasn't a dangerous offer. "Why don't you sit on the floor and let me rub your shoulders for a while. That might help your headache."

"Can you really do that?" Regan asked, looking hopeful.

"Yeah. I'm very good at it." Regan practically dropped to get into position for Callie to rub her shoulders. She whipped off her T-shirt, unconscious, as usual, about being partially dressed. It was wrong in every way to think of Regan as more than a friend when she was so hurt and vulnerable. There would be time for that when she was more like herself. Callie was very proud of herself when she was able to give Regan a good massage, making her pliable and loose limbed. It was only nine o'clock, but when Regan stood up, Callie stood up with her and started to lead her towards the bedroom.

"Where are we going?"

"*You* are going to bed. I can tell how tired you are."

"But...!"

"But nothing. You'll be in a much better mood tomorrow if you get some rest. And I've got so many things to do tomorrow I should get to bed early too."

Regan turned and gave Callie a grateful hug. "Thanks. For everything."

"You're very welcome. I'm just glad I'm here this week."

"Go to sleep and dream about moving here. That's what will really make me happy."

When they were in Regan's bed—together—everything would be perfect. Moving to Boston was just the first part of the plan.

The next day Regan juggled a few things around and was able to leave work by three. She showed up just a few minutes later and found Callie sitting on the deck working on a website she was trying to complete. "Hi. What's the chance of me stealing you away to go for a run to see something I think you'd enjoy."

Callie jumped to her feet and started to close down her computer. "I'd say it's about one hundred percent. But I'd like to get a few hours work done later."

"We can be home by..." She glanced at her watch. "Eight o'clock. How's that?"

"That's great. Let me get my running clothes on."

They got into Regan's car and drove about forty minutes, entering a state park with signs identifying it as "Miles Standish." "Oooh! History. This is really cool," Callie said excitedly. "We can run in a historic place."

"I did a little research, too," Regan said smugly. "You're not the only one who knows how to prepare for a trip."

They got out of the car and took off for a trail that Regan had decided upon. They'd only been running a few minutes when Callie said, "You're being really generous to find trails for me to run on. But we could go on a track, too. I know that's what you like."

They were running on an unpaved road on the edge of a good-sized forest and it was cool and shaded and filled with dozens of natural aromas. Regan took in a breath and let it out slowly. "To be honest, I'm liking this. Normally when I run, I turn off my mind and just concentrate on breathing and relaxing. But when I run over varied surfaces I stay more in touch with my senses. It's a nice change."

"I should probably run on a track once in awhile. It'd be easier to focus on my form if I wasn't trying to make sure I didn't trip on a tree root or something."

"When you move here I'll take you over to the high school where I run sometimes."

Callie turned her head so she could see Regan's face. "How serious are you about this?

"I'm a hundred percent serious. Given everything I know about you, I think you'd love living in New England. And I'd love to have you here. Preferably sharing my home."

"Don't play with me, 'cause I'm really thinking about doing it. I haven't seen one thing that I'm not completely charmed by. This area is just what I thought it would be, and that's all good." *And you're the prize of the whole region.*

"You haven't been here in the winter..."

"That's true. I've never really experienced a cold winter. I've been skiing and snowboarding, but I have a feeling that's different."

"Yeah, that's very different. Trying to get the ice off your windshield so you can see to drive home on slick streets isn't much fun. And don't even get me started on how I hate shoveling snow."

"Well, we could always change apartments. Very little snow in Dallas."

"Thanks for the offer, but no. I'm a New Englander and I like it that way. It surprised the heck out of me when my parents moved to Florida for half the year. I wouldn't ever want to do that."

"I have no doubts that I could be perfectly happy here."

"You haven't even seen Boston. After living in Cambridge, I realized how much I wasn't using the city. Now I try to go in at least every month and do something fun."

"But there's lots to do right around here. Have you ever been to John Adams' home? Let me tell you all about it…"

When they got home they ate a big Caesar salad topped with a good-sized portion of salmon that Alana had prepared for them. Callie ate her half and Regan commented, "It's been hard for me to get a handle on how much you normally eat. In P'town you were putting away four thousand calories a day, but you're very moderate here. What's the real you?"

"The real me is the way I've been since we've been here in Scituate. But when I'm on vacation all I think of is food. I want to try everything that's unique or local or different from what I usually have."

"That's one of the things I like best about you," Regan said, smiling at her warmly. "You like to experiment and go out of your comfort zone."

"Yeah, I do. I guess I wouldn't have taken a chance on Marina if I didn't mind going out of my comfort zone."

"I'm glad you did. We're always looking for good lesbians." Regan got up and took the plates over to the sink while Callie watched her and dreamed about one day being able to walk up behind her, throw her arms around her and kiss her. She'd never, ever had an attraction sneak up on her like this one had, but it was glorious. Normally, she knew if she was interested in someone within the first five minutes of meeting them. But they'd both been so wounded when they met that there wasn't any sexual chemistry between them. There was now. Enough to blow the house up.

To divert herself she went into the guest room and got out her computer then came back in the living room. "It won't bother you if I work, will it?"

Regan shot a quick look at the TV, then said, "No, I can read."

"Do what you want. Watch TV, listen to music, whatever. I always put headphones on and listen to music while I work, so whatever you're doing won't bother me."

"Really? There's a basketball game that I'd like to see. The Celtics are deep in the playoffs…"

"Go for it. Actually I like it when sports are on TV. I can look up and watch the game for a couple of minutes to give myself a break."

"Do you like the NBA?"

"I've never been to a game, but I like watching any kind of sports. It's like white noise."

Regan grabbed the remote and found the game she was looking for. "See how easy it would be to live together?" Callie just smiled at her, but as soon as Regan was engrossed, Callie found herself sneaking a glance at her much more often than she should have. There was something fascinating about watching Regan watch TV. That was almost a ridiculous thought, but it was true. Just watching Regan's beautiful eyes dart back and forth as she watched the players run up and down the court was mesmerizing. She was as fascinating as a 3-D movie with surround sound.

They kept to that pattern until Friday when Regan came home at noon and announced, "How soon can you get packed?"

Callie looked up from her computer, eyes wide. "Are you throwing me out?"

"No, but someone else is moving in and we have to leave."

"Regan! What are you talking about?"

"I arranged to swap apartments with someone in Boston. They're coming this afternoon and we're going to stay in their place. We won't come back here before I take you to the airport, so pack everything."

"I'm on it. I'm really excited, by the way."

"Me too."

"Where are we staying? Not that I know anything about Boston."

"We're staying near the Fens. It's a little apartment, just one bedroom, but I know you don't mind sharing."

Callie got up and went to her room to start packing while Regan stood in the doorway and watched her.

"Is this something you've done before?"

"No, I never have. But there are a lot of people in the city who like to come down to the South Shore for the weekend. The Irish Riviera is quite desirable," she said waggling her eyebrows.

"I can see why. It's great around here."

"I bet you're gonna think Boston is even better."

Callie grasped and squeezed Regan's arm when they reached the apartment building. "This is so great! What should we do first?"

"Have you had any exercise today?"

"Nope. I started working as soon as I got up. I thought we'd go for a jog when you got home."

"Then we'll go for a jog. Up for twenty-six point two miles?"

"God, no! Oh! The Boston Marathon. I can do half of it…I think."

"Let's just do around a quarter. I can show you some of the highlights."

"Have you run the marathon?" Callie asked, amazed that Regan could possess such an important piece of personal trivia that she hadn't pried out of her.

"Sure have. It's been a couple of years, but I ran it two years in a row. I've been thinking about joining a club and trying to qualify again. Us old middle-distance people have to have a goal, you know. We can't self-motivate like you trail runners can."

"I know how you people are," Callie said, smiling broadly at her friend, while trying not to get caught staring. Patience had to carry the day. Only when Regan was over Angela could anything happen. Trying too soon would be disastrous. This was too important to screw it up.

Regan worked the key to get it to slip into the lock of the door at their swap, the third and top floor of an older building in the Back Bay. She finally got the key to turn and they entered while simultaneously giving each other suspicious looks. "Garbage?"

"I hope so. We can throw garbage out." They went towards the smell, and Callie leaned over the trash can in the small kitchen. "Oh, lord!" She fanned the air above the can. "Figure out where we can dump this. It smells like rancid fish."

"A scent I'm all too familiar with." Regan got on her phone and called the tenant, showing remarkable restraint when she casually commented that she hadn't asked where to throw the trash when they left on Sunday. As soon as she hung up she took the bag and dashed for the door. "Open the windows. All of them!"

By the time Regan returned, her cheeks were pink and she still wore a pained look on her face. "We've gotta get out of here. I hate the smell of rancid food."

"Do you think there's anyone who likes it?" Callie asked, giving her a playful grin. "Let's get changed and not come back until we're so tired we'd be able to sleep anywhere."

They went into the bedroom and eyed the double bed. "This would only be a queen in Munchkinland. Damn," Regan mumbled. "I should have checked the place out first."

"It's fine. Really. I swear it's nicer than my apartment, so don't say anything too disparaging."

Regan's smile returned and she nodded. "It's fine. You're right. And it's always nice to save a few hundred bucks."

"Absolutely." Callie started to change. She was just a little dismayed when Regan shimmied out of her jeans and started to slip into a tiny pair of navy nylon shorts. She looked sensational in them…and that was the problem. Callie was used to running in baggy shorts over compression shorts. That's how just about everyone dressed in Dallas. But things were different in New England, she'd learned. A lot of people wore the kinds of outfits Olympic runners wore, showing off their lean bodies. The last thing she needed was to see Regan's lithe body displayed any more clearly!

But Regan evidently didn't know about Callie's burgeoning desire. She took off her shirt and put on a slim-fitting red singlet that advertised a running club from the South Shore, then tucked the singlet into her shorts, sat on the bed and put her shoes back on. Callie watched the long muscles of Regan's back flex and twist as she worked, then stood and clapped her hands together. "Let's move!" Regan demanded, luckily not asking why Callie was standing there with her khakis in her hand, no running clothes in sight.

Callie walked out of the bedroom a few minutes later, dressed in her usual grungy running clothes. "Where's the khakis?" Regan asked.

"Khakis?"

"Yeah. We need the khakis to get to Hopkinton."

"What do my pants have to do with anything?" Callie asked, completely puzzled.

"Just teasing." Regan picked up her keys and dangled them. "If you find someone with a thick enough accent, that's how they ask for their keys. "Where's my khakis?" she repeated, grinning.

Callie pinched her cheek. "Let's go see Bah-ston."

Regan had devised an ingenious way to see the highlights of the marathon course. It involved short runs of four or five miles, then a short car ride to the next spot. By the time they'd finished they'd been to the start, up and down Heartbreak Hill and cruised to the Hancock Building where they'd playfully waved to the imaginary crowds.

Afterwards, they headed out to one of Regan's favorite restaurants for dinner, and Callie was surprised that she'd chosen to return to Cambridge. "Aren't you afraid of running into Angela?"

"No. I'm not going to lose Cambridge. I like it and I've lost enough." She smiled thinly. "Besides, she's not the type to go out to dinner alone, and she's not dating anyone. She's probably living on Lean Cuisine."

"Uhm, how do you know for sure she's not dating anyone?"

They were riding on the T, Boston's subway, and it was noisy and fairly crowded. Regan leaned over and spoke right into Callie's ear. "I believe her. She's not generally a liar."

Callie nodded, not asking any more questions. When they exited the station, Regan said, "I believe everything she told me the other night."

Callie slipped her hand around Regan's arm, holding it close. "But..."

"It's like I told you. I believe she's sincere about wanting me back. I believe she's working hard in therapy, something she swore she'd never do, to figure out why she was unfaithful. I even believe she's serious about going to couples counseling to figure out why we had such a bad sex life."

"But..." Callie led again when Regan stopped talking.

"But...it's too late. It shouldn't have taken my breaking up with her to motivate her to do something that I truly believed would have helped us be happier." She looked so earnest and hurt that Callie felt her eyes well up with tears. "If I'm important to her now, I should have been important to her then."

Squeezing her arm, Callie said, "I'm sure you were always important to her. Maybe she didn't realize how bad things were. Some people aren't very psychologically aware."

"Yeah, I know that." Regan had her hands in her pockets, and she was walking with her head down, an unusual posture for her. "I might have been able to forgive her for a one time slip, even though that would have been *very* hard. But to know she was cheating for over a year?" She made a slicing motion across her throat. "That's the death sentence."

"Do you think this was mostly about sex for her?"

"Yeah." Regan nodded. "I'm sure of that. We were happy together, Callie. Really happy. The only thing we didn't have was a good sex life."

"Wasn't that important to you?" Callie asked, a little afraid of the answer.

Regan thought for a moment. "Yes," she said carefully. "Sex is important. But it's not the top thing on my list. It's not in the top five, to be honest."

"Mmm." It was in her top two, and she wasn't even sure what its competition was. Regan couldn't have been the one who didn't have the goods when it came to sex. That had to have been Angela. Maybe they'd never been compatible sexually and neither one had known how to get closer. It had to be that. A woman as warm and tactile as Regan had to be a good lover. She just had to be.

CHAPTER SEVENTEEN

EVEN THOUGH REGAN said she was determined to reclaim Cambridge, Callie didn't see any of her usual sparkle at dinner. Despite going to one of her favorite restaurants, Regan picked at her food and their conversation wasn't the usual fast-paced tennis-match that Callie had grown to love.

It was after eleven when they got back to their swap and Regan immediately went into the bathroom to get ready for bed. They'd had all of the windows open as well as the window air conditioner on, and now the place smelled relatively normal. Callie closed the windows in the living room, leaving the air conditioner on since she knew Regan liked a cool room to sleep in.

They switched places when Regan was finished in the bathroom and a few minutes later Callie emerged to find Regan in bed, her hands laced behind her head, knees tenting the sheet. She didn't seem to notice when Callie slipped into bed, but a few moments later she turned to her and said, "I'm really sad."

The sorrow in her beautiful eyes made Callie's heart ache. Instinctively, she opened her arms and Regan burrowed into her embrace like a child. They lay there for a long time, thoughts drifting in and out like the breeze of the air conditioner ruffling the curtains. The question had been rumbling around in her head, but it slipped out with no warning. She heard herself ask, "What's more important than sex?"

"What?" Regan's voice was muffled because she was pressed against Callie's t-shirt.

It was too late to turn back. Acting like the question was just a continuation of an earlier conversation was the only thing that made sense. "You said that sex wasn't in your top five things. What is?"

"Hmm." Regan pulled away and rolled onto her back. She was quiet for a while, clearly thinking. "I'm not sure in general. But I can tell you what I loved best about Angela."

"I'm interested." And that was the truth. Right then it was immeasurably important to know what was most important to Regan.

"Okay. I…uhm…" She cleared her throat. "It's still hard to think about her. About the good side of her."

Callie reached over and put a hand on Regan's arm. "You don't have to…"

"No, it's okay. I think it's good to talk about her. It might help me get some stuff off my chest."

"Okay. But don't think you have to talk just for my sake."

"Gotcha." She was quiet for a time, then said, "She was generous. With her money and her time. Did you know we met when we both worked on a Habitat for Humanity project?"

"No. You've never said how you met."

Callie could see Regan's thin smile by the light of the moon. "We both volunteered on a project about halfway between my house and hers. She has a tough job and she travels a lot, but she still volunteers for things." She took a breath. "Not just doing stuff to make the company look good, either. None of that community service crap a lot of people participate in because their firms make them."

"Like Marina," Callie quietly said.

"Oh, I'm sorry..."

Callie touched her gently. "No need to apologize. I'm just speaking the truth."

"Okay. Well, she belonged to a church and she did a lot of stuff with them. Tutoring and things like that."

"Interesting. Are you religious?"

"No, that was her thing. It was good for her and kept her involved in her community. It was hard for her being a black woman in a white industry. Belonging to her church centered her."

"That's cool. Very cool."

"She's a good person," Regan said, her voice shaking again. "She was scrupulously honest—except for the cheating. The type of person who'd go back to a store if she found out they'd undercharged her."

"Wow. Marina would have called her friends to boast."

"No comment."

Callie patted her. "It's fine with me if you speak your mind about Marina. You can't think worse of her than I do."

"Don't count on that."

"Tell me more about Angela."

"'Kay. Uhm, I guess the things I liked best about her were her honesty and her work ethic and her desire to do the right thing. She was just...someone I looked up to."

"Do you think that had anything to do with why things didn't work well...sexually?"

"Why would that be involved? Aren't you supposed to respect the person you love?"

"Well, yeah, but maybe you weren't on the same level, you know?"

"No, I don't. No idea."

"I'm not sure if this is nonsense, but the best sex I had was with Marina and I didn't respect her much. Maybe hot sex goes with...I don't know...not caring too much? Does that sound crazy?"

Regan didn't say anything for a while, but when she did her voice was soft and low. "I'd rather love a good person I wasn't into sexually than have great sex with a bad one. Maybe you've got a point, but I hope you can have sex and love and respect for someone. If you can't, I know which one I'd give up."

Callie didn't say another word. She felt like she'd revealed too much. If Regan felt so strongly about being with a good person what would she think of having killer sex with a dirtbag like Marina? But after just a minute or two Regan curled up against her again. Callie held her tightly, occasionally stroking her hair or back and, after just a few minutes, she felt Regan not only relax, but fall asleep. Callie continued to touch her gently, sharing in Regan's sorrow even as she slept. She held her for a long time, savoring this chance to caress the woman she was falling for. But she didn't feel a sexual charge, even though their bodies were nearly entwined. Regan needed a friend tonight, and that was a role that Callie relished as much as she did the newly discovered sexual pull, and it was a role she would never violate.

The next morning Regan was staring at Callie when her eyes first opened. She jerked awake. "You scared me!"

"It's because we're about three inches apart in this little bed." She backed up as much as she could. "Better?"

"It wasn't how close you were. It was those big blue eyes locked on me. You look happy this morning. Are you always this alert when you wake up?"

"No. But I have something planned and I wanna get going."

Cassie slapped at her lightly. "Then wake me up!"

"I did. By staring at you." She adopted a dramatic, creepy tone. "The intensity of my gaze burned right through your eyelids."

"I think it might have." Callie sat up and rubbed her eyes. "What are we doing?"

"We're sitting in bed, not progressing."

"Fine." Callie stood up and headed for the bathroom. "You could have showered first and then we'd be ready sooner."

"Now you tell me!" Regan called out to Callie's laughter. "Where were you when I needed you?"

⸻

They both hustled to get ready and were soon in line at a local coffee bar. Regan said, "I made reservations for something cool, but it's kind of expensive."

"Under five hundred dollars?"

Gasping, Regan said, "Of course!"

"Then I'm fine. I haven't had to spend much money this week. I've got five hundred dollars left in my budget for the trip and it's burning a hole in my pocket."

"This will take less than twenty percent of your bankroll." She chuckled. "Roll. That's appropriate."

"Are you gonna let me in on the joke?"

"Sure will. As soon as we get there, I'll tell you where we are."

Callie gently pulled Regan's ponytail. "I'm glad. I like surprises."

With a tender expression that somehow let Callie see into her soul, Regan said, "I wouldn't do them if you didn't like them." Then Callie turned to look at the pastries, so that Regan wouldn't see the longing in her eyes.

⸻

An hour later, they were tooling around the Freedom Trail on a Segway tour. Callie had heard of Segways, but she'd never seen one. Nevertheless, she loved the experience and she kept sidling up to Regan and saying, "Thank you for this. It's outstanding!" before she'd dart away, giggling.

⸻

At 1:35 p.m. the first pitch was thrown at what Callie hoped would be the first of many games she'd see at Fenway Park. The day was warm and clear, the fans were incredibly enthusiastic, the game was a complete sellout, and the Red Sox won with a walk-off homer in the ninth inning.

As they filed out of the stadium, Regan said, "Would you like to go to the second best sports bar in the country?"

"Uhm, okay, but why don't we go to the best one?"

"I have no idea where that is. I just know this one claims it's the second-best. And the beers are a third the price they are in the stadium."

"I should hope so! I don't usually pay that much for dinner! I made that one beer last six innings. It was warm, but they weren't gonna get that kinda money off me twice."

The bar was just around the corner and it seemed like most of the fans were heading there. "This place gets really crowded, but it's a lot of fun."

"I like fun. And I like crowded bars. Remember how crowded the place in Provincetown was?"

Regan grasped her arm and pulled her to stop, making hundreds of people veer around them. "Would you rather go to a lesbian bar?"

Callie guided Regan to stand behind a light pole, giving them some breathing room from the crush of people streaming by. "A sports bar is great. It's like a doubleheader."

"Are you sure? You seemed to really enjoy the place in Provincetown."

"I did. But that was then and this is now. Now we're in a baseball mood."

Regan took her by the elbow and started to walk towards the bar. "If you're sure."

"I'm positive." They put their heads down and fought like a pair of salmon to get in the door, but they finally managed.

Regan went towards the bar and returned a mere twenty minutes later with four beers. "Drink up," she said, grinning slyly. "Next time, you're buying. Then we can compare notes on how many people put their hands on your ass."

Callie had just gotten back from her turn to buy and she declared, "One guy rubbed his shoulder against my boob, and another one blatantly put his hand on my butt while leering at me. Not too bad." She chuckled, shaking her head. "Some guys turn into predators when they get into a place like this. Women are a little more subtle."

Regan winced. "That's why I thought you might prefer a lesbian bar. That and the other thing," she added, grinning.

"What other thing?"

"Chasing girls. You seem to be really good at it."

Callie let out a squawk of dissent. "I've never chased a woman or a man. I don't do that."

Regan laughed at her reply. "I saw you with six or seven different women in P'town. Not to mention the one you were playing tonsil hockey with."

Looking haughty, Callie said, "I didn't ask one person to dance. I never do. And I didn't kiss her, she kissed *me*. She pulled me onto *her* lap, not the other way around."

"Oh, I see. You just flash those dimples and women chase you. I can see how that would happen. You're too cute to ignore."

"I'm not exactly shy, but I've never had the nerve to put myself out there. I just wait for an invitation." She smiled sweetly, her devilish side showing through.

Regan tried not to stare, but it wasn't easy. Those dimples could make a grown woman weep. And when that smile flashed and those white teeth gleamed, it was enthralling. Where had the glum mood gone? Impossible to say, but no one could stay in a bad mood when Callie was around. Lying in her arms the night before had miraculously made the day dawn brighter and sweeter. How could that be? It must be the aura she gave off. Calming and nurturing but also playful and almost giddy. What a double play.

It was late when they finally stumbled into their swap. Neither knew where the light switch was, and they fumbled and bumped into each other for a few minutes, giggling the whole time. Regan tried to flip Callie's nose to get the light on and Callie stood in the center of the room and clapped loudly, several times, before grumbling, "The Clapper is a wonderful addition to any home. We should leave one as a gift."

Regan finally located the switch on a tiny bit of wall between two door frames. When the bright, unflattering light clicked on, she immediately shut it off. "Whoa! This is why lighting in bars is always soft and flattering."

"Hey! Was that intended for me?"

Regan switched it on again. "Of course not. But it's harsh and it hurts my eyes. I'm gonna find some candles." She hunted around the place, finding a pair of poorly used pillars. "Some people don't know how to use a candle properly," she muttered, before lighting both and setting them on the breakfast bar. When she turned off the overhead lights, she sighed with pleasure. "That's better."

The dim light did make the place look much nicer and it cast a golden glow on Callie's features that Regan found impossible to ignore. She slapped her hands on the bar to snap herself out of her musings. "One more for the road." She went to the refrigerator and pulled two beers out, handing one to Callie. "Are you woman enough?"

Taking the challenge, Callie twisted the top off and slugged down a healthy amount. Regan matched her, holding the bottle to her lips and letting it drain for a few *glugs*.

"Well played. You, my friend, know how to pound the brewskis."

"I don't do it often, but I've got the touch," she admitted, grinning goofily. "Now let's get back to our discussion."

"It was an argument," Callie decreed. "And I won."

"It wasn't an argument, and if it was, I won. I know when a woman's interested in me, and the woman in question was most definitely not."

"She was looking at you every time I peeked at her. Every time," Callie emphasized.

"Not buying it. And if she was, she must have thought she recognized me. Maybe she had her wedding at the Inn. She was married, you know. She had a big, big diamond on her left hand and the guy with her had a ring on too."

'Well," Callie said, banging her bottle on the table, "he might as well start looking for a lawyer, because she was into you. Big time."

"Was not. Not, not, not, not, not. I always know when a woman is into me. It's a sixth sense."

"You *always* know?"

"Always."

"You've never, ever, not even once, been wrong?"

"Never. Not once. Never will be wrong." Regan slammed her bottle onto the table hard enough to break it, but the glass held and she stood there, looking smug.

"Where did you get this power?"

"I don't know. But I guarantee I have it." A flurry of thoughts raced through her mind. She knew she was right, so it was time to gut it up and spill it. She looked vaguely triumphant when she added, "My powers tell me that there *is* someone who's interested in me."

Callie looked like she'd fallen into a hole. Her eyes blinked a few times, showing what looked like fear. "Who might that be?"

"Someone I know. She just started looking at me like this. It's only been a few days, but I'm sure I'm right."

"Tell me more," Callie said, swallowing audibly.

Regan moved to stand at the end of the bar. She leaned over, rested her arms on the Formica and gazed deeply into Callie's eyes. "You, Callie Emerson, have been looking at me in a certain way for a few days now."

"I have?" Callie choked out.

Regan tapped the neck of her bottle against Callie's. "You have. You've been looking at me like you want to kiss me." She put her bottle down and rested her chin atop a fist, holding her head just a few inches from Callie's. "Am I right?"

"Uhm…I…well…"

"I'm right," Regan said, practically purring. There was no way to back out now. It'd been a long time since she'd tried to seduce a woman, but she knew what worked. People loved confidence and she could bring it. "You actually look like you want *me* to kiss *you*." Her voice dropped down to a timbre meant to weaken knees. "I'm right, aren't I? This is how you get women to make the first move."

Callie could only nod. She looked frightened, but she leaned in. A sure sign. Regan moved even closer and their lips touched—delicately and fleetingly.

Regan took in a breath and slipped her hand across Callie's cheek, letting it rest just under her ear. One finger slid across the lobe, then down her neck, making goosebumps break out. Regan tilted her head and gazed deeply into Callie's eyes, then moved towards her again, letting their lips brush tenderly, then insistently.

They moved into each other, their lungs expanding as their bodies touched from breasts to hips. Each place their bodies met switched on a sensor. Energy throbbed in Regan's breasts, her belly, her thighs. Everywhere that Callie's warmth pervaded was alive in a new way.

Regan's head tilted back and her mouth opened to Callie's daintily probing tongue. As soon as that warm tongue entered her mouth, Regan was gone. Callie could have pushed her to the bar, the chair, the floor…any sturdy surface would have been just fine. She laced her arms around Callie's neck and pulled her in, hoping she didn't take a bite out of the luscious woman.

Her body wanted more. More than she could fathom. She needed Callie's hands to touch every part of her. Every part that had been yearning so insistently for the magic she knew those hands could create. Just as that thought registered, Callie's hands slid to her ass and pulled her forward forcefully. Their bodies pressed hard into each other, and Regan's head felt as though it would explode from the overload of sensation flooding her mind.

Then her hand was on Callie's breast and the moan that welled up from her made Regan weak. But she held on, opening her mouth a little wider to let Callie's delectable tongue anchor them together.

But the pull to merge was just too strong. Regan had to be horizontal. With their mouths still locked together they fumbled and banged their way into the bedroom, falling onto the bed with a *thump*. Regan pulled away and reached for her shirt, pulling it over her head so that Callie could reach her breasts. Lingering for just a moment she looked down and saw fervid desire in those green eyes. Just like Callie had planned the whole thing. No hesitation. Not tentative in the least. Just like she'd looked at Marina…at God knew how many other women. Other women while she'd been with Marina. Any woman on the list. Nothing more than animal passion. No love. No respect. No consideration for the consequences. And she'd agreed to all of that before she'd ever set foot in Marina's apartment.

"No," she whispered, almost too quietly to hear. "It's not right. I didn't think this through." Panic exploded in her chest and she couldn't get a full breath.

Callie placed her hands on either side of Regan's face, searching her eyes. "What? What is it?"

"It's not right," she repeated dully, not having any idea what else to say.

Slowly, Callie scooted out from under her leg and sat up. She slid her fingers into her hair and pushed it from where it had fallen into her face. She looked calm, almost resigned. The way she'd probably looked when a woman she'd wanted didn't pan out.

But Callie sat there, looking into Regan's eyes. "Is it too soon?"

The concerned voice was a warm hug. That was it. That was something to hold on to. Who was the real Callie? The woman who looked like she'd combust if they didn't have sex or the gentle friend who, she knew, would take a bullet for her? It was impossible to tell. They'd only had two weeks together. The panic started to ebb. They could figure this out. She nodded quickly and decisively. "Yes. That's it. It's too soon."

"You're still conflicted about Angela?"

Regan dropped her head and nodded. "I guess I am. I'm definitely confused."

Callie wrapped her in a comforting hug, murmuring into her ear, "It's okay. Really. It's okay. I don't want you to feel uncomfortable. It's fine, Regan. It's fine."

Regan had no idea how she was able to switch gears so quickly, but she'd never been more grateful to anyone. Callie had diffused a terrible situation with just a few words and a gentle hug. The temptation was fierce to fall back into her arms and kiss her until dawn, but it was too confusing. Nothing made sense, and she'd never have sex with someone she wasn't sure of.

Regan gazed into Callie's eyes for a long time. "Are you sure? I never, ever want to do anything to hurt you or our friendship." That was the truth. That was one thing that couldn't change, no matter what.

"You haven't hurt a thing. We'll just chalk this up to…" She laughed softly. "Something, and put it away. No pressure."

"Are you sure?"

"Yes. We'll slow down. Give you time to catch up to where I am."

They kissed tenderly, the pull so strong it hurt deep in Regan's chest. Who had leaned in first? It was impossible to say. When she pulled away, Callie's lips followed her, and the longing in her eyes made Regan's heart begin to thump quickly. "The worst thing we could do is try and fail to make it as a couple. That would devastate me," she said, meaning every word.

"You're right. It's too important to make a mistake. You've got to be ready."

"Yes, yes!" Regan took her by the shoulders and pressed harder than she should have. "That would be awful! As bad as it was for me when I left Angela." Callie burrowed against her body and Regan felt the reassuring safety of Callie's warmth.

"It means so much to me to have you feel like that about our friendship. It's a wonderful feeling."

"I won't hurt you, Callie. I promise I won't."

~

After brushing their teeth, they deliberately got back into bed, each of them almost hanging off her respective side. Callie tried to clear her mind of the swirling emotions that could have kept her up all night. She finally calmed herself with the obvious truth. Regan *was* attracted to her. There was no doubt about that. All she had to do was wait for her to flush the remains of Angela from her system, and they would be able to kiss and never stop. Never, ever stop. It would take some time, but she had plenty of that. Waiting for something wonderful was always worth it. Regan just needed to clear her head of bad memories.

She replayed in her mind the fantastic sensations that Regan had just gifted her with. Thinking of those soft, insistent lips, and the power she felt in that lithe body, Callie imagined the day when they'd share a bed with not a hairsbreadth between them. There was no question. Regan would be the partner she'd always wanted. Honest, loyal, compelling, alluring. Every lovely attribute she could want. That was Regan.

The next morning the alarm woke them long before either was ready to get out of bed. Regan was grumbling to herself when she shuffled into the bathroom, and Callie got up and started packing so they could stop and get a cup of coffee before they went to the airport.

When Regan came out of the bath, she stood in the doorway of the bedroom and seemed unusually unsure of herself. Callie looked up and saw her bloodshot eyes and the dark smudges under them. "Are you okay?" She tried not to be too obvious about how bad Regan looked.

"No." She walked over to the bed and sat down right next to Callie. "I couldn't sleep. I…I want to make something clear," she said, as Callie noticed her hands were shaking.

"About last night?"

Regan looked up, giving her a relieved gaze. "Yeah. I want to explain, but I don't know how. I acted really impulsively and that's not like me. I just hope…"

Callie put a hand on her shoulder. "I told you last night that it was fine. I meant that."

"But I want to make sure you know…"

"I know you care about me, right?" Callie asked gently.

Regan's eyes closed and she looked terribly sad, like she would start crying at any second. "Yeah." Her voice was hoarse and rough. "Very much."

"And you know how much I care about you too, right?"

A faint smile turned up the corners of her mouth. "Yeah," she nodded, looking down.

"But you're still grieving." She squatted down so she was at eye-level with Regan and she stared deeply into her eyes. "Our friendship has to come first, right?"

Regan looked like she wanted to say something, but she shook her head the faintest amount and returned Callie's gaze. "Right."

"And we both have to be ready, right?"

Now looking more sure, Regan nodded forcefully. "Right. That's critical." She stood up and put her hands on Callie's shoulders. "I'll try to be the best friend you've ever had…I promise that."

CHAPTER EIGHTEEN

CALLIE WAS ON the phone with Terri during the entire drive from DFW airport to her apartment. She lost the signal for a few minutes, but called her back once she was in her room. "So…I think I'm going to move there."

"That's crazy! You moved to Dallas for Marina and now you're going to move to Boston for Regan. I hope you don't meet someone from Cuba. You can't legally move there, you know."

"I moved to Dallas for Marina. That's the truth. But I'm moving to Boston for more than Regan. I can't even begin to tell you how much I loved it, Terri. You've been there…you know."

"I liked it, but I didn't love it. It's too big of a city for me."

"Ooo, not for me. We walked from one end to the other and it only took a couple of hours. It didn't seem that big to me. Not at all. And you can get by without a car. Try that in Phoenix."

"You could do it. The Anasazi didn't have cars." It was clear Terri was teasing, but Callie knew her friend would never share her need for lots of activities and changing weather.

"I'm going to do it, Ter. I should have done something like this years ago. Then I might have avoided wasting a year and a half of my life with Marina."

"I wish you hadn't had that fiasco, but it let you know you could be with a woman."

"I think I always knew that. But now I *want* to be with one. I want it so badly I can taste it."

"But you don't know she wants the same thing. It'd probably be smarter to wait until she's ready to take that next step."

"Maybe," she agreed. "But I've wasted too many years living someplace I didn't love. I can't let Regan decide where I live and when I live there. Besides, if I'm there, she'll slip again and next time she won't want to bail out. I'm certain of that."

That night, Regan called, and Callie could tell she wasn't quite herself as soon as she said, "Hello."

"Hi. Did you get a nap today?"

"No, I went in to work. Delaney needed a day off, and since she took up some of my slack this week, I thought I'd better return the favor."

"You sound grouchy. Did you have a bad day?"

"No, it was fine. But there's something on my mind. It's been gnawing at me. I guess that makes me a little…off."

"What is it?"

"It's…it's about what happened last night."

"Hey," Callie soothed. "I promise you that was nothing to worry about."

"I'm not worried," she began, but stopped herself short. "Maybe I am. I'm not real clear right now."

"Tell me what's going on. Come on. You can tell me anything. Promise."

Regan hesitated for a few seconds, then said, "I really want you to move here. I know you'd love it, and I know I'd love to see you a lot more often. But I don't think it's a good idea to have you live with me."

It felt as though she'd been kicked. Regan didn't sound cold, but her tone made clear that her mind was made up. It seemed impossible to talk without betraying her hurt, but she had to try. "I don't have to come at all. Maybe it's best."

"No, that's not it. I'd love to have you here. I just don't think living together is good."

"Well, we don't live together now…so I guess we don't have to in Boston." She was trying to sound lighthearted, but she was sure it wasn't working.

"I want to be clear about something. I'm not a person who says things just to make someone feel better. I try to be honest, even when I wish I didn't have to be. I *truly* want you to move here. I'm one hundred percent certain about that. I just think I need the experience of living alone. I don't like it, but I think it's good for me. I think it's helping me mature."

"You're more mature than anyone I know. But I think you know yourself really well, and if you think you need this, you probably do."

"I think I do. But that's obviously not the only reason. I really don't act impulsively very often, and what I did last night puzzles the heck out of me. I need to figure out what's going on in my head and I think that'd be hard for me with you right here. I promised you I wouldn't hurt you, and I have to live alone to make sure I can keep that promise."

Callie felt an ache welling up in her chest. "You're a good friend. I know it wasn't easy for you to tell me this, but I admire you for doing it."

"I don't want you to admire me, I want you to believe me."

Callie could feel the depth of Regan's sincerity and she found herself smiling when she said, "I think I'll do both."

⁂

Later that night Callie reached Terri after she'd gotten off work. After they'd talked for a long time Terri said, "Tell me again what she said. Try to think of the exact words."

"She said she was confused when we kissed. She needs to figure out how she feels and she's worried she can't do that with me living with her."

"That sounds…not great."

"Why?" Callie felt her ire rise. Terri wasn't going to ruin her high. "She's being honest. That's good."

"Yeah, it is, but that sounds like what an honest woman would say when she's done something she wishes she hadn't done. I hate to be negative, but it sounds to me like she wants to keep things at the friendship level."

"You wouldn't say that if you'd been in my shoes on Saturday night," Callie said, still tingling from their kisses. "She wants me. There's no doubt about it. She just has to flush Angela out of her system."

"Couldn't she want you but still decide not to be with you? I can't guess why someone wouldn't want you, but…" She was silent for a moment. "I love you, and I'm single. But I'd rather be your friend than your lover. Could she be like me?"

"No. No way. You and I have never even kissed. It's never been that way between us. But with Regan…we did more than kiss. She wanted me. Badly. But then something crept into her head and made her pull back. It's temporary. I'm sure of that."

"I hope you're right, 'cause she sounds like a keeper. A mature, honest woman who's good looking is as rare as a virgin in a whorehouse. Hell, mature, honest women who'd break mirrors are rare. A good looking one is unheard of!"

⁂

The next morning Delaney walked into Regan's office to find her leaning back in her chair, feet up on her desk, a large cup of coffee in her hands. "Don't you look like the cock of the walk?"

"Hrmpf." Taking her feet off the desk, Regan sat up straight and focused on her computer screen.

"How was your day off, Delaney? Did you do anything interesting?" Delaney asked, continuing to load on the sarcasm.

"Glad you're back. The Fleming-DiFillipos just added another ten people to the guest list. You're gonna have to come up with some creative ideas to shoehorn another soul into the hall."

Delaney sat down opposite her sister. "What's going on with you? You look like your favorite pet died."

"Nothin'." Regan continued to stare at her screen, paging through a document.

"Don't bullshit me. You were upset after you saw Angela, but you got over it really quickly. Now you're down in the dumps again." She narrowed her eyes as she scanned Regan's face. "Did you have a fight with Callie?"

Regan snorted. "No. We've never had a fight."

"You know," Delaney said, propping her feet up on the desk as she settled in, "I never asked how you know Callie."

Now the blue eyes focused even more fervently on the screen. "She used to go out with someone Angela worked with. We hit it off."

"Right." Delaney was still looking at her critically. "If you ask me—"

"I didn't." Regan finally looked at her. "I'm swamped. Can we chat later?"

"No, I'll be swamped later." She gave her the patented superior smile she'd been using since the day Regan was born. "If you ask me, you and Callie should hook up."

With her mouth set in a grimace, Regan snapped, "I didn't ask you. I'm perfectly able to find a girlfriend on my own."

"You didn't do so well last time, but I hate to say I told you so."

Scowling, Regan said, "You love to say you told me so."

"True. But Callie's just your type. She's your age, she's a lot of fun, and she's prettier than you are. You're a solid seven, but she's a nine. She's a step up."

"Thanks."

"I mean it." She sat there for a few seconds. "Oh, I know what's wrong. You want to go out with her, but she shot you down."

"Not true. Not even a little."

"Why not ask her out?"

Regan squeezed her eyes shut and tried to control her temper. "We're friends. Just friends."

"Hmm, there's something there. I can't tell if you want her and can't have her or if she wants you. But there's definitely something there." She took a pencil from the desk and tapped her chin with it. "I wonder which it is?"

"Fine! Here's the whole story. I'm attracted to her, like any sane woman would be. But it's not gonna happen and I'm pissed off about it."

"So she shot you down."

"No!" She lowered her voice and repeated, "No. That's not how it is. I'd love to be with her, but we're not looking for the same thing."

"What's she looking for? Another nine?" She snickered when Regan glared at her.

"Do you want me to answer or do you just want to torture me?"

"Both, but I'll take the answer."

Regan stood up and fussed with her hair for a moment, checking it out in a mirrored sign on the wall. Then she sat on the edge of the desk and looked down at her boat shoes while she swung her feet back and forth. "I'm ready to settle down, and Callie's shown that she's not there yet."

"How has she shown that?"

"I don't wanna get into it, but trust me, she's made some choices that show she isn't looking for the same kind of commitment I am."

"You're looking for perfection, Regan. You'll never find it. If you're into her, go out with her. You can work around most problems."

"Not ones like this." Regan didn't say anything else, but her statement had such authority to it that Delaney got up and quietly walked out of the office, knowing when she'd heard the last word.

Callie spent the next couple of weeks talking to family and friends about her plans. When she called her father, he let the news sink in for a moment. "I want to be on your side and congratulate you, Chicklet, but I'm really gonna miss you. I've loved having you here in Texas."

"I've loved being close to you, Dad. But I know I'm going to be happier in New England. It's the right place for me."

"Then I'll get over my disappointment and look forward to you visiting me. How's that?"

"That's good. How about you coming to Boston?"

"In the summer. I'd definitely come in the summer. But you won't get me out there in the winter. Don't even try."

"I wouldn't ask. I know how you hate the cold."

"Now, you'll probably tell me it's none of my business, but I still think there must be something between you and Regan."

Callie paused a second. There was something, but it didn't have a name yet. It felt like it might jinx it to talk about it before things were clear, so she kept it vague. "There might be something between us. But it's nothing concrete."

"I've seen your pictures from the Bahamas, honey. If you're going to be with women, I can't see why you wouldn't want to be with her. She's really cute."

"I think she's hot," Callie said, chuckling.

"I was gonna say that, but I didn't want to make you mad." He laughed, sounding a little embarrassed. "I haven't had a lot of time to get used to you being a lesbian. I'm still not sure of the rules."

"I'm not either, Dad. But I'm going to move to Boston even if nothing happens between Regan and me."

"Is she…does she…do you want another relationship like you had with Marina?"

"No. Not in any way."

"That was decisive. You defended your lifestyle pretty adamantly the last time we talked about it. Second thoughts?"

"I still think an open relationship can work. But it can't work with a liar. And a cheater. And a self-involved jerk. And a cheapskate. And a moody bitch."

"Got that out of your system?" His smile was so familiar she could see it in her mind.

"No, I have a lot more ways to describe her. But I'll save some for later. I like to have some gems to pull out when I need them."

A month later, Regan left a message and as soon as she had a minute, Callie called her back. "What's this I hear about a life-changing opportunity?"

"It's epic! Here's your new address." She started to rattle off a street number when Callie stopped her.

"Hold on there. Aren't you going to tell me about it?"

"I could, but wouldn't it be easier if you just started to pack?"

Callie lowered her voice and sounded like a chiding schoolteacher. "Regan…"

"Okay, but we're wasting valuable time. A guy who lives close to where I lived in Cambridge got a grant to do research in China. He has a very nice apartment, but he doesn't want to sublet it since he needs to come home every couple of months for a few days. So he's willing to rent it to you for well below market rate. He just wants to be able to use it a few times over the course of a year."

"He's going to be gone a whole year? That sounds ideal."

"It is. And it's well within your budget. When he wants to come home, you can come stay with me. *Now* will you start packing?"

Callie laughed. "I started as soon as you told me to. I just didn't want you to see how malleable I am. Now give me the address again so I can start sending out change of address notices. I'm coming home to Boston!"

~

Over the next few days Callie learned that Alana was the conduit that provided the information about the apartment via Angela. But Regan insisted that didn't bother her, and that she'd be very happy to visit Callie in Cambridge. Callie took her at her word and after exchanging e-mails and a few phone calls with Bruce, her new landlord, she got down to business and started making firm plans. Since she had no furniture to speak of, and the apartment was fully furnished, all she had to do was pack her personal items and clothes. To save money, she started sending one or two boxes a day to Regan at the restaurant. It was a fairly expensive way to move, but she figured it was cheaper than renting a truck or buying everything new.

Ready to go by the first of July, she'd taken Regan's advice and sold her car and was eagerly looking forward to using the money to buy a new computer when she got to Boston.

~

Delaney caught Regan on the way out the door of The Scituate Inn. "What's this I hear about Callie moving to Cambridge?"

Regan kept walking, making Delaney follow her out to her car. "She's coming on Friday," she said, looking very happy. "I can't wait."

"So, you're gonna stop being so hard-headed and start dating?"

Regan stopped and looked at her for a few seconds. This was dangerous. Delaney loved to get involved but she didn't know the whole story. And she didn't need to. "I don't have any plans to go out with her."

"What? Then why's she moving here?"

Regan shrugged. When she got to her car, she tossed her briefcase in the back and slid her long frame into the low-slung car. "She likes Boston."

Delaney stood so Regan couldn't close the door. "Is she into you?"

Sitting stock still, it took a few seconds for Regan to answer. "Uhm, yeah. Kinda. But I was as clear as I could be that we didn't have a romantic future."

"Regan." She dragged the name out, reverting to her "I'm gonna tell Mom" voice.

"I did," Regan said defensively.

"What did you say? Exactly."

"I don't remember. Something like we both had to want the same thing and have the same goals. Things like that."

Delaney thumped her on the head. "That's not being clear! She's probably moving here to be with you."

"No, no, she really loves it here. She's a big history buff and she loves the weather."

Crouching down so they were at the same level, Delaney said, "Don't screw around with her. Tell her you're not interested if you're not."

Lightly banging her head against the wheel, Regan moaned, "I can't do that. I *am* interested. I'm *very* interested. And if there's any chance that I'm wrong about her..." She trailed off, almost crying when Delaney patted her gently on the head. It would have been so nice to be able to spit it all out. To tell how much she cared for Callie, how wonderful it felt to be close to her, how she thought about her hundreds of times a day. But Delaney had zero tolerance for cheaters, and she'd think Callie was just that if she knew the truth. And Callie was too good a person to have Delaney think badly of her.

"I don't think you're over Angela yet. Just take it slow."

"I will." It would have been nice if that had been true. But Angela was in the past. Now Callie was all she thought of. She looked up as her older sister stood. "Thanks. I know I don't make it easy, but I love that you care about me."

Delaney tugged on her dark hair. "I care about Callie. You're on your own."

CHAPTER NINETEEN

ON HER FLIGHT to Logan Airport, Callie was giddy with freedom. That was a funny word to use, but it was the right one. Just the thought of making a conscious choice about where she lived was massively freeing. This wasn't about Regan. It wasn't *solely* about Regan. Living in Cambridge was going to be great. A world-class university, lots of tech people, history, seasons. Everything she'd ever wanted in a home. And being there would help keep her mind clear. Regan wouldn't be in the next room, clouding her mind with thoughts of forbidden fruit. She'd have her own life, make her own plans, eat dinner when she wanted to, and not depend on another person for the roof over her head. This would be her first experience living completely on her own. It was about time.

The apartment was actually nicer than Regan described. Bruce either had the skills of an interior designer, or he had hired one. Callie followed the rather meek-looking economics professor around the small apartment as he pointed out all of its features. From the way Regan interacted with him, Callie could tell that they had not been close friends. But they seemed at ease with one another and he never mentioned Angela's name, which Callie was happy about. Bruce was leaving the next morning, so Regan invited her down to the South Shore for the night.

They were both hungry, and as they left Cambridge Callie said, "Let's go someplace fun. My treat."

"Uhm...I was gonna go to the restaurant. My sisters want to see you."

"I can see them tomorrow, right?"

Regan's eyes shifted uneasily, the way Callie noticed they did when she was unsure about forcing an issue. "Yeah, you can, but...if you don't mind I'd rather go there. I like the food there better than any place else."

"Done," Callie said, pleased that Regan knew how to ask for what she wanted.

They had a great time relaxing with the extended family and a few of the regulars who were dining there that evening. She'd been around these people for just hours, but they'd welcomed her like one of their own. It already felt like home. And it was only going to get better. Afterwards, when they were going to Regan's house, Callie said, "I'm beginning to see why you feel comfortable at the restaurant. It's nice to be able to go behind the bar and take what you want and make your own drinks."

"Yeah. I tried that at a couple other places and it doesn't go over too well. I also like to be able to go into the kitchen and make sure my sister makes my hamburger the way I like it. She under cooks it if I don't keep an eye on her."

"She's a wonderful cook. I should be her apprentice for a few months to learn some tricks."

"The dinner you made for me when you were staying with me was great. I don't think you need any help. I'm the one who's hopeless."

"Alana can cook for you in Scituate and I'll cook for you in Cambridge. You don't have to learn a thing."

The next morning they loaded all the stored boxes into a Scituate Inn van and drove them up to Cambridge. The entire endeavor was completed by two o'clock, and both women collapsed onto the sectional sofa that filled the living room. "Somebody should walk down to the liquor store and get some cold beer," Regan said.

"It would be nice. Maybe I could toss money down to somebody on the street and have them go."

"You could do that, but you wouldn't get any beer in the deal. This is Boston, not heaven."

Callie forced herself to her feet and raised her hands above her head to stretch for a few moments. "I can't complain about buying beer in exchange for a strong woman and a truck. Want anything special?"

"Surprise me. You know what I like."

"I do. You like lagers and ales and you'll drink a stout in a pinch, but only one. Your tastes are a lot like mine."

Regan smiled her most impish grin. "That's why I think you have good taste. Hurry up now, the mover is thirsty."

Callie had been in town less than a week when she called Regan to tell her some news. "I found a good running club here in Cambridge. I'm going for a five k run on Sunday morning at nine. Will you be there?"

"You don't even know where to order in a good pizza," Regan teased. "And you're already joining a club?"

"Yep. I want to run the marathon for my fortieth birthday, so I don't have a moment to waste."

"You've got over four years!"

"I know, but I want to increase my mileage slowly. Then, once I can run twenty-six miles, I need to do a couple of marathons to get my qualifying time. I only want to run one a year so…"

"It sounds like you've thought this out pretty carefully. If I follow your lead I can run one for my thirty-fifth."

"Don't rub your youth in. I'll do what I can to keep up with you with my decrepit self."

Regan laughed. "I don't think that'll be a problem with you. You're one determined cookie."

"So? Will you be here?"

"Sure will. Can I come on Saturday?"

"You can come on Friday if you want. Then we'll have two nights to test out pizza places."

"Now that's my kind of thinking. Have pizza two nights in a row, then go running. It's a date."

In another week Callie had found a group of women who played pool on Thursday nights. And a few more days had her signing up for a monthly meeting of website developers and graphic artists.

That Friday night she walked into the Scituate Inn and was greeted by another new friend, an eighty-year-old man who had taken quite a shine to her. "Callie!" Jerry McMullen called, hoisting a beer in her direction. "Let me buy you a beer."

She smiled and sat down next to him at the small bar. "How could I resist?" She nodded to the night bartender, Alex. "A short draft, please."

Alex slid the glass down the bar and she sat happily chatting with the elderly man for a few minutes. Regan poked her head out of the office and did a double take when she saw her. "How long have you been here?"

"One beer's worth," Jerry said. "We're just getting started."

Callie could tell from Regan's questioning expression that she was asking if Callie was comfortable. A short nod was the reply and Regan said, "We might as well have dinner, huh?"

"Works for me," Callie said. "Caesar salad with salmon, please."

"Done. Be right back."

"So how's Cambridge treating you, honey?" Jerry said. "All of those pointy heads driving you nuts yet?"

"Not yet." She knew she could live in Cambridge for the rest of her life and be completely happy…as long as Regan was near.

They left the restaurant at around nine, and Callie could tell that Regan wasn't herself. Deciding to give her a little while to decompress after a long day at work, she didn't speak much on the way to the townhouse. But after Callie stored her overnight bag in the guest bedroom, she found Regan wandering around the apartment, looking like she was either thinking or blowing off some nervous energy.

"How about a walk?" Callie asked.

"A walk?" Regan's response was almost rote. It was as though she hadn't fully understood the question.

"Do you need some time alone?"

That seemed to snap her out of her fugue and she nodded. "No, I changed my mind. A walk would be good."

"Sure?"

"Yeah. It might help to get something off my chest."

They left the apartment and walked in silence down to the harbor. It was fully dark now and the only sounds were the muted thump of rubber fenders protecting boats from the docks, the lapping of the water at the hulls, and a few distant horns. There wasn't another person in sight, and after they started to walk along one of the piers, Regan let out a heavy sigh. She threw her head back and took in a deep breath, then said, "Angela called me today."

"Oh." Callie didn't need to say more. It was clear the call had upset Regan, so it was a waste of energy to ask her to restate the obvious.

"It really took me by surprise, oddly enough. I guess…I guess I underestimated her perseverance."

"You don't get her job without having a lot of that."

"True. But she's not the kind of woman to risk humiliation. Coming back after the last time really took a lot for her." She gazed at Callie. "I respect her for that."

Callie's heartbeat started to quicken. A nagging fear she'd been consciously ignoring made her stomach flip. Angela was a woman Regan had dearly loved, and if she wanted her back that was how it had to be. That's what true friends did, and no matter what, being a good friend had to be paramount.

Luckily, the next words out of Regan's mouth put her mind at ease. "It hurt to tell her no again, but it didn't hurt as much as last time." She gave Callie a sad, lopsided smile. "Practice pays off."

"Aww." Callie put her hand around Regan's arm and they walked closely together, slowly making their way up and down every dock. A speeding bullet-dodged. Angela's bad fortune was cause for a guilty, silent celebration. "How are you feeling now?"

"Okay. Kinda." They walked a few more steps. "Sad. Really sad."

Callie held her arm more tightly while they strolled along at a slow pace. "I'm happy to listen to anything you want to say. But if you want quiet, you've got it."

"Thanks." Regan disentangled and slung her arm around Callie's shoulders. Just as she did every time this happened, Callie took in a breath, hoping to catch just a bit of Regan's scent. It reminded her of a dusky red rose that grew in a yard near her apartment, and she assumed it was from a lotion or powder or some product she used. But she secretly hoped that Regan just naturally smelled like a beautiful flower.

They walked for at least half an hour, with Callie listening to the quiet sounds of the water and the occasional metallic clink from rigging hitting a mast or the groan of a tightening line. Regan broke the quiet. "Sit down with me?"

"Sure." They went out to the jetty, a long, built-up profusion of rocks that stretched out into the water. It was wide enough to walk on, and now, at low tide, it was safe to sit and dangle their feet in the cool water.

Once they were settled, Regan said, "There's a feeling I've been fighting."

"Fighting? That sounds serious."

"It is, kinda. It's the feeling that Angela really might be able to make some of the changes I wanted her to make."

"Uhm, what's there to fight about?" Her heart started to beat wildly again.

Regan was looking out at the water, her eyes focused beyond the horizon. "Even if she can, I don't want to give her another chance."

She said this with such cold detachment that Callie strangely felt sorry for Angela. But then Regan looked at her and Callie could see the sorrow in her eyes. "Does that make me coldhearted?"

"No, of course not." Callie put her hand on Regan's bare thigh, tamping down her desire to squeeze the solid muscles she'd developed from running. "She broke your trust. It's perfectly understandable that you don't want to give her another chance to hurt you again."

"It's not that," Regan said immediately. "Mostly."

Callie sat, poised, waiting for more.

"It's partly about sex."

"Go on."

"Even when we were having sex pretty often…like in the first year… it was never quite right." She grew quiet again, and her gaze returned to the void.

Callie wasn't about to start peppering her with questions, so she started to gently pat Regan's leg, settling into a soothing cadence.

After a few minutes, Regan seemed to open up and she talked with renewed energy. "We were too much alike. That's the problem in as few words as possible."

"Too alike how?"

"We both like to be in control." She grinned shyly and her hooded eyes showed she was embarrassed. "Know what I mean?"

"Yeah, of course. I'm the opposite. I'm the rabbit, always looking for a cute fox to catch me." She leaned against Regan and they both laughed.

"I'm naturally the fox. But I can adapt if I'm with someone who also likes to chase. But Angela didn't have one bit of rabbit in her. Not even one of those cute little whiskers."

"Ooo. And that made you always be the bunny."

"Yeah. And that would have been okay if it was only our sex life that was like that. But it was a lot more. She wanted me to be the rabbit all of the time, in every part of our lives. She wanted to pay for me, to keep our checkbook, to make our social plans, to make a decision to refinance the house…without telling me," she grumbled, obviously still miffed about that decision. "She wanted me to be her wife. The kind of wife my grandmother is to my grandfather."

Callie looked at her, letting her eyes wander from her strong features and set jaw down to her square shoulders, wiry, muscled arms and strong legs. "You don't seem like that type to me. At all."

"I'm not. I never was. I never will be. It was a low-grade struggle that went on in the background. She'd do something and I'd push back. We didn't actually fight very often, but it was always there, buzzing in the distance. I had to fight for every bit of autonomy I had, and frankly, it was tiring."

"I wonder…" Callie closed her mouth quickly. "Never mind."

"What?" Regan leaned against her.

"I was wondering how Marina and Angela…did it. They both have to be in control. Maybe that's why Marina claimed she wasn't into her."

"Ugh! I hate to think of them together. And not just because of the cheating. Thinking of Angela with another woman drives me crazy."

"Never mind." Callie put a hand on her leg and rubbed it quickly.

"No, you've got me thinking about it now. It's lodged inside." She slapped the side of her head as though she could knock the thought out. "Marina was never passive?"

"Noo." Callie laughed. "That's not in her repertory."

"You've got me. Maybe Angela was…" She stopped and thought for a few moments, then shook her head. "Nope. I can't see it."

"I wouldn't have believed that Marina could fake it, but she must have. Angela wouldn't have come back for more if Marina didn't put on an act."

"She sounds like a real winner."

That hurt. There was something so derisive about the comment and her tone that she allowed the words to get in for the first time. No matter how she might tear Marina down, she'd chosen her and having Regan talk about her so disparagingly cut too close to the core. She didn't want to hear another dig so she changed the topic. "Do you think your need for autonomy is the real reason you won't give her another chance?"

"It's all wrapped up together. Even if Angela could let go of her need to be in control, it would never be the real her. It's an elemental part of her personality. I guess I don't believe a tiger can change her spots. She'd be faking it."

"Probably. But if the behavior is what you want…"

"I don't want a girlfriend who's letting me chase her. I want things to be spontaneous. It would take so much effort for her to be the rabbit that we'd never be able to just be ourselves."

"The negotiating would wear me out." She leaned on Regan again and whispered, "It's much easier to find a girlfriend who wants to boss you around than it is to find one who wants to share equally. Luckily, I don't mind a bit if my lover wants to make the decisions. If she wants to do all the work, I can relax and do my own thing."

"That's what I need," Regan said longingly. She jerked noticeably, and Callie felt her muscles tighten. "I mean, you know…when I'm ready…later on…after I…" She looked at Callie with a pleading look in her eyes.

"I get that. Some day…waaaaay in the future." She held her hand out over her eyes, as though she were trying to see across the ocean. "Weeks or months or years or decades from now, you'd like a relationship where you can be yourself. Right?" She smiled at her, trying to look as non-threatening as possible.

Regan leaned heavily against her and let out a sigh of relief. "Yeah. That's exactly right. Thanks."

"Don't mention it."

"I won't," Regan said, then started to giggle, sounding more girlish than Callie had ever heard her.

CHAPTER TWENTY

THAT NIGHT, IN her bed, Callie spent a long time reflecting on what Regan had said. It was almost more than she could bear: to know that Regan was not only a good, moral, thoughtful, beautiful woman, but that she was a true top was enough to make her swoon. She'd been thinking about the issue with an almost detached perspective, but when she couldn't stop thinking, she decided she had to release some tension to get to sleep. She slipped her hand between her bare legs and was amused to discover her body had been thinking about sex, even when her mind hadn't. Her fingers slipped around her clit, so thoroughly lubricated she had to stroke herself firmly to get any friction. But she didn't mind. Thinking about Regan lying on top of her, bearing down with her weight, making Callie squirm under her was all she needed to propel herself to climax after climax until her wrist hurt and the tips of her fingers pruned. *Please make it soon*, she pleaded, as she drifted off. *I know you want it as much as I do.*

On the fourth of July, Callie was trying to lift a heavy cooler full of water and soft drinks. She only had to take it a few hundred feet, but the sand was hot and she hadn't kept her flip-flops on, even though

Regan had warned her to. She made it across the sand by jumping into the air every second or third step, and she could hear Regan laughing all the way across the beach.

"Told you so."

"Experience is the best teacher." She flopped down on the blanket making sure no part of her was in the sun. "It's crowded!"

"It's the fourth of July. You expected just a few Mannings out here?"

"Well, no…but how do I know? I've never been on the beach for fireworks. There must be four times as many people as on a regular weekend."

"Everybody comes for fireworks. You're gonna love 'em. I just hope my nephews don't cry the whole time like they did last year. Kinda ruined it."

"They're a year older now."

"Yeah, but they still cry a lot. Max especially. He's a drama queen."

"Don't let Delaney hear you say that!"

"Ahh, you've noticed that no one in the family can critique anything the boys do?"

"I'm not going to answer that. I want everyone to like me."

"Ha! I'd like to see the fool that doesn't like you." Regan smiled so genuinely that Callie felt herself fall in love with her for the thousandth time.

Hours later, when it was dark and everyone was tired from their long day in the surf and sun, the first big "pop" went off. Minutes later, Delaney and Ray gathered up their two bundles of tears and picked their way through the crowd, headed home.

"Maybe next year," Regan said.

"Shouldn't we help them? They've got a lot of stuff."

"Nah. If she wants help she'll order us around. Other than that, you'll just be standing there, looking stupid."

"I wish they hadn't taken all of those blankets. I'm cold!"

"Cold? It's probably seventy degrees."

"Oh, okay, I'll tell my goose bumps they're mistaken."

"Come here." Regan was sitting in a sand chair and she wiggled a finger to indicate Callie should sit in front of her. "Lean up against my legs and then you can pull my blanket up over yourself."

Thinking this was a fine idea, Callie ditched her own chair and settled herself right in front of Regan. She pulled the blanket up over her feet and legs, and was able to rest against Regan's shins, letting her lean her head back to see the explosions. "The boys might have liked it better if we hadn't been so close," Callie said. "We're about one inch away from the barrier."

"When they're here before me they can choose the spot." Regan tugged on a lock of Callie's hair, then grasped another handful. "Boy, your hair is really thick."

"Really?" she said, disingenuously. "I'm not sure you're right. Maybe you should experiment more to make sure."

"Oh, you like your head rubbed, huh?" Regan started running her fingers across Callie's scalp, making her purr with delight.

"I love that. But I also like just having bits of it pulled. Gently, of course."

"Of course."

Callie let her head rest against Regan's knees, watching the fireworks explode over their heads while Regan gently tugged on bits of her hair. "How's that?" she asked, leaning over to speak directly into Callie's ear.

"God," she moaned. "I mean…good. Really good." She dearly hoped Regan couldn't see her looking like she was about to drool.

One beautiful August afternoon they lay on the grass of the Boston Common, stretching out their legs after a fifteen-mile run. It was a perfect day and Callie knew they would probably stay outside until they were so hungry they had to give in and go back to her apartment for dinner.

Regan got up and jogged over to a vendor who was selling ice cream. She ran back with two chocolate covered confections and smiled when Callie dug into hers as though she hadn't eaten in a week. When Regan finished gulping her own ice cream down she pointed the stick at Callie and said, "Do you know who we never talk about anymore? Marina," she said decisively before Callie could answer.

"Sounds like progress to me. I like not talking or thinking about her."

"I guess you don't want to talk about her now, but some things about your relationship have always puzzled me."

Callie lay down on the grass and stared at the deep blue sky. "Ask away. I'm feeling so good that I can tolerate thinking about Marina."

"Stop me if this is too personal, but I've always wondered why you agreed to having an open relationship."

"I think we talked about this one of the first times we spoke. Didn't we?" She lifted her head just enough to be able to see Regan's face.

"Yeah, I think it was one of the first times, but I didn't know you very well then and you didn't elaborate. I'm interested in how the whole thing played out, if you feel like talking about it."

"I don't have any secrets from you. If you're interested, I'll tell you anything."

"I've always gotten the impression that it was Marina's idea."

"Oh, yeah. It was *all* her idea. At first I dismissed it without even considering it. But she was really persistent. She was in Dallas and I was in Phoenix and she came to see me a *lot*." She emphasized the last word dramatically.

"That doesn't surprise me," Regan said smiling at her. "That smile of yours could make women weep."

"I think you're exaggerating." Callie couldn't help but show her best smile. It was fun to taunt her a little bit. Regan was so transparent about some things that it made toying with her irresistible. Her blue eyes opened wide, and she stared at the smile a moment longer than a friend would have. Desire infused her expression, but Callie didn't push. She knew the key to their future relationship was to wait for Regan to be ready. "She was very persistent. And she kept reminding me why Rob and I had broken up. Over time, she convinced me that having a little 'breathing room' as she liked to call it made fidelity much less of an issue." She rolled over onto her belly and rested her weight on her arms. "I know you probably don't see it this way, but our agreement isn't what caused us to break up. The fact that she was dishonest was the problem."

"If you say so."

"I do. Open relationships are really pretty common, especially for gay men. I think, if both people feel the same about it, it can work."

"Not for me it wouldn't. Never."

"I'm not the spokesperson for open relationships. It takes a certain kind of person and you're not that person." Callie smiled warmly at her. "I think you're the kind of person who would give her all to one woman. I'm just sorry the woman you chose wasn't able to accept everything you had to give her."

Looking hauntingly sad, Regan nodded her head. "Yeah. Me, too. Sometimes you can't help but fall for the wrong person. I guess the key is to learn from it so you don't have to repeat your mistake."

"You won't. I'm sure of that."

"So am I," Regan agreed firmly. "Never again. I'd rather have a girlfriend with no sex drive at all than have one who cheats on me."

"That's being a little extreme. Sex is too important to throw it away, girl."

"Not as important as honesty," Regan said, her pretty mouth set in a grim line. "Well, I guess the issue is fidelity. I could take an occasional lie about something that wasn't critical. But I would never, ever accept cheating. Never," she emphasized, her eyes almost glowing with fervor. "I'm one hundred percent monogamous, and if I'm going to be, so is my partner. No excuses."

Laughing, Callie said, "I think you might be the spokesperson for monogamy."

"We need one," she replied, frowning. "It's almost out of style."

Regan lay next to Callie that night, smelling her sweet scent and longing for her in a way that was physically painful. The words they'd both spoken in the park flitted around annoyingly. It wasn't possible to be any clearer. She was antagonistic to open relationships. Being in one was the same—exactly the same—as casually dating. But Callie claimed she'd loved Marina and that they'd been partners. She could call it whatever she liked, but that wasn't what a partnership was. The amazing thing was that Callie had taken the whole discussion very lightly, as though it hadn't pertained to her. There had to be a way to get more clarity. No matter the expense.

They were at Callie's apartment the next evening, trying to decide whether to order Chinese or Thai. They finally picked Thai, and after calling in the order, they settled onto the sectional to have a beer while they waited. Regan took a sip of her beer and said, "You know, there's something that's been niggling at the back of my head." Callie playfully tried to see the back of Regan's head but she was unsuccessful.

"I'm being serious."

Callie reached out and gently touched her on the leg. "I can see that. What is it?"

"Do you ever think I'm too narrow minded about fidelity? I wonder if you think that I'm immature or that I don't have a big enough worldview or something." She felt very uncomfortable, and knew that Callie could see that.

"I don't think that at all. Nothing like that has ever crossed my mind."

"You sure?"

"Yes. Really. I think you really have to want a certain kind of relationship to have it be open. And I try not to judge people about how they behave sexually. I learned that after I reacted so badly with Rob. People have different ways of getting their needs met, and if they're not hurting anyone I try not to be judgmental."

Regan nodded slowly. "I'm pretty judgmental."

"I've never noticed that."

"I am. If I know someone has cheated, I don't feel the same about them. I lose respect for them. I don't think I can change that, and to be honest, I don't think I want to change."

Callie looked at her quizzically. "You don't have to change. There's nothing wrong with feeling a certain way. You're not out on the streets punching people who you know have had affairs. It's cool."

"I guess. It just occurs to me once in a while that maybe I was too judgmental with Angela, but then I realize there are things I just can't change. And that's one of them."

"That's the last thing you should worry about. No one needs to put up with an unfaithful lover. No one."

"Uhm, wasn't it hard for you the first time that Marina was with someone else?"

"Oh, God, it was hard," Callie said quietly. "It was very hard. When we first got together we agreed that we'd be monogamous until we were both ready. But she got ready after about two months. She called me from somewhere, maybe Utah? And said she'd run into someone she'd been with before and she wondered if I minded if she was with her that night."

Regan's eyes were wide and she looked as though she were seeing a ghost. "What did you do?"

"After I tried to stop myself from throwing up?" Regan didn't reply, she just stared. "I had to follow through. It was part of the deal we made. I realized I wasn't going to feel any better about it in the future so I just bit the bullet."

Regan put her face into her open hands. "I would have gone berserk."

"Marina made it crystal clear that she could not and would not be in a relationship that wasn't open. I knew from the beginning that this was something she wouldn't negotiate. So I went into this with my eyes open. Yes, she pushed me faster than I was willing to go, but I think she had to push me." She shrugged, looking unconcerned.

"So how did you get past feeling jealous?"

"Well, this might be more than you want to know, but I have a uhm…I guess you'd call it…a voyeuristic streak." She was blushing by the time she got to the end of the sentence.

"If this is too much…"

"No, I don't mind talking about it, but I don't want to tell you more than you want to know."

"I'm interested. If you want to add something, go ahead."

"All right. I think it goes back to when I was fairly young. My mom was out for the night and we had a babysitter. That was pretty rare, so I remember it clearly. The girl was in high school and I got up to ask for a drink of water or something. She had her boyfriend there and they were having sex right in our living room."

"Damn!"

"I know. She had a lot of nerve, to be honest. My mom would have killed her if she knew she'd done that. But I was, I don't know, ten or eleven maybe and my knowledge of sex was rudimentary at best. All I knew was that there was a guy on top of Kathy and he was doing something very weird to her. I don't know how long I watched, but I was there until they finished. You couldn't have pried me away."

"And you think…"

"Yeah. I think that seeing that gave me a proclivity for watching other people. It's always been part of my orientation."

"Do you go looking for…"

Callie laughed and slapped at Regan hard. "No! I don't go peeping in windows. But when my first boyfriend and I started having sex we used to talk about bringing another girl into our bed. That got me off." She shrugged her shoulders again. "That's just what turns me on."

"That's…interesting."

"Interesting or upsetting? You don't look very happy. Should I have kept my mouth shut?"

"No, no, not at all." Regan put on a smile that looked forced. "I guess it just surprises me that you'd want to have threesomes. I can't imagine being drunk enough for that."

"We didn't ever *have* a threesome. We just talked about it."

"You *talked* about it?"

"Yeah. We talked about it rather than doing it. It was just a way to turn each other on."

"Huh." Regan moved around on the sofa, looking like she had an itch she couldn't get to. "Uhm, did you and Marina have threesomes?"

"No, no, I don't think we ever would have wanted the same person. Our tastes were very different. But she'd tell me what she did when she was away and I'd get off on that. I didn't think that would happen, but it did."

"That actually turned you on? Hearing about her having sex with someone else."

Callie paused, looking tentative. "Is this too much?"

"No. It's fine." It was so hard to look normal. How could you love a woman and get off on hearing about her having sex with other people?

"Okay." She peered at Regan carefully. "Sure?"

"Yeah. Absolutely." It hurt, but it had to come out. It was too important to ignore any longer.

"So, sexually, we were very, very compatible. I've never had sex with anybody who turned me on more than she did or who knew how to get to me. Our sex life was frankly tremendous."

Stunned, Regan chugged her beer and got up to head for the kitchen. "I'm getting another. Are you ready?"

Callie looked at her beer from which she'd taken two sips and said, "No. Not yet."

When Regan came back, she sat down and took another long drink. "I told Angela when we'd just started going out that I never wanted to hear about anyone she'd been with. I don't like to think of the person I'm with ever having been kissed by another person." She took another drink of her beer, still flustered. "I don't think you and I are made the same way."

"That's what I was referring to earlier. Everybody has stuff when it comes to sex. You just need to figure out how to make it work if it's important to you."

Regan took another drink, her eyes focused on the window. "Sex is *very* important," she said quietly. "Sex is how I show someone I love her. It's a great way to communicate. But if you don't have love and trust and respect and concern for each other the best sex in the world isn't going to hold your relationship together."

"I understand that. I really do. But that's the ideal. You don't always get the perfect lover. So you figure out how to make it work, even if it's outside of your comfort zone."

The front door buzzed and Regan got up to answer it, mulling over Callie's words. Her view seemed to be that you took people as you found them, then figured out how to make sex work. That was so ridiculous that it didn't merit a comment. You only let yourself fall for the right person. You didn't take every bit of trash you found by the road. But Marina was trash, and Callie would have still been with her if Marina had been more careful. And that was unconscionable.

They ate their food in relative silence. That wasn't odd for them, so Callie chalked it up to Regan's being tired. But she had an edgy energy that showed itself when she got up to clean the kitchen, telling Callie to stay where she was.

Callie watched her work, seeing the tense, rigid set to her shoulders. She knew something was up, and as soon as Regan came back into the room she could feel her stomach start to flip. Regan sat down beside her and said, "We need to talk."

Trying to create some moisture in her arid mouth, Callie merely nodded.

Regan looked as earnest and as nervous as Callie had ever seen her. The first words from her mouth caused Callie's mouth to drop open in astonishment. "I love you," she said, her voice shaking. "I love you so much it hurts. And I wish with all my heart that we could be together, but…we can't."

"What?" She jumped up so fast her head spun. "What are you talking about?"

"It wouldn't work. It just wouldn't."

"Regan!" she snapped. "Spit it out."

"I don't think it was wrong of you to be in a relationship like the one you were in with Marina, but… Oh, shit. I've gotta be honest. I do think it was wrong. I can't get that out of my mind. It's like you were cheating even though you weren't."

"Pardon me? You're saying you can't love me because I was in an open relationship?"

"Yeah. That's exactly what I'm saying."

"You don't know the first thing about how it was between Marina and me. Not the first thing."

"I know that I wouldn't do something that I thought was wrong, no matter how much my partner wanted it."

Callie was almost yelling. "You do what you need to do to make the person you love happy."

"Then I guess I'm not as giving as you are. I was willing to do almost anything. *Almost* anything. But I would never, ever have agreed to let Angela have sex with other people."

"And the fact that I let Marina means that I'm damaged goods?"

"Yes, that's bad enough. But the fact that *you* did it is worse. I hate to judge you, but the fact that you could be in love with her and sleep with other women—even though you had permission—freaks me out."

"I didn't sleep with other women!"

There was a moment of complete silence. Then, sounding less sure of herself, Regan said, "Of course you did."

"Shouldn't I be the one who knows? Our relationship was open, but I was monogamous. I could have slept with other people if I wanted to, but I didn't want to. I was with Marina. *Only* Marina."

"You're kidding."

"I don't find this very funny, so no, I'm not kidding. Why do you assume that I was sleeping around?"

"Why in the heck would you be in a relationship like that if you didn't want to sleep around?"

"I told you why. Because Marina needed it."

"We've talked about this before. In depth. Why didn't you ever tell me the whole truth?"

"You never asked me specifically. And, to be honest, I always felt like a bit of an idiot for letting her do it while I didn't want to."

"Wait. Just wait a second."

"I'm waiting," Callie said when Regan didn't comment for a full minute.

"You must have known that I would have thought you slept with other women. Why didn't you make it clear that you didn't?"

"I didn't *know* you'd think that. Actually, since I never mentioned being with anyone else I thought you'd assume I was monogamous."

"What? That's kinda out there. That's expecting a lot of me to guess that."

"No, it's not," she said softly. "If you really knew me you would have guessed that. I've told you how good things were between us sexually. I've told you how much she turned me on. I love sex but I'm not compulsive about it. Why would I want more when things worked so well?"

Regan sighed deeply. "I don't know. I just assumed—"

"You assumed wrong. I didn't need more sex. I didn't need variety. I'm a monogamous person who was in a relationship with a non-monogamous person. That's it."

"I should have guessed that. I should have known you're not the type —"

"Stop right there! I don't have to defend what I've done in the past. It's actually none of your business who I've slept with. If Marina and I had an open relationship, that's between us."

"You're right. That's none of my business." She stood up and looked around, her aimless gaze scanning all of the horizontal surfaces. "Do you know where I put my keys? I need to go home."

"Home? You can't drop a bomb like this and leave!"

"I can't think straight. I just can't. I need to go home and let this settle."

Callie reached down and took Regan's hand, holding it tightly. "Don't shut me out. Please."

"I'm not trying to, but I'm…really, really not sure of what's going on in my head. I need some time alone. Is that okay?"

Callie helped her to her feet. "Okay. Are you able to drive? You look pretty vacant."

"Yeah, I'll be fine. I just need to think."

"All right. Call me when you get home, okay? I'll worry."

Her smile was wan and looked very weary. "I will. G'night."

By the time Regan had walked out the door Callie was slumped down on the sectional. That had gone very, very badly. But it wasn't obvious what had happened. What was Regan so upset about? How did it affect her? It was massively confusing, but it was bad. It was clear that it was bad.

The next day Regan arrived unannounced at seven p.m. Callie buzzed her up and stood in the door, gazing at her questioningly. "You don't look good," she said, seeing her pale face and red-rimmed eyes.

"I didn't sleep."

"Come on in. Do you want some iced tea or something?"

"No." She moved into the room with a strange sort of tentativeness, like she wasn't entirely welcome. Stiffly, she sat on the edge of a chair and said, "I know what had me spooked last night."

Nervously, Callie sat on the couch and waited, not saying a word.

"It took me hours, but it finally got clear this afternoon. I went out for a long run and it all fell into place."

"Go on," Callie said, knowing it was awful news.

"Here's the truth." Regan's pale blue eyes were filled with sadness when they locked onto Callie's. "I thought the fact that you had sex with other women while you were with Marina was the thing that was stopping me from being with you." She looked down at her hands which were rapidly interlacing and breaking apart. "It wasn't."

"What was?" Callie asked, not wanting to hear the answer.

"The fact that you were monogamous almost makes it worse."

"What?" For the second day in a row Callie yelled at Regan, something she hadn't done in the year she had known her.

"That might sound weird, but it's true. I thought about what you said and you're right. It's been stupid of me to focus on your relationship with Marina. If you both wanted other partners and that worked for you—no big deal."

"But…" Callie supplied when Regan seemed to lose steam.

"But you settled for a relationship where she got everything and you got the leftovers. That makes me question how well you know yourself, how much self-esteem you have, how much you're willing to give up just to keep your partner happy." She clasped her hands together so forcefully that her knuckles turned white. "That's not the kind of partner I want." Her voice was so quiet that the cars going down the street outside almost overpowered it, but Callie was listening raptly and heard every word.

Callie's voice was low and harsh when she said, "And you've been thinking about this for the whole summer?"

"Yeah. It's never made sense to me. You just don't seem like the kind of woman who'd want a bunch of sex partners. I struggled with it, trying to make it make sense. Then, last night, it finally did. You've got the kind of moral code I need, but you don't have the…"

"The what? Come on. What don't I have?"

"I don't…I don't think you have the self-respect." She winced when she said it, and looked like she wanted to run from the apartment. But she stayed right where she was, even though she was shaking.

"You'd better go home." Callie used all of her self-control to sound calm. "Now."

Regan looked at her, her puzzled expression touchingly innocent. Callie put a hand under her arm and pulled her to her feet, then pushed her towards the door, opening it with one hand. She gave her a final shove and closed the door in her face, ignoring the soft knock and the gentle entreaties to open the door. Callie was leaning against the wood, knowing she was on the verge of tears, but not wanting to break down with Regan right on the other side.

"Go home now," she managed to say. "I need to be alone."

"Okay," Regan said, then Callie heard her light step descend the stairs as she slid down the door, engulfed in tears by the time the front door closed.

CHAPTER TWENTY-ONE

THE NEXT DAY, Callie called off a meeting with a new client, then crawled back into bed, where she stayed until hunger forced her to forage late in the afternoon. She didn't want to do it, since talking about it made it real, but she had to call Terri.

"Hi," she said when Terri mercifully answered.

"You sound bad. What happened?"

"That obvious, huh?"

"Callie, tell me. You're freaking me out."

"Regan made up her mind. It's taken her the whole summer, but she's made up her mind. She can't be with me because I have no self-esteem."

"What?" Terri shouted.

"That's it. She thought it was because of my being a whore, but it's not that. Now I'm just a loser."

"Callie, tell me what happened. That doesn't sound like the Regan you've been telling me about."

"No, it doesn't. But that's the Regan that really exists."

It took two days to let the feelings break through the sorrow. Two days of replaying the conversation over and over again. Regan had never seemed like it, but she was ridiculously judgmental. She wanted a woman who had never done anything she wouldn't have done, but even if a woman met that test, she had to never have been with a person who'd done something "bad."

She'd probably been upset about the voyeurism too, just hadn't had the nerve to admit it. But she'd finally come clean and let out everything she'd been holding in. All of the judgment she'd been afraid to reveal.

It didn't make much sense. Regan was very open-minded and she'd never seemed to care what other people did. But she'd cared deeply about this. And it would take a long time before they could get back to where they had been. There was no chance of ever having more. Not a chance in hell, and that hurt more than words could convey.

Two days later, Callie called Regan with a brief missive. "Hi," she said when she heard her voice.

"Hi," Regan breathed out, her relief evident. "I've been staring at my phone every minute."

"You don't have to do that. It'll take me a while, but I'll get over this."

"I want to see you. Please let me come over."

"No, that's not a good idea. I need some time alone. I just called to get our schedules organized. I'm going to run with our group on the Thursday night run and you can have Sunday. Is that all right?"

"Does it have to be like this?"

"Yes, it does. I promised I'd always be your friend, and I'm going to get there. But I'm not there now. I'll call when I feel like talking again."

"Please let it be soon."

"I can't promise that. It'll be when I feel like I can be myself around you. That's all I can do."

"I'm so sorry, Callie…"

"Great. Bye." She hung up before Regan could get another word in.

After three weeks, three long weeks, Callie finally called Regan and said, "I think I'm able to be friends if you want to be. At least I'm ready to give it a try. How about you?"

"Yes, yes, absolutely. I really want to see you. I miss you."

"Okay. Well, the running club is doing something crazy this weekend. Why don't you come up and join us?"

"Is that the six a.m. run?"

"Yeah." She started to sound more like herself when she added, "These delicate little Cambridge people seem to think it's going to be hot this weekend. They decided to move the run to early Saturday, since it's supposed to be less humid."

There was a long pause and Regan said, "Wow. Six in the morning. I'd have to get up really, really early."

"You can come on Friday. I have an airbed."

"I don't think that's going to work. I've got something planned for Friday. Down here."

Regan sounded very tense and stilted. There was a dead silence on her part and Callie felt like she was supposed to be able to guess what made Regan clam up. Callie felt her heart start to beat faster and she managed to get out, "Do you have a date?" Her voice was shaking, but she was doing her best to sound normal.

"Not technically, I don't think. Uhm, I don't think it's any big deal."

It was a warm day and Callie knew that the cold sweat running down her back was not from the weather. "Tell me."

"Like I said, it's no big deal. But some friends of mine are having some people over for dinner. I'm going," she added, ineloquently.

"Is it a party?" Her heart was hammering so hard in her chest she could almost hear it. "Lots of people?"

"No. Just four I think. Yeah, just four."

"Oh. Do you know all of the people?"

Regan's voice was so tight that she barely sounded like herself. "I know the people having the party. They're a couple."

"Well, I can see why you wouldn't want to have to get up so early on Saturday. I'll let you know how this goes. Maybe we can do it another time. Oh, my phone is ringing. I think I have another call. Yeah, I have another call. Talk to you later." She hung up and threw her phone across the room where it mercifully landed against her pillows. Then she went to her bed and picked up the saving pillow and started to swing it over her head, slamming it against the wall with all of her might. Her arms ached by the time she sat down and finally allowed herself to feel the ache in her heart. Regan had moved on. She was gone forever.

After a while Callie felt like she was able to think clearly so she called Terri, who answered her cell phone with a happy, "Hi there!"

"Hi."

"What's up?"

"Regan is going on a date." She could feel the emotion in the back of her throat like a knot. But she was determined not to cry.

"A date? Are you serious?"

"Don't I sound serious?"

"Oh, Callie, that sucks."

"Yeah. That's about the right word for it. Three weeks ago she tells me she loves me with all her heart but can't be with me, and now she's ready to start dating. Her heart must be a lot bigger than mine, because I'm barely able to feed myself."

That weekend was one of the loneliest Callie could ever recall having. She'd made friends in Cambridge, but no one that she yet considered a close confidant. That was a role she'd given exclusively to Regan. And now that she'd been unceremoniously shunted aside, she didn't have anyone local to turn to. She called her father, and he did his best to console her, but she needed more than he could give. She barely got out of bed on Sunday, a habit she found she reverted to when she was depressed. Regan called several times, but she wasn't in the mood to talk to her. She didn't have the stomach to hear about her date, and nothing else mattered at the moment.

The thought of Regan dating was repulsive. The conjured image of her with another woman made her brain hurt. Regan had revealed a part of herself that was so discordant, it had to be unreal. But it wasn't. This wasn't something imagined. These were Regan's words and actions, and they made her want to forget she'd ever known her and never think about her again. Both urges were impossible.

Callie was tempted to skip her weekly pool match, but she knew she had to get out and interact with people, so she went. They started at nine and by eleven she felt like the ice had finally thawed from the muscles in her face. She was smiling and even laughing a little at the vaguely ribald jokes that floated around the table. They were almost through for the night when the door opened and Regan entered. She stayed right in front of the door, her eyes darting around until they landed on Callie. For the first time since she'd known her, Regan looked not only nervous, but frightened. Callie's ire rose in her throat. She wanted nothing more than to stride across the room and slap her as hard as she could. She'd never felt a stronger urge to hurt someone than she did now.

At this point, all she had was her pride, and she was suddenly determined to regain what little she had left. "Hey," she called out, drawing her fellow players' attention. "My friend Regan's here."

The other women looked over and nodded or said hello. The relief on Regan's face was clear to anyone paying the slightest attention. She walked over to Callie and said, "How are you?"

"Good. Fine." She was using all of her self-respect to smile and look friendly. "I've had a busy week. Sorry I couldn't make time to talk." She shrugged her shoulders. "You know how it is."

Regan didn't respond. Her eyes were hooded and she clearly didn't share Callie's decision to act like everything was fine. "Do you have time for a drink?"

"Sure." They started to walk towards the bar. "I finished the project I was working on, so I'm breathing easier now." They sat on stools and Callie signaled the bartender. "Two more, Mallory," she said, holding up her empty. Her stomach was tied in knots, but she was determined to continue the facade of normalcy. "An ale's okay with you, right?"

"Sure." Regan didn't say another word until after their beers were delivered and she'd taken a first sip. "I wanted to talk to you, and since you wouldn't answer..."

"Hey," Callie interrupted. "I get busy. Don't take it personally. If you'd said it was an emergency, I would have called you right back."

"Okay." Regan's head was drooping, and she looked like she didn't know what to say.

"It's nice of you to come up here, but you didn't need to. We're fine." She pasted on a smile that she assumed looked false, but it was the best she could come up with.

"We are?" Regan tentatively met her eyes, doubt nearly glowing from them.

"Sure. Why wouldn't we be?" She'd thrown that little land mine out there, daring Regan to run or throw it back.

Choosing the safest path, Regan shook her head slightly. "Okay. You'll let me know if we're not, right?"

"Right." Callie picked up her hand and started to put it on Regan's shoulder, but it was as if a force field stopped her cold. It dropped limply to her side. "You look tired," she managed.

"Yeah. I am. I haven't been sleeping."

Suddenly, Callie was filled with regret. Regan hadn't done anything wrong. She'd never led her on. If anything, she'd been extremely cautious with Callie's feelings. All she'd promised was that she'd always be a good friend. Nothing more. Seeing her look so sad, so worn down, made Callie feel that she hadn't been the same. Without allowing herself time to stop her instinct she turned and slid her arms around Regan's waist and held her. She got to her feet, shoving the stool away to be able to grasp her firmly. Regan nearly fell into her arms, nuzzling her face against Callie's neck, wetting her skin with her tears. "It's all right," Callie crooned. "We'll be fine. We'll get through this."

"I don't want to hurt you. I swear that. I tried so hard not to."

"It's okay," Callie soothed, knowing in her soul that it wasn't, and never would be.

A new pattern emerged. Regan started calling in the middle of the week to propose a movie or a game or dinner. Each time caught Callie off guard. But she almost always accepted, and within a month they'd settled into the new scheme. Now they saw each other on Tuesday or Wednesday night and Sunday. Every Sunday, without fail, they met for their organized run with their club. And by the end of September, Callie was comfortable with what Regan was willing to give. It wasn't what she wanted, it wasn't what she needed, but one day, while talking to Terri, she realized she'd finally accepted the situation. "I guess I've got to get off my butt and try to find someone to go out with."

"Yep. You need to do that. It's the only way you're gonna perk up."

"I know. But I don't have much energy for it."

"You never have a hard time attracting people, so use some of that charm and start going on dates. They don't have to be life-changing. Just go out."

The more Callie thought about it, the more Terri's advice made sense. She needed to get a few dates under her belt to start feeling like herself. Regan had knocked her self-esteem into a pit, and she was going to have to dig her way out of it.

The first date was hard. Callie actually felt sorry for the poor woman, a friend of one of the women on her pool team. Melody seemed like a perfectly nice person, but Callie felt no spark, no excitement. She looked at her watch much more than was polite while they were having dinner, but she honestly just wanted it to be over. She was actually relieved when Melody pulled up to her apartment, didn't bother getting out of the car, and ended the date with a rather unenthusiastic "I guess I'll see you around,"

She watched the car pull away, feeling empty. The loss of an evening wasn't important, but it seemed like so much work to find a lover. And there was no guarantee she'd ever find one much better than Marina. And that thought was seriously depressing.

She wouldn't have predicted it, but Callie got past the first few dates and then started enjoying herself. There was something appealing about being free to have just what you wanted. A woman shows bad manners at a restaurant? Dump her. She tries to keep you out late on a Saturday night and thinks training for a marathon is silly? Don't return her calls. She thinks an evening at the symphony and discussing poetry is the peak of perfection? Lose her number. She might not find love, but she didn't have to waste more than one date with someone who didn't appeal to her in every way that was important. That was a small victory, but it had to be enough. It simply had to.

CHAPTER TWENTY-TWO

IN EARLY NOVEMBER, Regan called Callie to arrange where to meet for the Sunday run. "Hey, while I have you on the phone, I wanted to ask about your Thanksgiving plans."

"I don't think I have any. I'm going to go to Phoenix for Christmas, but Thanksgiving is always kind of a downer. My dad's got a new girlfriend and they're going on a cruise, so Dallas is out. Gretchen goes to her husband's family and now that Emily has a boyfriend she might be going with his."

"What about your mom?"

"Eww. That's the bad part. I hate to leave my mom alone, but she can spend it with her sister's family. I know I'm being selfish but I hate to spend the holiday feeling like I want to jump off a bridge."

"You shouldn't have to. We want you to come spend it with us. The restaurant's open, but we close really early. As soon as we get rid of the customers, we have our own celebration. It's always fun, and it would be even better if you were there."

Callie could feel herself choking up, but she managed to keep her voice level when she said, "I'd love to."

As Regan had promised most of the customers vacated the Scituate Inn by 5:00 on Thanksgiving day. The few stragglers were loyal customers who were on a first name basis with everybody. It was an odd way to celebrate a holiday, but Callie decided she really liked it. They moved tables around until they had three long ones. All of the Mannings were there and most of the servers and cooks brought their families. There must have been close to sixty people and with everyone making full use of the bar, it was a rowdy time.

Alana had finished cooking and came out to make herself a drink right when Callie was getting a beer. "How do you like our Thanksgiving?"

"I love it. I really love it. It's more like a party, and I love parties."

Alana leaned over and said softly, "So who are you dating? I can't get any information out of Regan."

Without thinking, Callie automatically said, "No one special. I'm just shopping."

Alana looked surprised. "I assumed you were seeing somebody seriously since you're not here on the weekends anymore."

"No, no one special. I'm just saying yes to any single woman in the greater Boston area."

Alana took a quick look at her sister across the room. "You guys are getting along, aren't you?"

"Yeah. Sure. We're getting along great."

Looking puzzled, Alana said, "Then come down more often. We all love having you here."

"Thanks. I feel very much at home here." That was true. Even with both of them dating other people, there was no one she felt more at home with than Regan. She was a fantastic friend, and the fact that she'd also be a fantastic partner if she would wise up couldn't negate that. She was who she was and that was enough.

The Friday after Thanksgiving was one of the slowest days of the year at The Scituate Inn. Very few deliveries were scheduled, since they expected a slow weekend too. Regan was trying to use the day to catch up, but she wasn't being very productive. She'd been in the kitchen a couple of times, looking for a snack that she didn't seem able to find, then she wandered around behind the bar, idly examining their liquor supply.

She'd been back in her office for a half hour when Delaney came in and caught her shopping for running shoes. "Ha!" she said when Regan tried to close the window. "I've finally caught you goofing off!" She stood behind Regan's chair and put her hands on her shoulders. "When are you going to talk to one of us about what's going on with Callie?"

Wanting to escape her sister's questions, Regan tried to push her chair backwards, but Delaney blocked the casters with her foot, effectively trapping her. "I have to go to the bathroom," she lied.

"You could have gone one of the twenty times you've been wandering around. Now tell me what's going on."

"Nothing." She said this with such finality that Delaney moved around to the front of the desk and sat down so she could see Regan's face.

"Mom and Alana and I talked about you last night and it's obvious to us that things aren't the same between you two. Add that to the fact that she doesn't come down on the weekends anymore and something's up. Did you fight?"

"No." She paused. "Well, yes, but not recently."

"More details, please."

Sighing dramatically, Regan said, "You know I don't like to talk about my love life."

"I know that. We all know that. But you've been in a funk for weeks. Tell me what's got you so down."

Regan picked up her stapler and started to examine it like she was going to build a scale model as soon as Delaney left the room. "I'm not really down. I'm…I guess I'm resolved."

"Resolved to be grouchy and moody?"

She shot her sister a glare. "No, finally resolved that Callie isn't right for me."

"I'm perplexed. Didn't we have this discussion before?"

"Yes, we did. But I'm still stuck on her."

"Weird. Mom and I think you're just not over Angela yet."

Regan put the stapler down and lazily flipped her hand in the air. "She's barely crossed my mind. Other than to use her as a reminder to never get into a situation where I could hook up with another cheater."

"And you think Callie's a cheater?"

With her head rapidly shaking, Regan said, "No, she's not. There's other stuff. Stuff I don't want to talk about."

"Well, Mom and I both know you pretty well, and we think you're just gun-shy. It didn't dawn on me that you'd crossed Callie off your list. Especially when she stares at you like you're a circus act when you move around the room."

"She does not. I finally got up the nerve to tell her we don't have a future. It's over between us."

Delaney stood up and moved over to the doorway. "Well, at least you were honest. I'm glad you got it over with."

"Yeah." She felt like she'd eaten something very acidic, the way her stomach felt much of the time recently. "At least I did that."

"Well, did our little talk help?"

"Yeah." Regan's lack of enthusiasm was pronounced. "I feel great now."

"Any time. No charge. Just quit moping!"

Regan wasn't able to stop thinking about Callie, but she was able to keep her heartache to herself. She accepted a few more blind dates just to stay in the game, and hustled out of the restaurant as soon as she could each day, resolved to keep her feelings where they belonged—in her heart. She wanted Callie as much as she ever had, but she couldn't bear the thought of pledging her heart to a woman who'd settled for so little. Callie seemed like a well-adjusted person. But no one who had her head on straight would have gotten into the arrangement she had. No matter how great she seemed, Regan couldn't marry and have children with someone who wasn't a good role model. It wasn't fair to anyone involved. It would take time, but next time she'd get it right. Next time it would be for life. As soon as she could flush Callie from her system, she'd get busy and find her mate.

Callie and Regan decided to celebrate Christmas on December twenty-third. Because it was a Saturday and Regan had the day off, she came up to Cambridge to spend the day until she took Callie to the airport for her evening flight to Phoenix.

Callie opened the door with a big kitchen towel tucked into her slacks, an improvised apron. "Come on in."

"I smell something good. I was wondering what we were going to do for food," she teased. "Pizza doesn't seem very Christmassy."

"No, it isn't. I know this isn't a New England specialty, but I know you'll like it."

Regan went into the kitchen and started lifting the tops off pans and sniffing at them. "This looks and smells great."

"I know you like Mexican food, so I thought we would have kind of a traditional Mexican Christmas feast. One thing I learned in Dallas is how to cook Tex-Mex."

"That's really thoughtful of you. I thought we'd just go out and grab a burger."

"No way. You've done so much for me this year, the least I can do for you is make you a nice meal. That didn't sound right," she said, laughing. "A meal won't make up for all that you've helped me do."

"Hey, if I'd been paying for a therapist I'd be in the hole for about twenty thousand dollars. You helped me get through the toughest time of my life so far."

"Well, then let's call it even. But helping me move to a place that feels like home for the first time in my life was a really big gift."

"I knew you'd like it here." Regan was grinning happily. "You seem like you've really settled in."

"I have. My business is going great and I've met a lot of nice people. I'm happy."

"Good. Knowing that you're doing well makes me happy."

Callie wasn't sure what it was, but when those last words left Regan's mouth she could see tears starting to form in her eyes.

They'd stopped touching each other, not even hugging any more. Callie had to force herself not to wrap her arms around Regan and comfort her. "Don't get all sentimental on me."

"I'm a sentimental person." Regan shrugged her shoulders, looking young and a little embarrassed. She went back into the living room and got her bag, then wrestled around for a moment and came back with a nicely wrapped box. "I got you a little gift."

"Put it under the tree," Callie directed. Regan went to the two-foot-tall artificial tree that was on the coffee table. It was attractively decorated but had only one present under it and that one was addressed to her. Callie was in the kitchen stirring a sauce when she saw Regan pick up the gift and read her name. She watched as her friend momentarily dropped her head into her hand, then quickly wiped her eyes. She shuddered, then seemed to gather herself and came back into the kitchen wearing her usual happy expression.

Since Callie wasn't driving, and she had a slight fear of flying, she helped herself to a little more than her share of the champagne Regan had brought. It actually didn't go well with the dinner, but she wanted to drink it with Regan there, so they enjoyed it with their spicy, flavor-filled meal.

Callie wasn't drunk by any means, but she was relaxed enough to be able to fly without too much trepidation. When they got to Logan, Regan offered to park in the short-term lot and go into the airport with her, but Callie wouldn't hear of it. "That's a huge waste of your time. Just drop me off at the departures level."

They got to the right destination, but there were so many people going on trips that there was nowhere to pull up. There were at least fifty cars in front of them, all trying to find a spot to drop off a loved one. "I've got almost two hours, so I'm not worried," Callie said. "This is my new attitude about travel. I'm going to relax and let what happens happen."

"That's one of the things I really like about you. You don't get excited about every little thing that happens."

"I try not to be too excitable. It doesn't pay."

"Actually, you're an optimist. That's one of your best traits. You always seem to try to find the bright spot in any situation. Given what you've told me about your family, I'm really glad you didn't get that defeatist streak it seems like your mom has."

Callie's smile faded as she mulled those words over. "I don't remember my mom being like that when I was young. I guess I'll never know if that's always who she was or if my dad's leaving changed her. I hope that's who she was anyway." She looked at Regan sadly. "It's too painful to think that his cheating changed her personality. I just hope the same thing never happens to me."

Regan reached over and squeezed her hand. "I don't think it will. I know you've had a couple of heartbreaks, but they don't seem to have made you a bitter person at all."

"No, not yet." Feeling herself start to choke up, Callie threw a joke in. "Give me time. I'm still young." She knew she was going to cry, she just knew it. But she didn't want to do that to Regan. Probably the holidays were making her more emotional. If only Regan would just let it slide.

But Regan didn't. She took Callie's hand and brought it to her face, then kissed the back of it tenderly. "Please don't let that happen." Callie shot a quick look at her and saw that Regan was crying. Her eyes were shut tightly and her whole body was shaking, and Callie knew she was right behind her.

"This is crazy," she managed to get out. "We've got to get past this or not see each other anymore."

"Please don't say that!" Regan's eyes popped open and she looked horror-struck. "I need you! I don't know what I'd do if I couldn't see you."

Callie reached over and grabbed her shoulder. "Then move on and quit making moon-eyes at me! You do it all the time. I see you looking at me when we're running and sometimes you look like you're fighting with yourself not to throw your arms around me." She shook her. "You've *got* to stop."

Regan let her head drop. "I'll try. I promise I'll try. It's just so hard. I love you so much…"

Callie brushed her cheek with her fingers. "If you loved me, you'd be with me. You're not. So no more of this nonsense! That has to be your New Year's resolution. Okay?"

Still crying, Regan nodded, looking absolutely miserable.

"Fine. It's settled." She grabbed her bag by the handles, opened the door and dodged cars to get to the terminal, not turning around when Regan called her name again and again.

She got into the terminal and flopped down into a chair. This made no sense. Regan was dating. She was dating. Why couldn't they let go? The ball had been in Regan's court for months. If she'd changed her mind, she'd be welcomed with open arms. But she hadn't given any sign of that. She just looked heart-sick when she thought no one could see her. The only way to get past this was to truly move on. That had to be the motto for the new year. Move on.

CHAPTER TWENTY-THREE

CALLIE THREW HERSELF into the quest for a girlfriend as she did anything that interested her. She talked to nearly everyone she'd met in Boston, then joined three more clubs. Meeting people who shared some of her interests was a big help, and by the end of January she'd had dates with three more women. None of them was quite right, but she was heartened that she'd eventually find someone. She just had to be patient.

Their running club had access to a good quarter mile indoor track and Regan went up to Cambridge one night a week to work on her form with one of their coaches. Callie didn't always meet her there since she had different issues she was working on, but they usually got together for a drink afterward.

One night Regan pulled into the parking lot by the gym and saw Callie getting out of a car. Her heart skipped a beat, as it always did, when she saw her. But when Callie walked over to the driver's side and leaned in for a kiss, it hit Regan like a blow to the gut.

Regan was tempted to go right back to her own car, but she'd slogged through traffic to get to Cambridge and she had a firm appointment with the coach. She had to stay, so she veered to the left and tried not to look. She really did try. But the masochistic part of her made her take one look, and now she felt like she'd taken a jab to the chin.

The woman had practically pulled Callie into the car. One of her feet was off the ground and she was laughing hard; that melodic, lighthearted laugh that no woman could defend against.

How could she do that? Regan hadn't had a good night's rest in months, but Callie was right back in the game, kissing a stranger like a lover. That thought made her double over in pain. They probably *were* lovers. That stranger had probably had her mouth and hands all over Callie's beautiful body. Something that Regan would never, ever have.

Delaney walked into Regan's office the next afternoon, closed and locked the door, then sat down in a chair. Regan looked up at her, eyes widening when Delaney slid a beer across the desk. "Drink up."

"What?"

"It's quitting time. Have a drink."

"I don't drink at work."

"You can today." She nodded at the beer. "Go ahead. We're gonna be here for a while."

Scowling, Regan said, "How do you know I don't have plans for tonight?"

"You never have plans. And even if you do, you have to cancel them. You're not leaving until you tell me what has you so down."

Reluctantly, Regan grasped the beer and took a long drink. She put the bottle down and nodded at her sister. "That's good. Thanks. But you can't hold me hostage."

"Mom said I could." She stuck her tongue out, just like she'd have done thirty years earlier. "If you won't talk to me, she said you have to go to Florida so she can straighten you out."

"Superb." Regan pouted while taking another drink. "I don't know what you want from me. I don't think I've been that bad."

"Yes, you have." Delaney leaned over a little so Regan couldn't avoid her pointed gaze. "You've been really bad. I've been worried about you, and I haven't had to do that very many times in my life. You're the stable one, remember? You're not yourself, Regan. You haven't been since Angela."

"I feel like I'm in a fog." She knew that lack of sleep was part of the problem, but no way would she tell Delaney about her insomnia. "I've never felt like this before. Sheila thinks I should go on antidepressants."

"You don't need drugs. But you haven't bounced back like you should have. I know breaking up is hard, but you've been taking this much harder than I would have predicted."

"This isn't about Angela," Regan insisted, her voice rising. "I'm lucky to be rid of her."

Delaney looked at her closely, her head tilting as though she could see better from an oblique angle. "You didn't say things like that at first. You said you'd just grown apart." She leaned closer. "That was a lie, wasn't it."

It was nice to know that Delaney cared, but she really, really didn't want to get into this. She looked up at the ceiling for a few seconds, then finally faced her sister and nodded. Screw it. Angela didn't deserve a pristine reputation. "She was having an affair."

"I knew it! I told Mom and Alana that you wouldn't have gone from happy-happy to broken up in a matter of weeks if she hadn't done something horrible."

"Yeah, you're right there." It was horrible. The whole mess was toxic. She wished she didn't have to talk about it at all, but she was in this far —she had to finish it off. She leaned back in the chair, then pushed it further away from her desk and put her feet on the top. "That's how I met Callie."

"Callie? How does she figure into this?"

"Angela and Callie's lover worked together. They slept together too. For a year and a half." It wasn't possible to just say those words. She literally spat them out.

Delaney's cheeks turned a bright pink and her eyes narrowed into slits. Her voice was so full of barely-controlled rage that sparks nearly flew from her words. "Does she still live in the same house?"

Finally! A benefit from telling your secrets to your family. "You don't need to go kick her ass. She feels bad about it. But it was tough for me to get over. I'll admit that."

"God damn it, Regan!" She stood up and walked over behind the desk. Sitting on the edge she put her hand on Regan's leg and patted it gently. "You got fucked over. Majorly fucked over. It's barely been a year. No wonder you're in a fog."

Shaking her head, Regan said, "I don't think that's what's bothering me. It's Callie. Not being able to be with her hurts just as much as having Angela fuck things up."

"No. Trust me on this." She gripped her leg and squeezed firmly. "I know you better than just about anyone. Your whole personality is different. You've been depressed since you left Cambridge. Now I understand why. Having someone you love cheat on you is like getting a compound fracture! It takes a long, long time to heal. Especially when it's someone you really love." She leaned over and spoke lovingly. "I know how much you loved her."

Swallowing hard to force the tears away, Regan took another sip of her beer. Delaney had more experience with bad love affairs. She'd had her heart broken at least twice. "You really think so?"

"Yes. You've lost your spark, your self-confidence. You haven't had any of that cockiness you usually show. That's not because of Callie. It's because of Angela. That miserable son of a bitch."

Regan showed a faint smile. "It was a horrible betrayal, but we probably weren't made for each other. I think we made a better couple on paper than we did in reality."

"She wasn't right for you, as I might have mentioned." Delaney smiled unrepentantly. "Did I ever bring that up?"

"Yeah, I think you did. Like a hundred times."

"But that doesn't mean you didn't love her."

"No, it doesn't. I was committed to her."

"Yeah, I could see that. And I know you thought I was dead wrong, but you never seemed crazy about her. It seemed more like an arranged marriage."

Regan let out a snicker. "Wanna float that past me again?"

"It seemed like you had a list of things you wanted in a partner and Angela had everything. Kinda like you'd used a matchmaker."

Regan leaned her head back and drained her beer. "Huh. That's an interesting perspective."

"A correct one."

"I'm not sure about that. But I'll consider it." And if you're right I'll never tell you. You'd hold it over my head forever.

"One day you'll see that I was right. And I won't make a big deal out of it when you apologize for doubting me."

Regan reached out and covered her sister's hand with her own. "Thanks. You're all heart." They shared a smile, then she got up. "Can I go now?"

"Yes. If you'll spend some time thinking about how right I am."

With a grin, Regan grabbed her briefcase and headed for the door. "I do that every night."

Accepting that Delaney had been right was not easy, but pondering her comments over the next week helped some of the fog lift. Admitting how much Angela had taken from her helped almost immediately, and each day brought a little more clarity. By the time Sunday rolled around, Regan jumped out of bed when her alarm went off, something she hadn't done in months. The day was cool and dreary, but she felt a burst of energy that had been lying dormant ever since she'd walked out the door of Angela's home. Now she needed to take another look at Callie's choices. Maybe things would look different without Angela's betrayal hanging over her.

Callie was also in fine fettle that day, and they ran together through the cool morning, taking in the first signs of spring. "What's that?" Callie demanded, dragging Regan to a stop in front of a shrub enfolded in an exuberant splash of yellow.

"My grandmother calls that the golden bells of spring."

"What is it?"

"Just a bush or a shrub. It's usually one of the first things to bloom." She looked into the sparse woods and pointed. "There's a few on the edge there. You can follow it up the coast as it blooms. Kinda like when the leaves turn."

"Excellent. I'm gonna learn the names of all of the plants this year. Spring is gonna rock. I'm totally ready for it."

They started running again, slowly speeding up to their former cadence. "The bloom isn't off the rose yet, huh?"

"Nope. I don't think it ever will be. I'm crazy for New England."

Suddenly, seeing spring through Callie's eyes was imperative. "Hey, you haven't had a chance to get out of town much. Why don't we drive up to Maine or Vermont?"

"Really?" Callie's smile grew wide. "When?"

That smile alone could have propelled Regan all the way to Nova Scotia. But plans had to be made. "How about next weekend? It's somebody's birthday on Friday."

"It's mine!"

"That too. How about it?"

"You're on. Where will we go?"

"I'll make plans. Leave it to me." Spring was suddenly vitally important. Callie loved it and that was enough to make it paramount.

They finished their ten miles and assembled as a group as their coaches gave them a few tips. Some of the runners were going to brunch, but Callie started to ease away from the others. Regan turned and started to follow her. "No brunch?"

"Can't. Meeting someone." Callie scanned the area and waved at a woman sitting on a bench. She smiled at Regan and shrugged. "Gotta go."

But Regan stayed right next to her. She wasn't sure why she followed along, even though Callie tried to discourage her by whispering "I've got a date" as they approached the woman.

"Hi," Regan said, holding her hand out to the perplexed-looking woman. "I'm Regan, Callie's friend."

"Hi. Allison."

Callie wasn't smiling. "Regan just wanted to say hi before she left," she said, staring a hole in her.

"Where are you two off to?" Regan heard herself ask. Who was the woman who'd taken over her body?

"We're gonna go have brunch," Allison said.

"Oh. Where are you going? We usually have brunch with our running group."

Callie put her hand on Regan's arm and turned her towards the dispersing group. "You'd better run if you want to catch them."

Regan took a quick look at the group. "Yeah. I guess I'd better. Uhm, how long have you two been going out?"

"First date," Callie said, giving a tense-looking smile. "Gotta go now."

"Okay." Regan stuck her hand out and shook Allison's hand again. "You guys have a great time."

Callie and Allison started to walk and when she got about twenty feet away, Callie turned back and gave Regan a very quizzical look. Regan waved, feeling more confused by her actions than Callie probably did. She'd never tried to insinuate herself into someone else's date, but she'd almost asked if she could go with them. That was beyond strange.

After putting on her sweats, Regan decided to walk over to her favorite bookstore. She could have taken her car, but it was only a mile and parking was always problematic on Mass. Ave., so she decided to walk. Eventually she found herself on her former street. She had to go several blocks out of her way to get there, and she hadn't even realized she'd chosen such a circuitous route, but some part of her needed to be there.

Angela was in the front yard, working on a small flower bed she'd planted each of the years they'd lived together. She was in her usual gardening clothes: a nice pair of old khakis and a blouse that most people would think still had a lot of life left in it. But she was out there digging in the soil she'd built up with plenty of amendment to aid in the drainage. She gardened the way she did everything: carefully and properly. Regan stood on the corner, feeling exposed and vulnerable. Angela was just a hundred feet away, close enough to be able to hear a call. But Regan was never going to call her name again. Looking at Angela brought none of the heart-fluttering excitement she'd felt the first time she'd touched Callie's cheek. Angela was a good woman. She'd made a terrible mistake, and Regan was sure she'd do more than her share of penance over it. But there was nothing left. No animosity, no rancor, no pull. The relationship was dead. The time for grieving was over. It was spring. The time of rebirth and renewal, and Regan was going to start her life again—unencumbered by the past.

Regan picked Callie up on Friday night. It was a cold and clear night, and the weekend was supposed to be the same.

Callie came running towards the car, carrying a big backpack. She was practically skipping, and Regan felt the familiar and now welcome thrumming of her heart when they made eye contact.

"I'm so excited!" Callie tossed her bag into the back and settled down in her seat. "Where are we going?"

"Tonight we're going to New Hampshire. I found a nice place up I-95 that's supposed to have great breakfasts. I know that eating is your favorite part of road trips, so I was very careful to take that into consideration."

Out of the corner of her eye, she could see Callie's hand hover for a second over her leg, then retreat. They'd abandoned almost all of their physical affection, and it hurt to see that beautiful hand slip into the pocket of her coat.

"I didn't eat anything, hoping we could stop somewhere cool. Will we have time?"

"We've got nothing but time. Our only agenda is to have fun."

"That's my favorite agenda." Callie smiled and the warmth of her smile made the car feel cozy.

CHAPTER TWENTY-FOUR

THEY STAYED ON the interstate until they were halfway through New Hampshire. Regan pulled off the highway and followed some dim signs that indicated they were heading for U.S. 1.

After a mile or two they arrived at the inn, a small, tidy place that dripped New England charm. Regan looked around, very pleased with her choice. They checked in and went to their room, a spare but clean one with a very tall queen sized bed and a fire crackling in the small fireplace. When the innkeeper left them, Callie said, "This is probably the cutest place I've ever stayed. Would anyone notice if we knocked off the owner and just took her place?"

"Probably not." Seeing the happiness in Callie's eyes made her hours of work searching for perfection seem like a very good investment.

"Only one problem. Where can we eat? We didn't pass a place for the last fifty miles."

"We can eat right here." Regan shucked her coat and tossed her big bag on the bed. Slowly she pulled out a couple of bags and a bottle of wine, presenting everything to Callie. "We're going to have a little birthday repast right here."

Callie squealed with delight. "Wonderful! What have we got?"

"A bunch of stuff you like." They pulled a pair of comfy chairs up to the fire and put the bags on a small table. Regan opened them and placed cheeses, apples, pears, crackers and a tin of caviar before Callie.

Eyes wide, Callie took the tin and examined it. "I don't think we've ever had caviar. How do you know I like it?"

"Because I like it," Regan teased. "You like everything that's good, so I assumed you liked it. And if you don't…I'll eat it all."

"I love it!" Callie held the tin to her chest. "This is a great birthday."

"Don't forget the wine." She pulled a corkscrew out and started to open a bottle of white wine. "This will go really well with the cheese and the caviar."

Callie reached out and put her hand on Regan's shoulder, then obviously thought better of the idea. She brushed her hand over her shirt. "Some lint," she explained. "I'm glad I'm having my birthday with you. That makes it special."

Regan wondered who had first backed away from showing the slightest physical affection? They'd lost so much of their precious familiarity. They *had* to be able to reclaim it, if only Callie was willing.

Regan got the cork out and poured two glasses half full. "To very happy birthdays," she said, clinking their glasses together. "I hope you have a hundred more."

"Only if you promise to come to my hundred and thirty-sixth birthday party."

"I'll put in on my calendar the minute I get home." They touched their glasses together once again and each took a sip.

"That's good," Callie said, watching the wine coat the glass as she swirled it.

They dug into their meal, demolishing the cheese and caviar with ferocity. When they didn't have a single cracker left, they slowly sipped their wine, slumped back into their chairs and watched the fire dance.

"Nice meal," Callie said, her voice softer and slower than usual. "Very... nice...birthday."

"Oh! I forgot your presents."

"Presents? I get presents?"

"Absolutely." Regan got up and went to her bag, pulling out three gifts, each nicely wrapped. Handing them to Callie, she sat back down. "I hope they fit." She peered at the flat rectangles, each about an inch think. "You wear a seven and a half, right?"

Callie rolled her eyes, then tore into the first one. "Awesome! A guide to plants in New England." She started to thumb through the book, exclaiming over some striking examples of plants and flowers. "I'm crazy for reference books."

"Then you'll like the other two."

She hugged the book to her body and spent a moment gazing at Regan. "The other two could be travel guides to Phoenix and I'd love them. The fact that you cared enough to bring me here is remarkably generous. Thanks, Regan. You made my day really special."

"Aw, shucks. T'weren't nuthin." She grinned sheepishly.

"It's a lot, and I'll always remember this weekend." She handed her the book. "Write the date and where we are in there. I like keepsakes."

"Will do." Regan got up and fetched a pen from her bag, sharing a smile with Callie as she sat down and started to write.

Their high, very fluffy featherbed made lying on it feel like being cuddled. Driving had obviously tired Regan out, since she fell asleep just minutes after lying down. But Callie lay there for quite a while, watching Regan sleep. The fire was almost out, throwing off just enough light to highlight Regan's skin with a warm glow. She looked so pretty lying there. It was all Callie could do to stay on her side of the bed. Being with Regan was its own sweet torture. It was unfathomable that they'd never be lovers. But it was hard to hold out hope since they didn't even hug any more. There was a hole in her heart that Regan could easily fill if only she would. But that was hoping for too much…even though that had been her only wish when she'd blown out the candle on her cupcake.

They traveled along the coast, spying glimpses of the sea, tiny islands in the distance, and craggy rocks being punished by the crashing waves. Callie was staring out the window so intently that she flinched when Regan spoke. "I was wondering how dating was going for you."

"Huh? Were we talking about dating?"

"Uhm, no, but I was just wondering how it was going for you." *Damn! Could I have made that any more awkward? No, that's about as bad as it could be.*

Callie didn't answer right away. With each tick of the clock Regan's jaw clenched tighter.

"Why do you want to know?"

That was unexpected. Not the lighthearted way Callie usually answered every query. "Well, I'm interested…in you…and how things are going for you. We haven't talked about this…at all…so I don't know."

"Don't know what?" Callie's gaze was level, unblinking.

"I don't know how things are for you. Are you seeing someone…a lot?"

"No. I just had a first date with someone last week. Remember?" Now her expression gentled and she showed a smile.

"Yeah, I remember. I might never forget that, as a matter of fact."

"How about you?" Her eyes narrowed again, making Regan feel like she was under a microscope.

"No, no one…special."

"How about unspecial? You never say what you've done on a Friday or Saturday night. I always assume you're despoiling some innocent down on the Riviera." Now her face bore its usual sunny smile, and her eyes twinkled like they always did when she was teasing.

"No, I haven't despoiled a single soul. I…uhm…haven't been on a date since, oh, probably November."

"What?" Callie slapped her on the shoulder. "You're lying!"

"No, I'm not. My friends stopped trying to set me up by November."

"Why?" Now Callie's expression showed the care and concern that was so easily tapped.

"Because I didn't show any interest in the women they introduced me to."

"Hmm." She sat there, not speaking, not giving a thing away.

"Why haven't you found anyone special yet? I know you've been… busy."

"How do you know that?" The question wasn't sharply spoken, but there was a slight narrowing of the eyes.

"Uhm…I've seen you at the gym a couple of times…with one woman in particular."

"Oh, you have, have you? I've never taken anyone *into* the gym. How did you see me?"

She was busted. Well and truly busted. "I have to drive there, you know. I saw you getting out of a car." The worst night of her life had been seeing Callie kiss that woman.

"Interesting. Anything else?"

"Well, I saw you saying goodbye to a woman once before we went for our Sunday run." And had spent the rest of the day trying to ignore the only good reason she had to be with a woman so early on a Sunday morning.

"I've made some friends. But I'm still looking." Her eyes narrowed briefly and she added, "I'm still wondering why you ask. You've never come anywhere near the topic."

Regan took in a breath and tried to keep her voice from shaking. It was time to do it. But she couldn't. It felt like yanking up on the stick right before the plane crashed into a mountain. She was flushed with relief…and disappointment in herself. "I think it's time to start being more open…about things."

"Things, huh?" Callie's eyes were nearly burning a hole in her.

"Yeah. Uhm, things we've been thinking about."

"What have *you* been thinking about?"

"Well, about a month ago I made a huge discovery." Her voice sounded like a tightly strung violin string, and she felt a muscle twitch near her jaw. "I realized that I'd just gotten over Angela."

"What does that mean?"

What did it mean? It was so hard to make concrete statements about something as slippery as emotions. "Delaney was harassing me about my chronic bad mood and I found myself telling her about Angela and Marina."

"You've never told her?" Callie reached over and put her hand on Regan's arm. Just having her hand there made the world seem like a very safe place.

"Nope. I told a couple of my girlfriends about Angela, but not my family. So when I finally did, Delaney said it didn't surprise her that it'd taken me a year to get over Angela. That something like that always took a long time to heal."

Callie's expression bore the sad look she got whenever she talked about her heartbreaks. "It took me two years to get over Rob."

"Yeah. That's how long Delaney says it takes. A year or two."

"In my case I spent the second year trying to domesticate Marina so I didn't have time to think about losing Rob. I would have been better off by myself. I jumped from the frying pan into the fire."

"Yeah, I can see how that happened."

"You know, since we're talking about things we've been thinking about, I've been going to another group."

"Really? How do you have time?"

"It's not hard. It's actually easy to find time to do things that really matter."

"Sounds serious."

"Yeah, I suppose it is. It's a group for people who've had a cheating lover."

Regan snorted a laugh. "I bet it's not hard to fill up a room."

Joining in her laugh, Callie said, "Not hard at all. It's been really good, to be honest. It's led by someone getting her Ph.D. in psych at Harvard and everyone in the group wants to learn something. Know what I mean?"

"I guess so. Do you mean they're serious about it?"

"More than that. They're kinda fearless. We're all encouraged to point out things that people might not realize. Hearing things from people who aren't involved has been really helpful."

"What's been helpful for you?"

"There's a woman in the group who annoys me. She's perceptive, but kinda bitchy."

"You don't like bitchy."

Callie chuckled. "No, I really don't. But she pointed out something I needed to hear. She said she thought I tended to keep going when things were bad…even when I should stop and reassess."

"Like how?"

"I was talking about how hard it was for me after Rob and I broke up, and she said it sounded like I told myself that people would cheat, so I might as well find someone who was really good at cheating." She laughed, but it sounded sad. Regan snuck a quick look at her and saw the downcast look.

Gently, she said, "Do you think that's true?"

"Yeah. I do. I should have spent a long time licking my wounds. But I tried to brush it off and keep going. The rules had changed: fidelity wasn't going to happen, so I had to take what I could get and be happy with it."

"Wow. That's exactly what happened, isn't it."

"Yeah. She had a very good point."

"It must have been really hard for you to have Marina cheat. Especially since you hooked up with her just to avoid that."

"Yeah, it sucked, but it wasn't the same." Callie sounded strangely lighthearted.

"Why?"

"It should be obvious. I loved Rob. I would have happily married him and had kids. I wouldn't have bought a big block of cheese with Marina. I didn't do any long-term planning with her. None at all."

Regan shot a look at her. "But you loved her. You were planning on being together forever, right?"

"Forever?" Callie spit out a laugh. "God no. In my therapy group we have to try to be honest about the past. Not my favorite thing. But I've done it. Last week I admitted that I hooked up with Marina for two reasons: one, to get out of Phoenix and two, to see how I liked being with a woman."

"That's it?" Regan's voice broke.

"Yeah. That's pretty much it. Being with her was like having someone you had no-strings-attached sex with. I *wanted* to love her, and I set things up so I could, but I also had a very convenient escape hatch."

Regan's head spun. Now some things made sense. Like why Callie hadn't been devastated by the breakup. She'd anticipated it. "That sounds like a good group. What else have you learned?"

"I've learned that I know what I want in a partner, and I'm not going to take something that isn't right just to keep going."

It would have been a great time to make an overture. But it was terrifying. Too terrifying. Regan could only manage to nod her head at Callie's comments and hope she got another opportunity.

CHAPTER TWENTY-FIVE

THEY STOPPED IN front of a large, tall house, shingled in an attractive warm brown.

"Is this where we're staying?" The excitement in Callie's voice made the expense worth every dime. The inn belonged on an ad for the glories of Maine. It was old, but shone like it had been lovingly buffed.

"Yep. Looks good, doesn't it?"

"It looks awesome! Let's go."

A few minutes later Regan opened the door to their room. Sun spilled out of the room, and they had to shield their eyes to let them adjust from the darkness of the hallway. The place was gorgeous, beyond what she'd hoped for, and the room was expensive, much more than she'd ever paid for a hotel, but she wanted a place they'd always remember—one way or another.

The room had a large footprint, with a sloping ceiling where the roof dipped gracefully. A turret-style window looked out on the bay, and a pair of upholstered chairs flanked a large telescope on a wooden stand. The chairs were at the precise height to use the telescope to watch boats or birds or who knew what else might capture your attention.

The room was decorated only in white, and contained virtually no knick-knacks. But the wide-plank maple floors and the big windows made the space seem warm and open, yet still cozy.

Callie fell back onto the bed with her arms spread out. "This is the nicest bed in the nicest room I've ever been in." She rolled onto her belly, stretching like a cat. "Even though there are a hundred things I want to do, I feel like taking a nap."

Regan sat down next to her. "That's probably because you've eaten three times already. Your poor stomach doesn't know what hit it."

"I couldn't let you drive past a lobster shack with a long line, could I?"

"The place wasn't open," Regan said, looking at her fondly. "It wasn't eleven yet."

"I'm glad we stopped. That lobster roll was an A plus." She slipped out of her coat. "I'm slow and sleepy. I think I've gotta catch a quick nap."

"Have at it."

She started taking off her boots. "What will you do?"

"I might join you." Regan started to remove her own boots. "I like to be lazy on vacation. There's something decadent about staying in a nice place and lying in bed looking at the view."

Callie pulled her sweater off and took a T-shirt from her bag. Then she tossed it back in and took out a kelly green t-shirt and a pair of flannel pajama bottoms, pale yellow with images of pies, cakes and sundaes covering them. "Might as well do it right." She walked into the bathroom with her pajamas and her toiletries, leaving Regan to gaze out at the water, considering her plans for the afternoon.

After a few minutes Callie came barreling out of the bathroom and jumped onto the bed. "Perfect!" she proclaimed, the bed still shaking from her assault.

"You don't seem very tired now."

"Yes I am. I'm just in a hurry to get to sleep." She grinned so adorably that Regan's heart was hammering in her chest while she tried to change into a T-shirt. There would never be a better time to tell Callie how she felt, but actually doing it seemed like jumping off a cliff. Her hands were shaking as she wrestled out of her bra, slipped her arms back into her shirt and got into bed. Callie was lying on her side, her remarkably appealing face just inches away. The sun warmed the bed and shot a few beams onto her hair, making it look like a cascade of gold and copper and blonde. And when she slipped her hand into it and tossed her head back Regan almost gasped. That simple act was so incredibly sexy. The way she did it exposed her neck, the pale skin so luscious that Regan was tempted to put her mouth right on the spot and take a bite.

"This is kinda weird, isn't it?"

Regan emerged from her reverie, blinking. "What?"

"It's kinda weird lying in bed on such a beautiful day. I don't take naps very often, and when I do, I never take my clothes off." Rolling onto her back she reached behind herself to fluff her pillow.

"We're on vacation. We're paying for the bed, so we might as well use it."

"Good point. I'm helping you get your money's worth." She grinned, looking like a teenager who was getting away with something.

Regan didn't reply. She just closed her eyes and tried to lull herself to sleep by breathing slowly and deeply. Having Callie right next to her got under her skin like a mite. She itched from the closeness and finally had to open her eyes and think. But looking at Callie's unguarded face was anathema to rational thought. At least those perceptive eyes weren't staring back. That made it hard to think clearly under any circumstance. It was impossible to let this opportunity pass by. If Callie's feelings had changed—if the past six months had allowed her love to die—Regan might never have the chance to lie by her again. Once the issue was on the table again it would be impossible to go back to their easy familiarity. So she took her in fully, as though it was the final time. The sun showed the red undertones in Callie's brows and lashes, something one never saw indoors. Her skin was absolutely luminous. It was almost alabaster along her neck and the underside of the arm tossed casually over her head. But then it turned the palest pink upon her cheeks, and a darker, more sensuous pink on her full, beautifully shaped mouth.

Callie's eyes moved rapidly under her lids, and she twitched slightly from a dream. Then, as her body moved under the covers a gentle smile formed. It was mesmerizing. One dimple peeked out, showing a shallow parentheses of skin bracketing it. It was those dimples that had first caught and held Regan's attention when they'd met in the Bahamas. Now, one dimple was back to remind her of how far they'd come, and how she longed for more. Much, much more.

For nearly a half hour Regan lay there in silence, conjuring dreams of their future together. She flinched when one hazy eye peeked at her, then Callie rolled onto her side and scrunched her face up like a baby's. "Hi," she said, her voice a little raspy. "Did you sleep?"

"Not really. I was just lying here thinking."

Callie took her pillow and doubled it over, propping her head up a few more inches. "You look very serious." She squinted, as if she could see inside Regan's head if she tried hard enough. "What's going on?"

"Uhm." It wasn't too late to turn back, but it wouldn't be any easier later. "I was thinking about how I handled things…last summer."

Hazy eyes sharpened. "Last summer…when?"

"Uhm, when we were in Boston."

"Yeah? What about Boston?"

She wasn't going to make this easy. "When we…when I…"

"I know what you're referring to, Regan. Tell me what's on your mind."

Maybe she *would* make it a little easier. "Here's what happened. I'd been feeling awful. Really awful. I'd never felt so unattractive, unappealing, and rejected in my life."

Callie reached out and touched her arm, stroking it gently. "I understand."

"Yeah, I know you do. So I was kinda ruined emotionally when this gorgeous woman came into my life. I reacted to her like any sane person would have. I kissed her and almost let her magnetism lead me to do something that I wasn't ready for."

"*Let* her?" Callie's brow jumped up an inch.

"I didn't say that right. I was the one who wanted to be with her. I wanted it so badly."

"But..?"

"I was still too wrapped up in Angela and in how I felt about myself to be able to really open myself up. So I closed down. Really fast. Really tight."

"That's the truth. It was like a guillotine came down on your feelings."

"That was a mistake. I should have realized that *I* was the problem. But nothing like that had ever happened to me and I didn't realize how heartbreak could screw you up."

"That makes sense, I guess."

"I struggled with it for a couple of months. I was ridiculously into you, but I kept trying to figure out what was wrong. What kept me from grabbing you and running away together?"

Callie's eyes blinked slowly, and it looked like she was on the verge of tears. Her voice was rough when she said, "I would have gone anywhere you wanted to go."

"I know that." A wave of shame flowed over her. Callie had done nothing to deserve such harsh treatment. "I was stupid. Or unaware. I took two plus two and came up with five."

"And you said I was too screwed up for you to get involved with."

Regan's eyes closed again and she let regret burn in her heart. "That wasn't what I believed though."

"What was?"

"I don't know. I was too confused to think straight. But I'm sure that's what it sounded like."

"That was exactly what it sounded like. And you never said it was something else. What was I supposed to think?"

"That was definitely the stupidest calculation I've ever made. There was zero truth in that. The problem was all in here." She pointed at her heart. "It was still broken, but I didn't know it."

It looked like Callie was trying to stop herself from what she did next. She looked at her own hand reach out and settle atop Regan's heart.

How could a touch so innocent make her feel like she would explode? "I was wrong to even think that you didn't have self-esteem. But I was grasping for straws trying to figure out why I was afraid to be with you." She put her hand over Callie's and the warmth of her skin raced directly to her heart. "I'm not a judgmental person. But I tried to make myself believe you were…I don't know…not who you seemed? I guess I had to make myself believe you were flawed so it made sense that I was backing away."

"When did this get clear in your head?"

"I've known something was wrong for a couple of months. Nothing was making any sense. But it wasn't until I talked to Delaney that everything clicked into place. The day after we talked, I felt like a giant weight was lifted from my shoulders. And the day I saw Angela, I knew she'd been the stumbling block."

"You saw Angela? Good lord! On purpose?"

"Yeah. The day I tried to go on your date with you." It had been a week, but she was still mortified.

Callie chuckled softly. "That was seriously weird. I thought you'd been drinking."

"No. I just wanted to be with you. It didn't matter that some other woman had gotten there first." She smacked her face with her open hand. "Love can make you act like an idiot."

"Love?" Callie reached up and tucked a few strands of hair behind Regan's ear. That gentle touch nearly burned as every nerve rushed to that centimeter of skin. She barely heard Callie say, "Tell me about Angela."

Coming back to her senses, Regan said, "I walked over by our old house. She was outside puttering in her little garden." She took in a heavy breath. "It was hard to see her. But after watching her for a few minutes, I felt the last little bit of ice melt in my heart. I could feel the final bit of her hold on me loosen. Then it floated away." She blinked a few times, still feeling puzzled. "It sounds funny, but I could almost see it. By the time I walked away I was over her."

"That seems…sudden." Callie shook her head. "No, not sudden, but…it's hard to imagine your feelings just leaving in a rush like that."

"Not to me. That's kinda how I am."

"Unfathomable?" Callie asked, smiling again.

"Yeah. Kinda. Even to myself. I bumble along, knowing there's something wrong, then it snaps together. Once it does that, I can look back and see how I got there."

"So you're positive you're over Angela."

"Yes. I'm positive."

Callie's hand closed around Regan's bicep, and she looked into her eyes. "What does that mean?"

"That means I can finally let myself tell you how much I love you."

"And…"

"And that I want to be with you." The rest was easy. The feelings had been there for months. The words just had to explain them. "I love you and I want to be together." She reached out and grasped Callie's shoulder to try to pull her close. But Callie blocked her hand and leaned back, away from the touch.

"You said some harsh things. I have to know that you don't think my morals are weak. If you think I'm inferior to you—"

"No! I swear I don't think that."

Callie looked like she was going to cry. "What *do* you think? You aren't the kind of person to speak without thinking. Remember you took an extra day to come back and tell me I had no self-esteem."

"I know I did. And I did think it over before I said it." This was the most important thing she'd ever have to explain. Her whole future depended on doing this right. "I'll admit it took me a long time to get over your being in an open relationship."

"Get over?" Callie said frostily.

"Get over my negative feelings about it. I know it's none of my business, but if I have bad feelings about it that would hurt our relationship." She looked up and saw Callie glaring at her. "It's true, and you know it."

"Fine. It's none of your business, but if it bothers you it matters."

"Right. So I really worked on myself, and over time I finally came to believe that there wasn't anything immoral or illegal about it, and if it worked for you…"

"It was none of your business," Callie said, grinning slyly.

"Yeah, something like that. But I've gotta tell you, if I'd known you weren't trying to build a life with Marina, I would have gotten over it a lot sooner."

"Then I'm glad I didn't tell you." Callie's haughty smile was both adorable and infuriating.

"Thanks!"

"I mean it. Marina will always be a part of my past. It's much better to have worked that through on your own. But what about my lack of self-esteem?"

Regan laughed, her shoulders shaking from the effort. "I don't know what I was thinking. You've got tons of self-esteem. I must have just been thinking of excuses to explain why I couldn't make a play for you."

"So you've worked out all of your bad feelings about my checkered past?"

"Not all of them." Her smile disappeared. "You were playing around and seeing what would happen with Marina. But that was like playing with a loaded gun. It went off and I got wounded."

Callie closed her eyes. "I know you never would have had your heart broken if Marina hadn't met Angela. But don't forget they worked together before she met me."

"That's not it. This is hard for me to say, but I don't want to have any secrets from you."

"I don't want that either." She grasped Regan's hands. "Tell me anything."

"I think you made a very bad choice in being with Marina. I'm not talking about your relationship being open. I'm talking about her as a human being. Wasn't there some part of you that knew she wasn't a good person? Didn't you doubt her?" Callie was so perceptive. And she hadn't just learned that trait in the last year.

Callie's eyes closed and she flopped onto her back, taking in long, slow breaths. "I didn't trust her. That's why I didn't let myself get too emotionally involved." Tears appeared in the corners of her eyes and traveled down her cheeks. "I couldn't have stopped her from chasing Angela, but I was wrong to be involved with her." She sniffled a little and reached out blindly with her hand. It settled onto Regan's thigh and she squeezed it. "I shouldn't have been with her, but if I hadn't been, I wouldn't have met you." She rolled over and braced herself with her arm. "I don't like to admit this, but I can see why you'd doubt my morals. My mom used to tell me 'Know me, know my friends.' There's some truth to that."

"Yeah, there is. Why do you think you did it?"

"I've thought a lot about that in my therapy group. The only answer I've come up with is that she made me feel desired again."

"That's really it?"

"Partly. Rob made me distrust all men, so I was really open to being with a woman. Marina came along and swept me off my feet. She was really pretty and very much in demand. Her wanting me and flying to Phoenix a bunch of times to convince me made me want to take the chance."

"Even though you had to agree to let her sleep with other women."

"Yeah. I know it sounds stupid to you, but it felt more honest. She had a ridiculously high sex drive and she needed a release valve. Knowing that up front made me stupidly think I had some control." She shook her head hard, like she was trying to knock a bad thought from it. "She said something like that at the end. That she had to lie to make me think I had control over her sex drive. Maybe she knew me better than I knew myself."

"Would you do it again?"

Callie reached out and wrapped Regan in her arms. "I'm going to tell you the truth, even though you might try to run away." She swallowed and said, "I probably would if I were in the same situation. But this time I'd make it clear we were just dating. And when I found myself tip-toeing around the apartment to avoid annoying her… That's where my self-esteem was lacking."

"You're more sure of yourself now."

"Yep. Part of it is that I'm finally over Rob. Plus, making myself look at my actions is really good for me. I don't like it, but it's good."

Callie pulled away and gazed into Regan's eyes for a minute. "What do we do now?"

"I guess it's time to fish or cut bait." She grinned brightly. "I'm ready to fish."

"Are you sure you can trust me?" Callie sounded so hopeful it made Regan's heart ache.

"Yeah." She faced her and smiled. "I can."

"Are you positive?" Callie pulled back, her eyes scanning Regan's face quickly.

"Completely. You know me. I never take a big step unless I'm sure."

"That's true. If you're sure of that, then I know I can trust you."

"You can. I promise I'll never question your relationship with her again. Actually, let's never mention her name again. She's in the past. The distant past."

But Callie's head shook. "No. I don't want to have anything off limits. If something comes up, I want you to be able to talk to me about it." She reached over and grasped the tip of Regan's nose between her fingers. "It's gonna take some time to get used to the way you process things. You're a handful."

"We could just promise never to have problems." She knew her grin was so wide it probably made her look crazy, but she couldn't help it. It was hard to be serious for long with Callie. She made every problem seem like it was very temporary.

"How about this? Maybe you could try to talk about things as they come up. Then you don't have to walk around in a fog."

Regan took the hand away and kissed the back of it. "I'll try." Gazing at the lovely hand, she tentatively kissed it a few more times, heartened by the way Callie kept it right by her mouth. "Will you try to do something for me?"

"Of course."

She looked up and let their eyes meet. "Will you try to fall in love with me again?"

Callie's eyes closed as a beautiful smile bloomed on her face. "I've never stopped loving you. Not for a minute." The expression that Regan had seen many times but had never been able to define appeared. "Do you really think it would take me this long to find a lover if I was serious about it?"

"No." She moved another inch closer. "You could do it in five minutes. Maybe even four."

"I think five is right. No need to brag." She smiled and warmth filled Regan's entire body. The rush made every cell sing with pleasure.

"So, if I love you and you love me…"

"We should do something to commemorate this discovery. Any ideas?"

"Come here," Regan said softly. She raised her arm and Callie scooted the last inch to rest against her.

"Best place on earth." Callie sighed, shifting her shoulders and increasing the contact. "I haven't been here often, but each time makes me feel like all's right with the world."

"I feel best when I'm with you, and even better when we're touching. You ground me."

Callie turned her head and looked into Regan's eyes. "I can see my future."

"With me."

"Yes. Definitely with you."

Regan gently stroked her cheek. "Don't be nervous."

"Why do you think I'm nervous?"

"You're shivering." She ran a hand down her arm with goose bumps following.

Callie looked down at her arm. "I guess I am. I feel like we're about to take a *very* big step."

"Yeah. Very big." Regan put her hand on the back of Callie's head and brought it to her chest. She stroked her hair for a few seconds. "I feel like I'm right on the cusp of taking one of the biggest steps of my life, and I want to make sure I do everything right."

"You don't have to worry about that."

"Oh, I think I do." Regan moved back enough to let Callie see her grin. "I've got a lot more on the line than you do. I'll never get another chance for a woman as good as you."

"That's true. But that's the great thing about being in love. You're not alone. We're making this choice together and we'll always have each other for support."

"Isn't that fantastic?" The mere thought made Regan's head spin.

"Completely. There's nothing better than being loved."

"I love you," Regan declared, sure and confident. "I love you, Callie, and I'm going to love you for as long as I live."

"Then kiss me. A whole lot."

Regan caressed the back of Callie's neck until she saw her beautiful eyes blink slowly. Leaning in, she pressed their lips together tenderly. It had been nine months since it had happened, but she'd thought of their first kiss thousands of times. As soon as their lips touched that first frantic kiss was gone from her memory. Her body flooded with sensation. The soft firmness of Callie's lips, the sweet scent of her hair, a hint of peppermint from her mouth, even the down in the pillow she lay on suffused her senses. She stilled and let her body speak to her. Consciously opening herself to whatever came, she let Callie into her soul.

"This is wonderful," Callie murmured when they broke apart for a moment.

"So, so nice. Just like my dreams."

"Just like mine." She nuzzled her face into Regan's shoulder. "When I was taking my nap I had a dream about you." She batted her eyes. "It made me happy."

Regan gently stroked her cheek, amazed by its softness. "Tell me about it."

"I don't remember the whole thing. But we were in bed together and I knew we were going to make love." Tears sprang to her eyes and she blinked them away. "I dream about you all of the time, and I usually wake up sad when I realize it was just a dream." A brilliant smile slowly formed on her lips. "I never have to have that feeling again." She pulled Regan close and hugged her tightly. "I'll always have you."

CHAPTER TWENTY-SIX

BREAKING APART FOR a moment, Callie looked into Regan's eyes, her gaze a little unfocused. "Are we going to make love?"

"Definitely."

Callie's head spun when Regan grasped her firmly and placed a dozen hot kisses on her lips. "Wow!" Callie lay on her back, with Regan sprawled atop her. "You're really good at that." She grasped Regan's chin between her fingers. "Have you been practicing on the girls in Scituate?"

"Nope." She shook her head, her dark hair slipping over a shoulder. "Pent up demand." She took a few nibbles along Callie's neck, stopping only when her squirming blocked access. "You know," she said deliberately, "I was full of it when I said sex wasn't very important to me. It is."

"Good news for me. How'd you figure that out?"

"It wasn't hard." She looked a little embarrassed when she held her hand out and shook it. "I think I've got a repetitive motion injury from thinking about you."

Callie took her hand and inspected it carefully. "You can give it a nice long rest." Kissing it gently she placed it over her heart. "So, you've been fantasizing about us?"

"Not us. You. I think about any part of you and I'm gone." Her downcast eyes and slight flush made her more adorable than ever. She was so eminently teasable.

"When did this start? After you talked to Delaney?"

"God, no. It was probably a month or so after we got back from the Bahamas." A guilty-looking grin stole across her face.

Callie playfully slapped at her. "That long?"

"Yeah. I felt guilty about it for a long time, since I was still really heartbroken, but I got over it." She shook her hand again. "Obviously."

"Why'd you feel guilty?"

"It seemed wrong somehow to start thinking about another woman when I wasn't over Angela."

"Oh, Regan." Callie lay on her back, staring up at the ceiling. "You're so precious."

"Is that a compliment?"

"Yeah. Of course it is. I just think it's precious that you're so monogamous that you think it's wrong to fantasize about other women *after* you've broken up. That's intense!"

"I'm really, really monogamous, but I know that's not the norm."

"I will never, ever complain about you being too monogamous. That's one of your most endearing qualities."

"Monogamy is the only way for me. But I let that get out of hand with Angela. Once we were together I honestly thought I had to just live with our shitty sex life. That was dumb. Really dumb. Thinking that way got my heart broken."

"What would you do differently?"

"I should have paid attention to the way we related sexually. It wasn't great even before we moved in together." She slapped herself in the forehead with the flat of her hand. "So dumb. I kept telling myself that she had ninety percent of what I wanted in a partner."

"That last ten percent is pretty important."

"Yeah, tell me about it. That last ten percent made Angela cheat."

"No, I don't think so. She cheated because she was afraid to be honest. She knew she wanted someone she could top in and out of bed, but she's obviously attracted to assertive women. She never would have been interested in Marina if that wasn't so."

"Yeah, you're probably right. But she's the last person I want to talk about today." She smiled impishly. "No, as usual, Marina's the last. But Angela's second to last."

"It's a deal. No more of either of those knuckleheads."

"I only brought it up because I want you to know I'll never let something like that happen again." She took Callie's hand and stared deep into her eyes. "I'll do anything I can to make sure you're sexually satisfied. Sex is too important to be an afterthought."

"It is. But the other things are too important to ignore. Trust and honesty are requirements, not options. I learned that from my eighteen months with she who will not be named."

"Sounds like we both learned something important. It sucks to learn things, doesn't it?" She laughed and rolled onto her back. "I'd much rather read things like that in a book."

"Me too." Callie put her hand on Regan's shirt and tugged on it. "Books can't replace some experiences though." She pulled the shirt up a few inches and tickled along the edge of Regan's panties. "Some things have to be experienced in the flesh."

Regan turned her head and looked into Callie's eyes for a few seconds. Then she shifted onto her side and took over. With the first possessive kiss, Callie knew she'd found a home. Regan kissed like she knew exactly what she wanted, and that she knew exactly how to get it. Her body hovered over Callie for a moment, then she settled her full weight onto her, making her feel wonderfully trapped. Their breasts compressed against each other, softness upon softness. Then Regan's knee slid between her thighs and settled boldly against her. It was divine.

After a few long minutes of intensifying kisses, Callie looked deep into Regan's eyes. The love she saw there filled her with emotion. She'd been waiting for this woman all of her life.

As they gazed at each other longingly, Regan rolled off and decisively said, "I'm going to undress you."

Callie blinked at her while a thrill raced down her spine as she waited for instructions.

"Let me take off your shirt." She grasped the hem, then smoothly pulled it off. Callie looked down at herself as Regan did. Suddenly, she felt a little shy, being so intimately revealed. But Regan looked positively joyous and that made the little bout of shyness disappear. "I'll never get tired of looking at you," Regan whispered. She gently kissed one hard nipple. "You're more beautiful than I'd dreamt." She placed her hands on the swell of Callie's hips, letting her hands rest there for a moment. Her thumbs chafed the waistband of her pajamas, then she slid them down, smiling. The desire burning in Regan's eyes made Callie's heart beat hard in her chest. Regan needed her, wanted her, lusted for her, and nothing had ever made her happier.

Regan hugged her, squeezing almost to the point of pain. "I love you with all my heart." She slid her hands around Callie's back and let them roam all over her skin. "You're so warm and soft." She sniffed delicately along her neck. "And you smell fantastic. So clean and fresh. It used to drive me crazy when we stayed at each other's houses. I wanted to put my face on every sweet smelling spot. You're such a beautiful woman," she whispered. Her hands started at Callie's shoulders and slipped down her body, making a small turn at her hips before coming to rest on her ass. "I can't believe how lucky I am. You're almost too beautiful to touch." Those beautiful blue eyes twinkled when she grinned rakishly. "Almost."

Callie grabbed and held her tightly, nuzzling her face into Regan's shoulder. Once again, Regan's decisiveness made her feel a little shy. It was like there was a finite amount of confidence they shared and the more Regan showed, the less she felt.

"Let me see you," Regan whispered. "Come on. Let me see how beautiful you are."

That was it. Regan sensed the key to her sexual desire. Having a woman she lusted for tell her exactly what to do. Callie slowly pulled the covers away, revealing her nakedness. Her arm started to rise to cover her breasts, but Regan grasped her hand and held it. Then she dipped her head and kissed a warm path up her breastbone, ending at her lips.

Regan's body shifted onto Callie's again, possessing her delightfully. Callie took in a deep breath at the glorious feeling of having Regan's luscious body atop her. It was heady in a way that almost made her weak. Her desire was at such a fever pitch she couldn't stop her hands from roaming, touching Regan's back and her muscular ass. "You're amazing," she murmured.

"No, you are." Regan slid back onto her side and gazed at Callie's body, whispering exclamations of pleasure so soft that no one could have heard them. Then with a gentle hand on her shoulder she turned Callie onto her belly. She sat up, as though she needed to see more, and ran her hand all over her back, then down to her ass, her thighs. Her fingers gently followed the curve of Callie's spine, then returned once more to settle on her ass. Then she turned her again and slid onto her, enveloping her in an incendiary kiss—one Callie felt in her core. Callie's need, her desire, her passion were all wrapped up in one wet kiss that seemed to go on and on.

Lying on their sides, legs entwined, Regan murmured. "I knew you were beautiful, but I had no idea you were as beautiful as you are." When she pulled away her grin showed her playful side. "How do you ever walk away from a full length mirror? I know you must spend a lot of time touching yourself. Nobody could ignore a body like this for long. Show me how you do it."

Now that Regan was nearly daring her, she felt bolder. Slowly, she began to trail her hand down her arm, then caressed her breast, a bolt of sensation hitting her when Regan's eyes went big and she bit her lower lip.

"That feels good, doesn't it?" Regan asked, thickly. "It's making me crazy and I'm not even getting to touch you. Just watching you is about all I can take."

"You look like you know just what you're doing."

"Are you comfortable?"

"Yeah, I am."

"You look it. You look like you like doing this. Actually," she said slowly, "you look like you're about to burst. Do you know your hips are pushing into me?" She looked down at Callie's hips, which were, in fact, circling and pressing in time to some silent beat.

"No."

"I like that," Regan purred. "I like having you grind against me. I want you to get what you want, whenever you want it."

"All I want is to love you."

"I want that more than I'll ever be able to say. Will you undress me?"

Callie dove for her, nearly tearing her shirt as she wrestled it off her. "Easy," Regan whispered. "We've got the rest of our lives together. I'm not going anywhere."

It took just seconds to pull the shirt from her body and slide her panties down her long legs. "You look just like I'd imagined," Callie murmured, looking at her with ill-disguised longing. "Your skin is flawless. And your breasts…" She took one in her hand and gazed at it for a few seconds before she sucked it into her mouth, laving the hardening nipple against her teeth.

"Touch me," Regan said. "Touch me all over. Get to know my body any way you want."

That was the most welcome invitation she'd ever received. She sucked a breast into her mouth while her hands roamed everywhere. Regan's body was the most wondrous thing she'd ever touched in her life. Every part of it made her throb, and she didn't have enough hands to satiate herself. Regan arched her back, pressing her breast harder against Callie's mouth. "That's so nice. Do whatever you want. Anything you want."

All of a sudden there was too much to do. Too much Regan to caress, to explore. Instinctively, Regan stepped in and took over again. "Lie down and let me show you something."

Letting go, Callie placed one last kiss on the pink nipple and rolled onto her side. Regan sat up and started to touch herself just as Callie had. "My breasts are very sensitive," she said, casually stroking them while staring into Callie's laser-like gaze. "But you can play with them any way you want. Soft, hard, any way at all. If you like it, I'll like it."

Nodding intently like an A plus student, Callie continued to stare at Regan's hands as they slid down her body. "And my ass is very sensitive too." She was lying on her side now, stroking her skin until she looked like she'd combust. "I'd love it if you'd grab it and squeeze it when you go down on me." She rolled up against Callie and kissed her hotly. "I can't wait until you do that. I've been thinking of how your tongue will feel when it touches every part of my pussy." She shivered roughly. "It makes me come every time."

"I…" Callie cleared her throat, trying to form words. "I want to do that."

"Do you?" The deep timbre of Regan's voice was hardly recognizable. It was a sultry, sexy purr Callie never would have expected to come out of her. A sexy, welcome surprise.

"Yes. So much. Now?"

"Do you want to do it now?"

"Yeah…Yeah." She knew she sounded like she'd lost her mind, but it didn't matter.

"Would you like it," Regan said, "if I put myself over your mouth and touched my breasts while I told you how I felt?"

"God, yes!"

Regan slung one leg across Callie's shoulder and sat lightly upon her chest. She looked down at her, eyes filled with love. "Am I too heavy?"

"You're perfect. Come closer." As Regan hovered over her she wanted to leap up and bury her face. But her patience was rewarded when Regan very slowly moved forward and Callie's tongue pressed against gossamer soft skin.

Regan hissed out a stream of air as she started to move. "Your tongue is so fantastic. Watch me," And Callie followed her hands as she squeezed her breasts hard. "Ooo," she murmured. "I love to squeeze them hard," she got out through gritted teeth. "Your tongue is…it's… perfect. Just perfect. Right there." She thrust her hips gently. "Stay right there and let me move." She reached down and held onto Callie's hands, then moved against her tongue, her eyes shut tightly, her breathing elevated. Then she shuddered and flexed her legs just enough to lift herself a few inches. "I almost went over the edge," she said, shivering. "But I'm not ready. I need more."

"Let me, let me," Callie begged. "Come back." Her arms wrapped around Regan's thighs, halting her.

Regan caressed her hair, murmuring, "I will. Just let me move away from the edge of that cliff."

"Touch your breasts again. Let me watch you do that."

Staying well away from Callie's mouth, Regan rose to put all of her weight on her knees, then she started to play with her breasts again. She pinched her nipples until they grew dark pink, then shook her shoulders, making them move. Cupping and squeezing them again and again, she finally said, "I can't wait. All I can think of is your tongue." She lowered herself onto Callie's eagerly awaiting mouth. In just a few seconds she snapped her hips then held herself still, while Callie let her tongue glide all over the firming flesh. "That's it. That's it. Just that way. Oh, so good!" Then she shook and twitched, letting out bursts of air before falling like a tree, landing on her side. Surprised by her tumble, Callie scooted over to be able to lie face to face with her. Then they kissed, leisurely, until she could feel Regan's racing heart slow. Her skin was moist and very warm and she shook just a little, but her smile was angelic. Callie held her and kissed her hungrily, desperate for kisses, even though they'd shared hundreds.

They lay still for a few moments, then Regan stretched her body out and squirmed around on the big bed. "This is fun," she said, grinning euphorically. "Isn't it?'

Callie grabbed her and kissed her. "God, yes! I don't think I've ever had this much fun in my whole life!" She was still a little giddy, but she didn't care that she didn't sound cool and collected. She didn't have to project an image with Regan.

"It's been so-o-o long since I could be myself."

Callie's hand rested on her belly and she stroked her gently. "Poor thing."

She closed her eyes and shivered. "God, it's been four, four and a half years since I really clicked sexually with someone. I've had an awfully long dry spell." Then her smile flashed and she added, "That's over."

"You bet it is." Callie moved to straddle her. "We really click. Isn't that a relief?"

"It'd be a damn shame if I had to pack up and head home by myself, but I swear I would have if we didn't have some spark. I will never be in another relationship where my partner isn't into sex."

"Not a problem. Your partner's very into sex. You just have to keep up with me."

She shrugged, still grinning. "I'm good."

Regan was so ridiculously charming. It was amazing she wasn't completely full of herself. But she wasn't. "You know, it usually takes a while to really sync with someone. It's gonna be cool when we're really rockin' this, isn't it?"

"That might have been my best work. Don't expect a lot more."

"Ha! If you believed that you wouldn't be grinning like you are. Admit it. You're a natural."

"I don't want to brag…"

"You're entitled to. I love being guided exactly like you did it. I don't want to think one single thought when we make love."

"You think," Regan said, chuckling. "Maybe you think with your body because you give off plenty of cues."

"If I give off cues, you read them." She rolled her head around like she was woozy. "Nobody's ever talked to me quite like that. It was divine." She collapsed onto her chest, her new favorite place. "Just divine."

"I thought about your voyeuristic streak and I thought it might turn you on to watch me touch myself and talk about it." She wrapped her arms around Callie and hugged her. "I guess it turned me on, too."

"You did that for me? I kinda thought you were…funny when I told you about that. Like you thought it was perverted."

"No way. If something turns you on, I'm into it."

"Really? I…I wasn't sure you'd be…adventurous."

"I'm open to just about anything. When you promise that you'll never be with anyone else, I've got to make sure you never *need* to go elsewhere."

"I never will. I'd die before I'd betray you."

"I know." Regan closed her eyes and rested her forehead against Callie's. "I know that's true. But you're giving up a lot to be with me. I have to make it worth it for you."

"I'm not giving up a thing. I'm getting the world."

"I feel the same. But I'm gonna take this responsibility very seriously. I'm going to do whatever I can to make you never want another woman. So let me know whatever turns you on. I'm game."

"I will if you'll do the same."

"You've done well so far," she teased.

"Yeah. About that," Callie said, taking Regan's hand and sliding it along the back of her thigh. "Weren't you trying to turn *me* on?"

"Yeah, but you begged to be able to taste me. I was just following orders." She laughed and rolled Callie onto her back. "Now it's my turn to beg."

"Yeah. That's right. I'm gonna make you grovel." She looked into Regan's bright eyes and said, drolly, "I could take it or leave it, but I'll do it for you."

"Let's see." Regan clambered down the bed, keeping their eyes locked together. When she got to Callie's pelvis, she gently spread her legs and settled down on her forearms, her face just inches away from her sex. Delicately, she opened Callie with her thumbs and smiled, an incredibly satisfied look on her face. "You're beautiful. Really beautiful. Like a gorgeous flower." Without warning, she pressed her lips against Callie's sex and stayed right there, nuzzling her lips and her tongue into every fold.

"Fantastic," Callie murmured. "Do that…forever."

Eyes shining, Regan lifted her head. "I could. I really could." She turned her attention back to Callie's body, exploring like a scientist, while Callie tried to just breathe and feel. Regan kept her hands atop her hips, and she started to press them into the bed, trapping her. That was exactly what Callie craved. The more helpless she felt the more her body cried for release. But Regan didn't let her move. The more she mewed and squirmed, the tighter Regan held her.

Her desire built and waned, with Regan repositioning her to drive her just a little more crazy. Finally, her legs were draped over Regan's shoulders with those strong, gentle hands holding them in place. As Regan greedily lapped her, she knew she'd lost all control. She writhed and tossed around on the bed, wanting more. Then her vulva started to pulse against Regan's mouth. Waves of pleasure hit her hard, but Regan stayed right with her, hanging on to wrest the last bit of sensation from her.

"My god," Callie murmured after she caught her breath. "Get up here and kiss me."

Grinning, Regan climbed up and flopped down next to her then placed a gentle kiss on her lips. "I'm gonna have to stay on top of you," she said, looking very self-satisfied. "You're hard to hold onto."

"You've got my number, Regan Manning. You've got it good." She wrapped her arms around her and they wrestled for a few moments, with Regan winding up on top.

"You've got mine, too. I think this is gonna work out pretty well. How about you?"

"This is icing on the cake." Callie's expression turned serious as she said, "I mean that. You're the cake. I bet we don't spend more than…oh, three or four hours a day having otherworldly sex. The other twenty hours a day is the good part."

"Three or four hours might be what we do when we've been together for a while. But now we've gotta make up for lost time."

Callie wrapped her arms around Regan's shoulders and kissed her, relishing the still novel experience. "This is the best day of a pretty awesome life. But I can't wait for tomorrow 'cause I know every day will be better with you by my side."

Regan placed a long, tender kiss on Callie's lips, then gazed into her eyes, letting the feeling build. Then she took a deep breath, cleared her throat and said, "I want to marry you."

Callie blinked, eyes opening wide. "You want to marry me?"

"Yes, I want to marry you. I can't imagine my life without you. I want to tell everybody I love what you mean to me."

"Get married," Callie said, as though she were testing out how it sounded. "Married."

Regan jumped out of bed and dashed for her bag where she rooted around, grasped something and ran back to bed. She took a steadying breath while she fumbled under the covers. "I'm so glad you came to Boston. And I'm so glad we were the first state to legalize marriage between women. Isn't Massachusetts wonderful?"

Callie nodded slowly. "Yeah…it's the best place on earth. What are you hiding there?"

Regan's hand slipped out of the covers and held up an emerald ring set in gold. "Will you marry me?"

Tears welled up in Callie's eyes and she clutched Regan, holding on tightly. "Yes, yes. I'll marry you right this minute."

With trembling hands, Regan slipped the ring onto her finger, then kissed it tenderly.

"It's so beautiful. How did you know I'd love it?"

"You've told me you like Delaney's, but that you liked emeralds better than diamonds. I pay attention to every word you say." She knew she was gazing at her with a lovestruck expression, and that's just what she wanted. Callie needed to know what was in her heart. They kissed, gently, almost chastely.

When they broke apart, Regan gazed at her for a moment, marveling at her beauty. Callie grasped her face with both hands and began to kiss her in earnest. Her kisses were full and warm and covered Regan's lips completely, making her want more and more. After just a few moments, Regan could feel the desire burning in her heart, as insistent as any physical need she'd ever had. This was what true love felt like. There wasn't a doubt in her mind or in her body. She was Callie's.

Long moments later, they broke apart. "Did you say you'd marry me?" Regan asked lazily.

"Yes, yes, yes, yes. I'll marry you."

"That's good. Because I'd have to kill myself if I couldn't have you now."

"You've got me," Callie pledged, wiping away a few tears as they formed. "Forever."

TWO MONTHS LATER

CALLIE AND REGAN sat on a bench in front of a cafe on Commercial Street in Provincetown. The day was lovely, warm and dry. They'd been on a run, and were still in their running clothes. Callie reached over and tucked a few hairs behind Regan's ear. "I really made you work for your lunch, didn't I? Your hair couldn't stay in its ponytail."

"I think I did just fine." Regan leaned hard against the bench, stretching her arms straight in the air as she performed some of the unique exercises she indulged in after running. "One of these days I'm gonna beat you, and then you'll know how it feels to see me in the distance."

Leaning over to drape herself across Regan's lap Callie batted her eyes seductively. "That'd be great. I'd love to be behind you, watching your adorable butt. You know, sometimes I hold back just so I can leer at you."

"But you always find a way to pull out another gear and dust me."

Giggling, Callie sat up and flipped her hair over her shoulders. "I can see your butt at home."

"You know, it was just a year ago that we were here, watching people walk down the street. I remember not being able to look at other women because I was mesmerized by the sun shining on your hair."

With a bright grin, Callie patted her cheek. "And now you can't look at other women because I'd strangle you."

Regan's grin matched hers. "That's pretty harsh. Not to mention unfair." Whatever chart measured cuteness didn't have a number high enough for how Regan looked when she played like this. "Your last lover could have sex with other women. I can't even know they exist." Being able to tease each other about their exes was new. It was still a little touchy, but it felt healthy to toy around these possibly dangerous topics.

She leaned forward and cupped Regan's face in her hands. They were just a couple of inches from each other and Callie could see so many flecks of color in Regan's eyes she almost lost track of what she wanted to say. "It's perfectly fair. Marina could have had sex with my mom at ten and come home and be perfectly normal at noon. You, on the other hand…" She had to have a quick kiss. Lips that luscious couldn't be ignored for long. "Would feel guilty about looking at another woman's body for more than two seconds. When you feel guilty you behave differently. So…no checking out chicks for you." Another longer kiss followed, and she couldn't make herself pull away. Being close to Regan's sweet face was always a treat, and being able to kiss her openly was extra special.

"Is that really the reason?"

"Of course not. First off, I'd never tell you what you can or can't do. I just want you to know that if you looked at another woman it would slay me." Just thinking about it made her feel like she'd choke up.

"No worries." The certainty in Regan's eyes was enough. It spoke volumes. "How about you?"

"How about me what?" She'd forgotten what they were talking about. All she could concentrate on were Regan's tantalizing eyes.

"Can you look at other women? What's your rule?"

"Oh." She pulled away, flipping her runaway hair back again. "I've got the best looking woman in the world in my bed every night. I have no interest in looking at the runners up."

Regan took her hand and squeezed it against her chest. "So…should I be worried if I ever catch you looking?"

"That's a laugh. The only thing I look at is the clock to check when you're coming home. I start at about three and keep doing it every two minutes until you finally hit the front porch."

"I love that you come to the door to meet me every night. It makes me so happy."

Leaning into Regan's body, she said, "I'm really not kidding about the clock. I'm so addicted to you it amazes me."

"Same here." She buried her nose in Callie's hair and took a deep breath. "Every part of you turns me on."

Callie looked up and playfully asked, "Time to get our moneys worth from our room?"

"Have I ever said no?" Regan smirked, looking proud of herself.

"Not even once." She kissed her softly, staying very close. "You can, you know. You don't have to fulfill all of my needs."

"Of course I do! You fulfill all of mine, so it's only fair." She was grinning happily, showing she was barely kidding. "Besides, you've never suggested making love when I wasn't one hundred percent in favor of it."

"You make the first move more than I do." Turning to make eye contact she added, "I love that."

Increasing the strength of her hold, Regan murmured into Callie's ear, "I couldn't be happier."

"Goosebumps!" she giggled, showing Regan the evidence now covering her arms. "You know, coming here might not have been the best idea for a mini-vacation. We don't want to look at other women and we barely leave our apartment when we're at home, so we clearly aren't looking to meet people here."

"We'll start socializing. I just need a few months or years or decades to focus on you." Kissing Callie's ear, Regan asked, "What's longer than a decade?"

"Dunno. On second thought, I think it was good to come. We can kiss and hug in public here."

"We do that at home."

"Not like this, we don't." Callie slithered out of Regan's hold and put a hand on each shoulder. Looking at her with the full force of her sensuality, she pressed her hard against the bench and leaned in, compressing their lips together. She felt Regan twitch, the way she often did when the first flush of desire hit her. Callie stayed right there, opening her mouth just enough to let Regan's tongue make a dainty entrance. That did it for her. Regan's tongue had been on nearly every surface of her body, but feeling it enter her mouth turned her on each and every time.

Looking thunderstruck, her eyes slightly out of focus, Regan drawled, "I don't think we can make love on the street—even here."

"We're not making love. We're having foreplay."

"I love foreplay," Regan said, sounding oddly wistful. "It's one of my favorite things on earth."

Callie grinned mischievously. "I think I'll start you off in the shower today. I'll strip off all of your clothes as soon as we get into our room, then guide you into the bathroom. I'll get my clothes off while the water warms up, then I'll force you up against the glass and lather up my hands." She leaned close and whispered, "I love to take you from behind."

Glassy-eyed, Regan nodded. "I love when you do that. I can clear my mind and just feel. I'm not distracted by looking at your beautiful face." She blushed, looking prettier than Callie could fathom. "When I look into your eyes when we make love I can hardly think."

"You don't have to think today. I'll do all the thinking." Callie petted her dark hair, smiling when Regan automatically leaned into her touch. "You've been doing an awful lot of the heavy lifting around the bedroom. You can be on vacation this weekend."

Grinning, Regan shook her head. "That's not work. That's play, and you know I love to play."

"I'm learning. I'm definitely learning. I thought you were a pretty serious woman, but you're actually pretty goofy."

"Yeah, that's me. You had bad timing in meeting me at my low. But I'm back and better than ever!" She stood and grasped Callie by the forearms, lifting her to her feet. "Time to play." She led the way down the crowded street, calling out, "Make way. Gotta make love to my gorgeous fiance. Clear the path, please. Lovemaking in progress."

Callie laughed at her antics, turning to silently apologize to the women they'd blown past.

Turning onto a quiet street, Regan kept talking. "Did I ever tell you about the time I made love to a firefighter?"

"Why, no, I don't think you have." Callie smiled at her, feeling the love she had for Regan thrum through her body. This was Regan's new game, and it was adorable. She made up sexual experiences out of whole cloth and described them in detail. So far each had involved a woman in some sort of uniform, and required Regan to spend a while taking said uniform off—slowly and sexily. Callie assumed she would always have a fetish for voyeurism, but she hadn't felt the need to exercise it in the time they'd been together. Just being with Regan was enough to drive her desire. And having her put her efforts into thinking up new scenarios just for her was utterly charming.

"Well, I did. She'd just come from fighting a four-alarm fire, and she had every piece of equipment on. Hat, coat, big yellow suspenders... She was smokey and sweaty and tired, so I knew I'd have to get her in the shower before I had my way with her."

Callie thrilled at hearing the things that sprang to Regan's mind, and from the sparkle in her eyes she could tell that Regan loved the game. The stories were about things she doubted Regan would have ever done, but it let her flex her creative muscles and it never failed to turn Callie on. Regan usually started off playfully, then started to get into it when her imagination began to run wild.

They reached their bed and breakfast, chasing each other up the stairs to surprise the cleaning woman, who was just about to get to work on their room. "If you'd leave us a couple of towels, we're good," Callie said, slipping into the room and pulling Regan with her. "Actually, we can re-use the ones we have. Conserving water and energy is important." She closed the door and leaned against it, slapping her hand over her mouth to dampen her laugh. "How obvious was I?"

"Very." Regan leaned against her, pressing her against the wood. "She'll know just what we're doing when she hears your screams."

"Or yours." She looked into Regan's lovely face, pausing to admire the strong, elegant bone structure. It still amazed her that someone so compellingly beautiful loved her. But love her she did. Wonderfully. She wrapped her arms tightly around Regan's waist and hugged her until she grunted. "Save the firefighter for another day, will you? I want to take a quick shower and then go to bed. I have a huge need to put my hands on you and I don't want to use up all of the hot water." She kissed her tenderly. "This is going to take a while."

"Nice and slow?" Regan continued to press against her, and now her voice was low and sexy. Whenever Callie made the first move Regan tended to respond coyly. It was like she wanted to be seduced, and

Callie found this facet of her personality completely alluring. She looked into her eyes, which were now hooded and shy.

"I do. I want to make love to you." They kissed, gently, for a long time. "Sometimes I want to have sex with you, sometimes I want to make love and today I want to worship you. Get ready to have me kneeling at the altar of Regan."

In a split second Regan's eyes filled with determination. Even though she didn't look strong—she was. Very strong. Years of unloading deliveries at the restaurant had built an ample supply of wiry muscle. She swooped Callie into her arms and strode purposefully for the bath. Callie lay her head on her shoulder and relaxed completely. Regan was in charge and everything was perfect. Simply perfect.

The End

By Susan X Meagher

Novels

Arbor Vitae
All That Matters
Cherry Grove
Girl Meets Girl
The Lies That Bind
The Legacy
Doublecrossed

Serial Novels

I Found My Heart In San Francisco

Awakenings: Book One
Beginnings: Book Two
Coalescence: Book Three
Disclosures: Book Four
Entwined: Book Five
Fidelity: Book Six
Getaway: Book Seven
Honesty: Book Eight
Intentions: Book Nine
Journeys: Book Ten

Anthologies

Undercover Tales
Outsiders